VESUVIUS

JOHN D. FENNELL

Books by John D. Fennell

THE MYSTICAL MIRROR Trilogy:

Book 1: The Boy in the Mirror
Book 2: The Book of Mysteries
Book 3: Guardians of the Mirror

THE ROMAN TIME MACHINE Series:

Book 1: Vesuvius
Book 2: The Prophecy
Book 3: The Druid of Britannia

ISBN-13: 9798524372376

www.johndfennell.com

For Dad

Chapter I

The Great Earthquake

A villa outside Pompeii
62 AD

The earthquake struck with the suddenness of a thunderclap. One moment, birds were singing alongside the lazy splashing of the fountain, while a gentle breeze ruffled the trees in the garden. The next, the ground was quaking, the walls of the villa trembling. Rippling and rattling, tiles began to skitter down until, one by one, they shattered on the ground below.

Inside the villa, a large vase toppled from its stand and exploded into a hundred fragments. The electric lights in Janus' laboratory blinked off and on, while the many screens around the room flickered and crackled.

Janus dashed into the atrium. The water in the small, rectangular pool in the centre of the floor began to dance and jump as if it were suddenly boiling. A tile fell through the rectangular opening in the roof directly above the pool and dived into the water like a bird looking for a fish. A priceless statue of his friend Jupiter juddered off the end of a table and split apart on the unforgiving mosaic floor.

With growing unease, Janus stroked his thick beard. No doubt, he thought, many of those in nearby Pompeii would expect the earthquake to end soon. Such tremors were commonplace and were, after all, to be expected when one lived at the foot of a massive volcano like Vesuvius. But as Janus thrust a hand against the trembling walls to steady himself, he knew instantly that this time it was different. The battle had begun.

On and on the tremor continued, slowly gathering in force,

until the crash of roof tiles became a constant string of explosions. A loud clatter of falling pots and pans rang out from the kitchen, and then another statue in the corner of the atrium toppled from its pedestal and collapsed onto the mosaic, sending its decapitated head rolling across the floor.

Just when Janus was about to order the evacuation of his villa, the tremor ceased as abruptly as it had begun, and silence returned momentarily.

Janus' heart was pounding wildly in his chest. Standing as still as the remaining statues in the atrium, he braced himself, expecting the quake to return at any moment.

A loud knock on the front door echoed through the house, jolting him back to life. He heard footsteps. One of his servants hurried into the room, closely followed by a soldier, his hobnailed boots tapping loudly on the stone floor. The man stepped forward and saluted.

'What news of the fighting?' Janus asked.

'It is not good, my lord. Our losses have been great.'

When the soldier removed his helmet, Janus could see he was breathing heavily and sweat was glistening all over his grubby face. All over his body armour there were dents and scratches and what appeared to be scorch marks. Janus glanced from the man's ripped tunic to the bleeding scar on his right arm and tried to contain his unease.

'And Jupiter is dead,' added the soldier with a grimace.

'What? That cannot be.' Despite the sultry evening, Janus felt cold, felt his legs weaken. Had he not been still leaning against the wall, he knew he would have collapsed. 'You must surely be mistaken.'

'I wish I were. But, with respect, my lord, that is not why I was sent here. Lord Hercules and the Lady Minerva are rallying our remaining soldiers. They have succeeded in containing the main threat.' He was speaking fast now, the words spilling out in his haste to deliver the message. 'But a small group has managed to break out and is heading this way. We believe they are coming for you, my lord. And for your machine.'

Feeling an increasing anger and a thirst for revenge, Janus declared: 'Then we shall fight them off here.'

'That will not be possible, my lord. I have not come with my men. They are all dead. I am the only one left. You and I will not be able to hold them off for long.'

Janus felt the blood drain from his face, the fight flow out of his body. He slumped backwards onto a chair. This could not be happening. So many friends dead. And all because of one man's thirst for power.

'Then what is to be done?' he asked meekly.

'They said you should destroy your machine, and then run, my lord. I will keep them at bay as best I can while you do so.'

Janus closed his eyes, scratched his beard. He felt numb.

A deep, thunderous explosion tumbled through the air from the direction of Vesuvius. A few seconds later, the tremors began again, shaking the villa as never before. More tiles slid to the ground, exploding likes falling meteorites on the paths around the house. Another, much larger statue lost its balance and crashed to the floor. Cracks darted across the walls of the atrium like fast-moving snakes, and a large chunk of plaster thudded onto the mosaic.

'Come, my lord,' said the soldier, replacing his helmet and reaching out a hand to Janus. 'It is no longer safe to stay here.'

As they headed towards a door, several more tiles fell through the opening in the roof and crashed into the pool, spraying them both with water.

When the quake finally began to subside, a cry from one of the servants rang out through the house. 'Enemy soldiers are coming, my lord. A dozen of them.'

Janus looked into the soldier's eyes and knew what he must do. 'I need you to delay them, to buy me as much time as you can.'

The soldier paused for a moment, clenching his jaw, before replying: 'Of course, my lord.' He saluted once more, then turned on his heel.

'Primus!' cried Janus urgently.

Moments later, a short man in a simple tunic appeared, and bowed his head.

'Prepare the machine,' ordered Janus, striding towards the other end of the villa, expecting his servant to follow.

As they burst into another room, shouting could be heard behind them, followed closely by the clash of weapons and the familiar explosion of fire darts. Janus shot a nervous glance at his servant before clapping his hands to illuminate the room.

'What is to be done, my lord?' asked Primus.

Janus bent down over a cot and picked up a swaddled baby. 'Bring him, too,' he added, indicating an adjacent cot with his chin.

With the sounds of fighting growing ever closer, the two men rushed out of the room, each with a bundle in their arms. At the end of a dimly lit corridor, Janus halted before a door. He reached out a hand and placed his palm against a small rectangle on the wall. Immediately, the door slid silently open.

Once inside, Janus pointed to a corner of the room. 'Turn it on. I will enter the co-ordinates.'

By now, the child in Janus' arms had begun to cry. He set it down on a table against one wall and began tapping his fingers on a glass panel embedded in the table. Instantly, the panel became alive with tiny flashing lights, numbers and words flickering across the screen. Continuing to ignore the cries from both babies and the growing sounds of fighting outside, Janus worked his fingers furiously.

'The power is on,' said Primus, rushing over to his master. 'What now? What are you planning to do?'

'Place my daughter in the machine.'

'But my lord,' said the servant, a look of horror on his face.

'You said we were never to use it again.'

'Just do it!' Janus instantly regretted his show of temper and placed a hand on his servant's shoulder. 'Forgive me, my friend. But I have already lost my son. I will not lose my daughter, too. We must send her far away. Somewhere they ... somewhere *he* can never find her.'

Without warning, the earthquake returned, shaking the battered villa once more. All manner of objects clattered to the floor; chunks of plaster fell from the ceiling.

'They are here, my lord,' said a deep voice. The soldier had returned, his massive frame filling the doorway. His armour seemed to be even more battered, charred and blood-stained than before. 'I will hold them back as long as I can. But it will not be for long.' Without waiting for a response, he darted back out into the corridor.

'Quick,' ordered Janus, turning back to Primus. 'Put her in now. And the other child, too.'

'But my lord ...'

'We have no choice. Do it now.'

'Then you must go with them,' insisted Primus.

Janus smiled ruefully. 'No, my friend. We both know I can hold them off longer than you can. And besides, I must destroy everything after you have gone. I ask a great deal of you, for this is a one-way trip, I'm afraid.' He handed him a small wristband. 'And you will need this. Keep it safe.'

Primus looked at the object, then with barely a pause, he said: 'Then I go willingly.' He turned, picked up both bundles and headed for the corner of the room, where an ornate rectangular frame stood on a small platform. It resembled a doorframe, but contained no door and appeared to lead nowhere, with just the wall behind showing through. All around the frame, a tangle of cables was attached.

An explosion rent the air. Whether it had been caused by the firefight outside the room, or by part of the house collapsing from the earthquake was impossible to tell. But either way, the room shook even more violently than before. A tall cabinet toppled over, knocking Janus to the floor.

As he scrambled back to his feet, he saw three hooded men enter the room, their tattered crimson cloaks swaying as they moved. Janus pointed a clenched fist at them, and immediately, several finger-length bullets of flame shot towards them from his wristband. One of the fire darts burst into the shoulder of one of the men, sending him tumbling to the floor with a cry. The other two men ducked hurriedly out of harm's way, while the remaining darts fizzed past them and exploded into the wall behind.

Another violent tremor shook the house. A large section of the ceiling came tumbling down between Janus and his attackers. Through the clouds of dust filling the room, fire darts shot towards him. He flung himself to the floor, but not before one had struck him a glancing blow to his arm. The burning, searing pain took his breath away. Yet somehow, he managed to turn and unleash more darts of his own, before scrambling for cover behind the fallen cabinet.

As he lay gasping through the pain, he caught sight of Primus' anxious face. His servant was standing frozen in shock, the two screaming babies in his arms.

'Go, now!' screamed Janus, and leapt to his feet. He lunged towards the table against the side wall and began tapping furiously once more. He glanced over his shoulder, saw Primus turn and walk towards the structure in the corner of the room, and watched as a multi-coloured sphere emerged from the centre of the frame. The shimmering ball grew rapidly until it was taller than Primus, and then it swallowed the man, like a whale devouring a tiny fish. The sphere then burst into nothingness, leaving only the empty rectangular frame.

Janus felt a fire dart explode into his back. The pain was like nothing he had ever experienced. Fearing he was about to pass out, he strained with all his might to reach a hand across the screen in front of him and slammed his palm down onto the smooth glass. In response, a myriad of lights flickered across the screen. With that, he lost all control and slumped to the floor.

A swaying crimson cloak made its way towards him, its owner moving smoothly like a ghost, feet crunching on the debris littering the stone floor.

'Well, well, Janus. Look at you now,' said the figure in a chillingly calm voice, as it halted above him.

It was strange, but the pain was subsiding, although Janus could feel himself shaking violently. Or was it simply the earthquake continuing to rock the villa?

'You are too late, Bellona,' he hissed between clenched teeth. He did not need to see her face to know who it was. 'There's nothing left for you here.' He felt a strange sense of satisfaction wash over him.

'Get over here!' shouted the woman called Bellona. 'Make sure he lives.' She then dropped to her haunches, her face glaring down at Janus. 'Where is it? Where have you sent it this time?'

Janus turned to look up at her. Strands of her long hair had come loose and hung across her dirty but attractive face. 'You are a disgrace to our kind,' he said. Just a few seconds more and all the data on his computer would be erased, and all control would be passed to the *Temporum*.

She grabbed his chin in one of her long-fingered hands. 'Where is it?' she snarled.

'Somewhere you will never find it,' he replied. He forced himself to smile.

Bellona cursed and looked frantically around the room. Once more the ground shook, sending more objects to the floor and causing the lights in the room to wink and hum.

Janus could feel the energy draining from his body like water tumbling from a fallen bottle. One of Bellona's men was bent over him, examining his wounds, wiping away blood, running a small hand-held device across his body. By now, Janus could only move his eyes. He watched as Bellona bent down and picked up a long staff and then hurried back over to him.

'I believe this is yours,' she said, an ugly smile creasing her face.

Janus managed to summon a small chuckle. 'Without the *Temporum* that will not help you.'

As Janus' eyes began to close, he could see the fury return to the face of Bellona, and it made him smile one last time. *At least my daughter is now safe*, was the last ever thought that ran through the mind of Janus.

Chapter II

The Girl Who Did Not Belong

Present day

Spinning furiously, the wheels struggled to gain purchase on the dirt track. Mud and stones flew away from the rear of the car in a dirty cloud, until at last traction was gained and the vehicle shot off down the track, desperately trying to catch up with those in front.

From the comfort of his chair, Zak Scarlett stared intently at the screen in front of him, whilst simultaneously twisting the mini steering wheel left and right. The car he was controlling veered around obstacle after obstacle: a tree, a crash barrier, then another car.

'Zak!' called his mum from downstairs. 'Zak. Come on. You've got school.'

'Coming! I'll just be a minute.' Just a few more turns and he would be in front, then he would pause the game. He could always run to school if he had to. It was his birthday, after all, and he had been waiting months to get his hands on this particular game.

'Zak! Now!' ordered his mother. 'Arjun's here. Don't keep him waiting.'

In the next moment, Zak's car careered off the track, collided with a large tree and came to an abrupt halt.

'Oh, great!' Zak sighed. He then leapt out of his chair, picked up his school bag and hurried down the stairs, at the bottom of which he could see his best friend, Arjun, looking up at him with a grin on his face.

'Happy birthday, mate,' said Arjun, as they rushed out of the front door. 'So I take it you got it, then?'

'What?'

'*Ultimate Rally*, or whatever that new game's called.'

'Oh, yeah. It's great. I know racing games aren't your thing, but come round after school. I'll show you. I might even let you have a go, if you're lucky.'

Arjun laughed. 'I reckon there's no chance of that ... Hey, what's this bloke doing?'

As they strode along the street, a man was shuffling straight towards them. He was short with hunched shoulders and had an elderly, craggy face.

'Oh, not this guy again,' muttered Zak. 'I see him a lot, hanging round these streets, staring at me. Gives me the creeps. Let's cross over.'

Zak was about to cross the road, when the man stopped a few paces from him and called out. 'Zak. Zak Scarlett,' he said in a croaky voice.

Surprised and a little disconcerted to hear his name, Zak froze to the spot. The man had never spoken to him before. 'Yes. That's me. How do you know my name?'

'Happy birthday, Zak. I have a present for you.' Zak looked down as the man extended a hand towards him, holding a small package. 'Take it.'

Zak looked from the package to the man's oddly, leering face, which reminded him of a gargoyle. His eyes sparkled, either with warmth or madness, Zak could not decide which. 'Er, no thanks. Come on, Arjun. Let's go.'

The two boys were about to turn and walk away, when the man thrust the package even closer to Zak, preventing him from moving forwards. 'Take it, please. It is not mine. Now that you are thirteen, you have come of age. It belongs to you. I have guarded it safely all this time. But now you must have it, before my time is up.'

'Look, sorry, mate,' said Arjun, stepping between them. 'But my friend said he is not interested. No disrespect, but kindly leave us alone.'

The man shot Arjun a fierce look, before returning his unnerving gaze back towards Zak. 'At least see what it is. Let me show you.' Before Zak could respond, the man opened the package and took out what appeared to be a watch. He placed it in Zak's hand.

Zak was about to throw it back at the man when something stopped him. The moment the cold metal touched his palm, his curiosity was piqued. He studied the object. It was made of what looked like gold or bronze and was clearly very expensive. The face of the watch was almost the size of his palm and displayed the date and time in numbers rather than with the hands of a clock.

'What am I supposed to do with this?' asked Zak, without taking his eyes from the beautiful object in his hand.

'Keep it,' whispered the man. 'Keep it safe. When the time comes, you will know what to do.'

With his mouth open, unsure what to say, Zak stared at it. 'Who are you?' he asked at length. But when he looked up, the man was already shuffling away down the street.

'Well, that wasn't at all weird,' said Arjun. 'What are you going to do with it?'

Unable to take his eyes off the object and running a thumb over its smooth surface, Zak mumbled: 'Well, might as well keep it for now. Can't do any harm, can it?'

Later that morning, Zak had completely tuned out of Mrs Sullivan's history lesson. He was sitting towards the back of the classroom, studying the watch, which he had by now strapped around his wrist. The more he looked at it, the more he loved this mysterious present from a bizarre stranger. It was one of the coolest things he had ever seen. Somehow it seemed to be both very old and yet modern and stylish at the same time. The burnished metal with its intricate tiny patterns around the edge, together with the well-worn leather strap suggested it had been made long ago. Yet the digital display was like something he would have expected from the latest gadget to have come out of America. He could adjust the brightness just by tapping the smooth surface. And if he swiped a finger one way or the other, different menus could be accessed. Who on earth had made it? And why had it been given to him?

He was jolted back to the present by a friendly nudge to his elbow. He glanced across to Arjun, who was sitting next to him, grinning.

'Oi! Pay attention, birthday boy,' he whispered. He then leant over, looking at the watch. 'What is all that gibberish?'

Zak looked at his friend, puzzled. 'What do you mean?'

'All those weird symbols.'

Rather bemused, Zak looked from his friend to the watch face and back again. The display was pin-sharp, even in the bright light of the classroom. 'It says 19th of October, 10:17 a.m. Can't you read that?'

It was Arjun's turn to look askance at his friend. 'No, it doesn't. You're just making that up.'

Zak was about to reply, when Mrs Sullivan raised her voice and looked pointedly at the two boys. 'And so, when Vesuvius erupted on the 24th of October, 79 AD, Pompeii was buried under five metres of ash and pumice. All those people left in the city at the time would have died.' As she marched up and down in front of the class, she pressed her small remote control to change the pictures that appeared on the large screen behind her. Image after image of what looked like stone statues, as grey as ash, flashed up on the screen. 'These are plaster casts of just some of the many people who died that day. When their bodies decayed over time, they left an empty space in the ground, which archaeologists can fill with plaster. When the surrounding rock is then removed, we are left with these amazing statues of the people of Pompeii, frozen at the very moment of their deaths.'

'Seriously, why do we need to know about this stuff?' mumbled Zak, and returned his attention to the watch. The more he fiddled, the more functions he discovered, until suddenly a map appeared. Although the screen was barely five centimetres across, the map was somehow projecting beyond the edges of the watch, so that the image was much bigger and therefore easier to see. In the centre of the map was a tiny pulsing red dot. He soon realised this was indicating his current location, because when he pinched thumb and finger together across the map to zoom out, he recognised the UK, and the dot was still pulsing exactly where he was.

While Mrs Sullivan droned on and on about Pompeii this and Pompeii that, Zak absently moved the map about, drifting across Europe. As he did so, several other tiny red dots appeared on the map.

Whilst transfixed by the image on his wrist, his finger happened to rub against the side of the watch. The map vanished in an instant, making him jump. A thin ring of red appeared around the rim of the watch face and slowly began to pulse.

He heard gasps around the classroom and looked up. And there, standing next to Mrs Sullivan, was a girl his own age. A girl he had never seen before. She had not walked into the room, as far as he could tell, but had simply appeared from nowhere.

For a brief moment, both she and Mrs Sullivan looked as startled as one another. But then, much to Zak's amazement, both their faces relaxed.

'Go and sit back down, please, Maia,' said the teacher, matter-of-factly.

With a blank expression on her face, the girl called Maia walked down the aisle between desks and sat down in a spare chair near to Zak. He gawped at her, his mouth open.

'Now, where were we?' said Mrs Sullivan, turning back to her presentation. 'In the year 79 AD, the Emperor Titus had only just come to the throne ...'

Zak was incredulous. He looked around the room for signs that anyone else was as shocked as he was. But everyone else was just carrying on as though nothing had happened.

'Just a minute,' he said, and found himself rising to his feet.

'Zak Scarlett,' said the teacher, looking cross. 'Is there something you wish to say?'

'Well, yes, as a matter of fact there is. Am I the only one who saw what just happened? Is no one going to say anything?' He quickly became aware that everyone was staring at him as though he had gone mad. 'She,' he continued, pointing at the new girl, 'appears out of thin air—'

'Zak. Unless you have something important to add to this lesson, kindly sit back down.'

'But—'

'Sit down, or I will have no choice but to put you in detention.'

Realising he was getting nowhere, Zak slumped back onto his chair, aware of the faint sniggers around him.

'Are you all right, mate?' muttered Arjun.

'No, not really,' sighed Zak, shaking his head.

At the end of the lesson, Zak walked out of the classroom in a daze.

'What was that all about?' asked Arjun, as they sauntered along the corridor, which was crammed with other pupils.

Zak came to an abrupt stop and stared at his friend. 'Are you serious? That girl — Maia, was it? — appears out of nowhere, and you're all acting like nothing happened. Or like it happens all the time.'

'But nothing did happen,' replied Arjun with a confused frown.

Zak laughed, desperately looking for signs of mirth in his friend's face. But there were none. 'That girl — who is she and where did she come from?'

'You mean Maia Jones?'

'What? You know her?'

'What is this?' asked Arjun, his face contorting more and more. 'Are you playing some kind of weird joke? Because if you are, sorry, I don't get it.'

Zak grabbed his friend's sleeve. 'I have never seen that girl in my life.'

Arjun tried to respond, but just found himself laughing whenever he tried to speak. Eventually, he said: 'Of course you do. That's Maia Jones. We went to primary school with her. I seem to remember you tried to kiss her when you were about six.' Arjun laughed again.

A thought struck Zak. 'It must have something to do with that weird bloke giving me this watch this morning.' He looked at the puzzled expression on his friend's face. 'Oh, no! Don't tell me you don't remember that either.'

'Oh, I remember that all right. I just don't see what that has to do with Maia Jones. Look, if you fancy her that much just go and ask her out, simple as that.' Arjun's face had now hardened, his patience clearly running thin.

'What? No, it's not that. I just want to know where she came from.'

'Mate, I think I've had enough of this daft conversation for now. Come on, we've got maths to go to.'

And with that, Arjun turned and strode away, leaving Zak standing alone, his heart racing and his brain scrambled. It felt like the whole world around him had gone mad. Or was he the one who was now losing his mind?

It was breaktime and Zak was pacing up and down on his own at the edge of the playground. Arjun had already lost patience with him again and stormed off in a huff. But Zak refused to just let the subject drop. A girl had materialised out of nowhere in the middle of his history lesson and he was determined to figure out why.

He kept glancing over at Maia Jones, who stood a short distance away, chatting to two other girls. All three were smiling and laughing as though they had known one another for years. However, Zak knew the other two well, but had never once seen this new girl with them before.

There was nothing for it: he was going to have to confront her. As he strode towards her, he still had no idea what he was going to say.

'Oh, look, Maia,' said one of the girls. 'It's your new admirer.'

She turned to look at Zak with a wary frown. 'What do you want, Scarlett?'

He studied her for a moment, perplexed that she seemed to know who he was. She was clearly the same sort of age as he was and had dark hair held back in a ponytail. She was no more than average height and was wearing the correct school uniform. In short, there was nothing remarkable about her appearance at all. He kept staring, hoping that a moment of sudden recognition would fly into his head.

'Well, what is it you want?' she asked.

'I want to know who you are?'

'He wants to get to know you, Maia,' smirked one of the other girls. 'Look. His face is going scarlet.' The girl laughed at her own joke.

'That's not what I meant,' hissed Zak through bared teeth. 'Who are you and where did you come from? You may have fooled everyone else, but not me.'

'Oh, go away little boy,' she said. 'Go and bother someone else.'

Zak grabbed her arm. 'I know I have never seen you here before. So tell me: what is going on?'

'Ow! You're hurting me, you idiot!' She twisted her arm free, while her two friends stepped forward and pushed Zak away. Maia glared at him, red-faced. 'You need help, Scarlett. You need to see a doctor.'

Realising he was wasting his time, Zak turned and hurried away, with the girls' shouted taunts ringing in his ears.

It made no sense at all. Perhaps he *was* going mad. After all, he was the only one who seemed to think there was anything unusual going on.

Surely the day could not possibly get any weirder.

Chapter III

The Hooded Men

Later that day, Zak found he was daydreaming even more than he had been in the history lesson. Then again, he did have a lot to daydream about. A strange man had given him a mysterious watch on his way to school, and then an unknown girl had appeared out of the blue in the classroom. A girl that everyone seemed to know but him. The two events had to be connected. But how? And why?

While his mind was racing, the classroom fell completely silent.

At first, Zak just thought he had drifted off and blocked out the teacher's voice. But as the lack of noise began to encroach on his consciousness, he looked up towards the front of the classroom and started, almost falling off his chair. Mr Stokes, the teacher, was frozen like a statue with one arm stuck out. Not even his eyes were blinking.

Then, when he began looking around, he noticed that everyone else seemed to have frozen. It was like looking at a room full of wax dummies. Were they all playing some bizarre trick on him?

'What the ...?'

There was a gasp to his right, a girl's voice. When he jolted round to look, Maia Jones was looking around, horrified. 'What's happening?' she said, putting a hand to her mouth. She looked as startled as him.

'You!' said Zak. He stood up to take a closer look at his fellow pupils, then turned back to Maia. 'This is something to do with you, isn't it?'

'What?' she said, looking at him with what appeared to be genuine astonishment, even fear. 'What are you talking about?

What is going on?'

Zak snorted. 'You tell me.' She was feigning surprise, she had to be.

He walked out from behind his desk and headed towards Mr Stokes. 'Sir? Can you hear me, sir?' he waved a hand in front of the teacher's face, but there was no reaction, none at all. He felt for a pulse but could feel nothing. He then found he could move the teacher's arms and hands as easily as if the man were made of plasticine. So he proceeded to place one of his hands on a hip and thrust the other into the air, index finger pointing skyward. When he stood back to admire his handiwork, he chuckled at the teacher's newly acquired disco-pose.

'What are you doing?' asked Maia, moving alongside him. 'Are you not scared by all this?'

'I don't know. Should I be scared? You tell me.'

'Oh, you're insufferable,' said Maia, rolling her eyes and folding her arms.

Zak picked up a black marker pen from the teacher's desk and then drew a small square moustache on Mr Stokes's top lip. He chuckled again, then mumbled: 'I think I must be having the weirdest dream ever.'

'What has got into you, Zak? Why do you think this has anything to do with me?' asked Maia. Her voice sounded like she was fighting to suppress panic. 'Tell me, please.'

'Because first of all, this morning, some weird bloke gives me this thing,' he replied, thrusting his wrist with the watch on towards her. As he did so, he noticed the thin red ring around the watch face was still pulsing. 'Then you appear, someone I've never seen before, yet everyone else says I should know who you are. And now finally, everyone in the school freezes except you and me. So don't try to tell me these things are not related. And don't pretend you know me. I have never seen you before today. So what could you possibly know about me?'

She stared back at him coldly, her cheeks flushed. Then a

single tear rolled down her cheek, and immediately, Zak regretted his aggressive tone. He looked away.

'You're Zak Albert Scarlett,' she said suddenly. 'Albert after your uncle. You live in Mead Crescent, number 26 or 27 I seem to remember, with your mum and dad. Your mum's name is Pat. She used to be a T.A. at our primary school, but now works in an office in town. You've always been mad about cricket and play for the school and a local club. Your best friend since the age of five is Arjun Chaudhry. Oh, and when you were six or seven, you fell off a climbing frame. Everyone thought you'd broken your hand, but when you got to hospital, they couldn't find anything wrong.' She stood staring at him with arms folded defiantly.

It was all correct.

'What ...? How ...?'

Maia's face suddenly looked surprised. 'Look!' she said, pointing over his shoulder. She then rushed past him towards the windows.

He followed her and looked out. They were on the first floor, overlooking the empty playground below. Empty, save for a ball of blue and grey smoke that was growing and swirling rapidly, hovering just above the ground. When it had become the size of a small building, there was a momentary blinding flash, causing Zak to close his eyes.

When he reopened them, the sphere had vanished and there, standing in the middle of the playground, were five tall figures, wearing long crimson capes, which rippled in the breeze. Each person wore a hood pulled over the head. One of the figures was holding a pole as tall as the man himself. But it was not their striking appearance that caught Zak's attention, but rather their movement. All of them were moving their heads swiftly left and right, clearly surveying their surroundings, urgently looking for something or someone.

'Just when I thought the day couldn't get any crazier,' muttered Zak.

'How come they can move?' asked Maia.

Zak was about to suggest that maybe she should know, but he thought better of it. Maia had something to do with all this, he just knew it. But her reaction, the emotion in her face, suggested she genuinely knew nothing at all. Or was she just simply good at acting?

As they stared at the figures below, another man shuffled into view, short and hunched over.

'I know him,' cried Zak. 'It's the man who gave me this watch.'

The old man stopped a few metres away from the group of hooded figures and began waving his arms about and shouting at them. In response, one of the men pulled back part of his cloak and raised a bare, muscular arm towards the old man, pointing a balled fist at him at arm's length. With his arm perfectly rigid, and with the old man still croaking harsh words at him, the hooded man dipped his fist down a short distance. Instantly, what looked like a small dart of fire shot out from the wristband the man was wearing. It struck the old man, who froze for a fraction of a second, before disappearing into a puff of white mist.

Zak felt his chest go tight, his breathing stop for a moment or two, and heard Maia gasp beside him. Before he could speak, he saw the hooded figure with the tall staff raise it into the air and then point it straight up at the two of them. The five hooded figures then began marching swiftly towards the school building.

'I think we'd better hide,' said Zak.

He turned and scampered past Mr Stokes and his classmates, still frozen like statues, and out into the corridor. His legs felt like jelly, while his heart was pounding so fast it felt as though it might explode. What had started out feeling like a thoroughly bizarre dream was fast turning into a horrible nightmare. What on earth did those men want? And why had they killed the old man? Perhaps they were after the watch. Should he just throw it at them and run away? But what if it was not the watch they were after?

At the end of the corridor, he skidded to a halt, unsure which way to go next.

'We should go this way,' said a breathless Maia. 'Down to the teachers' offices. We can hide down there.' Without waiting for Zak to respond, she turned and raced towards the stairs.

'How do you know your way around this school?' asked Zak, catching up with her, as they hurtled down the steps.

'Oh, will you give it a rest!' she snapped. 'I've been at this school as long as you have.'

'No, you haven't,' mumbled Zak.

They stumbled out through the fire doors, into the corridor on the ground floor.

'Stop!' yelled a booming voice, which echoed behind them.

Zak turned to his left and saw the crimson-hooded figures emerging into the corridor, no more than twenty paces away. He froze in terror.

'We have been hunting you these past seventeen years,' continued the voice. 'You will not escape us again.'

As the figure strode towards them, Zak noticed he was pointing directly at Maia. And on his bare forearm, he could see the man had a large tattoo of what looked like a chunky hammer, the kind the Norse god Thor was always shown wielding.

Her face full of terror, Maia turned and ran. Zak quickly followed her. She may have been lying about who she was, but the men chasing her had just killed a defenceless old man. So it struck Zak in that moment, that if anyone was in the wrong, it was not Maia.

They burst through another set of fire doors. On the other side, Zak noticed an empty room, its door held open by a chair. He grabbed the chair and threw it against the fire doors, before sprinting off after Maia. Then, when he rounded a corner, he nearly collided with a trolley covered in books next to a teacher, as lifeless as an abandoned manikin. Quickly, he grabbed the handles of the trolley and swung it out into the middle of the corridor and ran some more.

Peering over his shoulder as he moved, he looked back just in time to see one of the hooded men stumble into the trolley, stagger and then right himself against the wall. As he did so, his hood fell back to reveal his face. Zak only saw it for a second or two, but the image stayed with him. The man was thirty or forty with short, black hair and stubble all over his chin. He had a tanned complexion, and although he looked somewhat ruggedly handsome, he wore an angry, sullen look, which Zak guessed was never far away.

A short distance ahead of him, Zak heard Maia yelp. Just in front of her, a door was opening and a crimson cape was beginning to appear. She and Zak both came to an abrupt halt in the middle of the corridor, their pursuers behind and now in front of them. There was only one thing left to do: try to barricade themselves into one of the rooms.

Zak grabbed Maia's arm and pulled her back. 'This way, quick!' He had just seen the unmistakable door of Mrs Sullivan's office, covered as it was in small badges, pictures and other assorted souvenirs from her travels. He knew that of all the small offices nearby, hers would be the most cluttered, the most crammed with boxes and other items they could use.

He pushed open the door and, still holding her forearm, dragged Maia through the doorway.

There was a dazzling explosion of light, like coming out of a dark cave into brilliant sunlight. Zak jammed his eyelids shut, and felt his balance failing, as though he were falling.

The next thing he knew, he could hear a seagull crying overhead, and voices, dozens of voices, chatting and laughing and shouting. When he opened his eyes, they were standing in a doorway, their backs to the door, looking out onto a cobbled street, which was bathed in bright sunshine. People were everywhere, walking past them on the pavement in both directions. A horse and cart clattered and creaked past on the cobbled road.

Whilst it was good to see ordinary people moving again after the frozen school, Zak immediately noticed that most of those around them were wearing tunics and sandals. One or two men ambled along in togas, whilst the women with them wore long, elegant, flowing dresses. And there were no cars or motorbikes or bicycles. Just people on foot, and horses, mules and carts.

'What on earth ...?' began Maia, but then words seemed to fail her.

'I'm either going completely mad,' said Zak, 'or Mrs Sullivan has a whole Roman town hidden in her office.'

Chapter IV

Pompeii

'Are you two actually going to buy anything?' demanded a voice from behind them. 'Because if you're not, kindly move along.'

Zak turned around and realised that he and Maia, in their state of utter bewilderment, had wandered out onto the pavement. They were now standing outside a bakery. A man was frowning at them from behind his counter, on which more than a dozen large, round loaves of bread were stacked in neat piles. His shop opened directly onto the street. Zak smiled nervously and mumbled an apology as they moved away from the bakery.

'If only we had the right money,' said Zak, inhaling the comforting smell of freshly baked bread.

'Yeah, and then at least we could buy some new clothes,' added Maia. Her eyes flitted about nervously.

No sooner had she spoken, than Zak, too, began to notice they were attracting a growing number of puzzled looks. More and more people were turning to stare at them. The dark blazers of their school uniform were, it seemed, making them stand out more than if they had been walking down the street naked.

'Come on,' said Zak. 'Let's cross over there, into the shade.'

To get from one side of the road to the other, there was a set of large stepping stones, the gaps between them wide enough to allow the wheels of the carts to pass through. As he stepped from one to another, Zak looked down and could immediately see why they needed such a crossing. As well as the curbs being much higher than he was used to back home, down in the road, a steady trickle of water was flowing across the flagstones and around all manner of debris: piles of horse manure, leaves, twigs, broken pots and other pieces of rubbish.

Once over the other side, Zak and Maia moved into the shade of an awning that was hanging over the pavement in front of a shop. At least in the shadows, their dark blazers were not quite so out of place.

Zak puffed out his cheeks. This was all too much to take in. 'Where do you suppose we are?' he asked.

'Well,' said Maia, leaning out to look all around, 'it looks like Pompeii to me. Look, that has to be Vesuvius in the distance.' She was pointing to a gap between two low buildings.

Zak followed her gaze, and there, rising high into the sky like a giant natural pyramid, was the unmistakable shape of a volcano, no more than a few miles away. The sheer size of it took his breath away.

He closed his eyes and rubbed his forehead. 'This doesn't make any sense. And what did that man mean, back at school, when he said he'd been hunting you for seventeen years?'

'Oh, Zak. I don't know. I really don't,' sighed Maia. She stared up into the sky, then closed her eyes. She looked close to tears. 'I'm only thirteen, like you. I've not been alive for seventeen years. He must have thought I was someone else.'

Zak looked at her but said nothing. Instead, he turned back to the street, trying to make sense of it all. There was a constant chatter from the dozens of shoppers ambling past, while others were shouting out the prices of their goods for sale. As he watched and listened, it occurred to him that, apart from the unusual clothing that everyone was wearing, it could have been the scene from any busy market back home.

But then everything went silent, everyone froze.

'Oh, no! Not again,' hissed Zak.

His eyes darted up and down the street. From what he could see, every living thing had stopped moving or making any sound. Even a seagull overhead was frozen in mid-flight. An eerie silence had descended. There was no noise, no wind, no movement. It was as though someone were able to pause time. Except that somehow Zak and Maia seemed to be immune.

As were their pursuers.

After only a few seconds of total silence, footsteps and voices could be heard, drawing ever closer. With all the frozen people around them, it was impossible to see where the voices were coming from. But Zak did not need to see them to know it was the men in crimson capes again. He and Maia turned and ran in the opposite direction.

With so many figures standing motionless on the narrow pavement, moving fast was impossible. They had to constantly dodge left and right around people who stood as still as clothed statues. There was a woman in a colourful, flowing dress holding a child's hand. Then two men in togas frozen in mid-conversation. And two more men next to a cart, paused at the moment they had been busy unloading large and clearly heavy clay pots.

Briefly, Zak contemplated jumping into the road to avoid the pedestrians. But even there, several carts and horses would have certainly made progress just as slow.

Realising they needed to speed up, Zak decided he had to start pushing people aside. Yet even though they were being chased, the last thing he wanted to do was start shoving people off the high curb and down into the road. But when he glanced behind him, he saw with horror that their pursuers were doing just that, ploughing their way along the pavement, toppling people over left and right.

'These shops are too small,' gasped Maia. 'There's nowhere to hide.'

'Let's try down here,' suggested Zak.

They had arrived at a crossroads, with much narrower roads spearing off at right angles. He turned left and darted down the road, which was largely in shadow. At least here, there were far fewer people standing in their way.

'I wish I'd paid more attention in Mrs Sullivan's class,' said

Zak between great gasps of air. 'If this really is Pompeii, I might have some idea where I was going.'

'Wait!' cried Maia, bending over to put her hands on her knees. 'We need to take our blazers off. We stand out like sore thumbs.'

It was true, realised Zak. All the people dotted around them were wearing mostly colourful clothing: light blue or green dresses; light brown or white tunics; red togas. No one was wearing anything remotely like their charcoal grey uniforms.

Zak agreed and whipped off his blazer and hurriedly draped it around the shoulders of a man nearby, while Maia did the same. With footsteps echoing behind them, they turned and sprinted away.

At the next junction they turned left, then left again.

'I think we should go back to the busy street,' suggested Zak, panting so hard he was struggling to speak. 'Might actually be easier to hide in the crowds.'

Anguish was written across Maia's red face. 'What if we run right back into them?'

'You got a better idea?'

Without waiting for a response, Zak ran as fast as he could towards the sunlight up ahead, which indicated the much wider main road. Once there, he paused for a moment to look in both directions. 'This way,' he said, and turned right.

He had only gone a few metres when he staggered to a halt.

'What is it?' asked Maia.

'Two of them coming this way. Back the other way, quick.'

They turned around and ran. By now, Zak's heart was hammering, his lungs and leg muscles screaming at him to stop.

Up ahead, he saw more people being toppled into the road, and glimpses of more crimson cloaks flying towards them like red dragons. He stopped abruptly, his eyes darting in all directions, frantically looking for a way out.

'Quick, down here,' he said, grabbing Maia's arm and pulling her off the high curb and into the road. They both nearly tripped and fell when they landed, but somehow managed to keep their balance. There were two carts close together outside a shop where several men were frozen in the middle of unloading their cargo. Zak pulled Maia down with him between the two wooden vehicles and, gasping for breath, pressed a finger to his lips.

As they sat there for several interminable seconds, they could hear the footsteps converging on them. Desperately, Zak tried to fill his lungs with air, whilst at the same time making no sound. He closed his eyes, fearing the worst.

Suddenly, noise filled his ears in a flood. Talking, shouting, hooves clopping on the flagstones, metal-rimmed wheels screeching, seagulls crying above. If a few minutes previously it had seemed as though someone had abruptly pressed pause, so now that person had apparently pressed play once more, and the town had sprung back into life. All around them was movement and sound, and the smell of cooking mingling with the odour from the muck in the road.

This was their chance. Zak peered through the spokes of the wheels. Just down the road a commotion had begun. People who had just been shoved over were now remonstrating with one of the hooded men. More and more people were joining in, others were turning to see what all the fuss was about.

'If we're quick,' said Zak, 'we can make that side street without being seen. Come on.'

Hunkering down low, they hurried out of their hiding place between the two carts and darted into the shadows of the side street. Once there, they ran again, swerving around people who were once more on the move.

Zak was hurtling along the pavement, not daring to look back. To his right was the narrow, cobbled road, to his left a long, plain brick wall. Without warning, two figures emerged out of a large doorway set into the wall. Zak was so close that he had to leap out of the way to avoid colliding with them. In so doing, he lost his balance and fell into the road, tumbling over and landing in a heap on his back.

'By Castor! Look where you're going,' said a rather snooty voice.

Maia jumped off the curb and crouched down next to Zak. 'Are you okay?' she asked.

Gingerly, Zak sat up and examined his hands, one of which was covered with blood. 'I think so,' he mumbled. He then looked up, past Maia and saw two people staring down at him. One was a girl of about their age, dressed in a long, pale green dress. With her blond hair hanging down in plaited ringlets, Zak would have considered her rather pretty, if it were not for the fact that she stood frowning down at him in a most superior fashion. Next to her, stood a slightly older, taller boy. He was black with close-cropped hair and wore a simple tunic and a rather indifferent expression.

'Are you all right?' asked the girl, though her face suggested she was not at all bothered one way or the other.

Zak smiled as warmly as he could. 'I'm fine.' He glanced nervously down the narrow road towards the busy street, which crossed at right angles a short distance away. A steady stream of people and carts was strolling past along the small section of sunlit road that was visible. At any second, he expected to see hooded men charging towards him.

'Look, is there any chance you could help us?' he continued, 'We need somewhere to hide.'

'Why? What in the name of Jupiter have you done?'

'We haven't done anything,' snapped a glaring Maia before Zak could reply. 'These ... these men are chasing us, and we don't know why.'

For a moment or two, the girl stood looking down at them, her proud chin in the air.

Maia pulled Zak to his feet. 'Come on, Zak. We haven't got time for this.'

But as Zak stared into the girl's sparkling blue eyes, her face broke into a mischievous grin. 'This sounds like fun. I think we shall help them, Dexter,' she said, without turning to look at the boy next to her.

'There they are!' cried a voice, echoing down the narrow street.

Zak turned his head in time to see three of the hooded men standing at the top of the road. As they moved out of the bright sunshine of the main thoroughfare and into the shade of the narrow side street, they became dark, phantom-like shapes, their capes billowing behind them.

The Roman girl turned sharply around and rapped on the door from which she had just come. 'Felix, open up. Dexter, do what you can to slow those men down. Whatever it takes.'

As the large wooden door in the wall in front of the girl slowly creaked inwards, the boy called Dexter leapt to a section of the windowless wall where several thin jars were stacked together vertically. As tall as a man's leg, each one bulged out in the middle, before tapering to a narrow point at the bottom. Dexter began knocking them over one by one, sending them rolling into the road in front of the oncoming men, who staggered to an abrupt halt. One of the jars smashed into many large fragments, spilling a dark liquid over the flagstones.

The girl ushered them all through the open doorway, before the man called Felix, a tall, muscled hulk of a man, slammed the sturdy wooden door in the faces of the crimson-cloaked men.

Only then did Zak realise he had been holding his breath for what had seemed like the last minute or two.

Stepping off the street and into the house was like passing through a gateway into an entirely different world. Outside there had just been a long, windowless brick wall, with nothing but a large wooden door in the middle of it. But inside, there was a vast house, with what seemed like an endless number of lavishly decorated rooms spread over two floors. And the whole house was arranged around a large central garden full of small trees and statues.

'So tell me: who exactly were those men chasing you?' asked the Roman girl.

She, Zak and Maia were sitting around a small table in the middle of the sunny garden. Dexter was standing, as sullen as before, at the girl's shoulder.

Several narrow paths radiated out from the small central area where they were sitting, meandering past numerous small trees and shrubs. A fountain was splashing its soothing music just behind them.

While a servant was busy bandaging Zak's cut hand, he could not help but keep looking at the glimpses of the house he could see through the trees and bushes. Having seen the strange and terrible weapon their pursuers had used on the old man in the playground, he was still nervous. He expected to see those hooded men come crashing through the walls at any moment.

'Don't worry,' smiled the girl, following his gaze. 'They won't get you in here. And if they did manage to knock the door down, my uncle is one of the *duoviri* who run the city council. He could have a hundred soldiers here in no time.'

But even that failed to comfort Zak. Whatever technology the hooded men possessed, it was clearly not from ancient Rome.

'As I told you,' said Maia, sipping the ice-cold cup of water brought to her by one of the girl's servants, 'we have no idea who they are, or why they were chasing us.'

The girl gave a thin smile as if she did not fully believe Maia. 'You're not from round here, are you?' she continued. 'Those are strange clothes you are wearing.'

Maia and Zak exchanged a nervous look. Zak was still wearing the white long-sleeved shirt and charcoal trousers, whilst Maia had the white blouse and pleated skirt of their school uniform. If these people really were ancient Romans, he realised, he and Maia must have looked very odd indeed.

The servant had finished tending to Zak's wounds and left.

'Thank you,' he called out to the woman's back as she hurried away. The woman did not respond and the girl gave Zak a queer look. 'We're ... er ... from ...' he began, not really knowing what to say.

'We're from Britain,' Maia cut in quickly.

'Ah, that explains it. I've heard the Britons have an odd way of dressing. But you speak excellent Latin, by the way. I detect no accent.'

'What?' said Zak. 'What do you mean, Latin? Hang on. How come you can understand English?'

'English? What's English?'

'You know, the language we're speaking now.'

'We're speaking Latin.'

'Latin? No, we're not. I don't speak a word of Latin.'

'What *is* the matter with you?' asked the girl, a frown creasing her forehead.

Zak felt Maia tap her foot several times against his under the table, apparently trying to get his attention. 'I'm sorry,' she said quickly. 'It's been a long and very frightening day. We're both a little tired and confused, aren't we, Zak?' She briefly caught Zak's eye, clearly trying to warn him to keep quiet.

'Er, yes, that's right,' he said, downing his drink. 'Sometimes I forget just how great I am at languages.'

Maia gave him a withering look.

The girl raised a hand, clicked her fingers and said: 'More water for our guests.'

Immediately, the boy behind her scurried off and returned moments later with a jug of fresh water. After Dexter had filled his cup, Zak looked at him, smiled and thanked him. The boy said nothing.

'Tell cook to prepare some food, Dexter,' ordered the girl. 'A light snack.'

As Zak watched the tall boy hurry off and disappear into the house, he said: 'Not very talkative your friend, is he?'

The girl chuckled. 'He's not my friend. That's Dexter. He's just a common slave.'

'A slave?' gasped Zak.

'Yes. My father's idea of a stupid joke. I said I was bored and wanted some friends of my own age to talk to. So he bought me a slave. A fifteen-year-old Nubian boy. Ridiculous.'

'Look, sorry for being stupid again,' said Zak. 'But where exactly are we?'

'This is the house of Aulus Cassius Fronto. I'm his daughter, Cassia.'

'Nice to meet you, Cassia. I'm Zak and this is Maia. But I meant, what town are we in?'

She laughed again. 'You Britons really are strange people, aren't you? This is Pompeii. Where else would we be?'

At that moment, the ground began to shake. The cups on the table before them started to rattle across the wooden surface, until one of them toppled over and fell to the floor. The trees around them shook, scattering autumnal leaves everywhere.

Terrified, Zak leapt to his feet, while Cassia remained calmly in her chair, watching him with an amused smile.

'Who is the emperor at the moment?' asked Maia.

Zak shot her a puzzled look. What an odd question to ask at a time like this, he thought. But then he noticed she looked just as anxious as him.

'Why, Titus of course. Vespasian died earlier this year. Hadn't you heard?'

Maia had gone as white as a sheet. 'And what is today's date?'

'Well, let me see. Today is the fourteenth day before the kalends of November, if I remember correctly.'

Though he could not explain it, Zak instantly knew that meant the 19th of October, his birthday. The same date as they had left the school.

Maia looked at Zak, her face horrified. 'Five days before the eruption,' she mumbled.

Chapter V

The Mysterious Watch

The tremor lasted no more than a minute or two. But when it had eventually finished, Zak was still shaking, his palms sweaty. Just what else was he going to experience that day? Some birthday this was turning into, he thought.

'There. It's finished now,' said Cassia, still in her chair looking up at Zak and Maia with the hint of a smile.

'You don't seem too concerned,' said Maia.

'Oh, you get used to them when you live around here. We've been getting a lot recently. Some worse than others. There was a really big one here seventeen years ago. Nearly destroyed the city apparently. I'm only thirteen, so it was before my time. But there's been nothing that bad since I've been alive. Anyway, let me go and see where that wastrel Dexter is. Wait here.'

Zak watched her glide elegantly towards the pillared colonnade, which ran around the edge of the entire garden. He then began pacing up and down, adrenaline still making his heart pound.

'What are we going to do, Zak?' asked Maia.

'I don't know,' he mumbled in reply. He felt scared and angry and confused. 'How come she can understand us?' he said, suddenly rounding on Maia. 'And how come we can understand her?'

'How should I know?' replied Maia with a shrug.

Zak snorted. 'I thought you might say that.'

'What's that supposed to mean?' said Maia, glaring back at him.

'When are you going to tell me what on earth is going on here?' he demanded, pointing at her aggressively.

'Look, I know as much as you do ...'

'Ha! You expect me to believe that? You're keeping something from me, I can tell.'

Maia turned away and crossed her arms. 'Well, you can think what you like.'

But that was just it: Zak no longer knew what to think. He just wanted to go to sleep, to wake up the next day and find it had all been a horrible dream.

After they had eaten a small meal of bread, olives, grapes, cheese and dates, Cassia found some clothes for Zak and Maia. If someone were indeed after them, she reasoned, they would need to change out of their highly conspicuous clothing.

Zak was surprised at the footwear. He had expected sandals with his toes exposed, but instead, one of the slaves gave him a pair of leather boots, which covered his ankles and were laced up at the front. They were surprisingly comfortable and well made. He was less impressed with the tunic.

'I feel like I'm wearing a dress,' he said, as he came out of a small room and met Maia under the roof of the covered walkway at the edge of the garden. He was wearing a plain, short-sleeved tunic which ended just above his knees. Around his waist was a thin leather belt with a small pouch attached to one side, which was barely visible under the folds of the loose-fitting tunic.

Maia grinned. 'It suits you. Now if you just grow your hair long, you'll look very pretty.'

'Oh, very funny. At least you look normal,' he added, looking at her new, sleeveless blue dress which flowed down to her ankles.

'Yeah, not ideal if we have to do any more running though, is it?' She then looked at Zak's bare arms. 'You might want to hide that,' she added, pointing at the strange, chunky watch on his wrist. 'If anyone sees that, they'll ask all sorts of awkward questions.'

'Yeah, you're probably right,' he replied, staring at it. 'At least it's stopped flashing for now. It had a red ring around it just before you and those men turned up.' He took it off and was about to tuck it into the leather pouch on his belt when Maia asked to have a look at it.

'It says 0079,' she said. 'It shows the 19th of October 16:27, which, looking at the angle of the sun, is probably about right. But what does 0079 mean?'

'Oh, I was fiddling with that in Mrs Sullivan's class. I changed ... Oh, crikey.'

'It's 79 AD, isn't it?' said Maia. 'That's the year we're in now. The year Pompeii gets destroyed.'

They looked at one another, eyes wide with shock. 'Mrs Sullivan was rabbiting on about Pompeii,' added Zak. 'I tuned out and began playing with this thing. I found I could change all the numbers, including what must be the year. Without really thinking, I must have changed it to 79. Probably because that was the year she kept mentioning.'

Maia laughed.

'What is it?' asked Zak.

'All this time you've been blaming me, demanding to know what's going on, when it was you and your watch all along that brought us here.'

Now it was Zak's turn to laugh, a dismissive, mirthless laugh. How stupid did she think he was? 'But then you've known that all along, haven't you?'

Maia's face dropped in an instant. 'What's that supposed to mean?'

'You tell me.'

'Oh, for goodness' sake. What is your problem, Zak?'

'What is my problem?' he began, raising his voice. But then he quickly stopped himself, glancing up and down the colonnade, and lowered his voice to a harsh whisper. 'I'm stuck here in Pompeii two thousand years ago, five days before Vesuvius is due to erupt with no way of getting back home. And it is all because of you and whatever it is you're not telling me.'

'I don't have time for this,' muttered Maia, turning away from him. She was about to storm off when Cassia appeared before them, her sweet smile quickly turning to a frown.

'For two friends, you two certainly argue a lot,' she said.

'We are not friends,' mumbled Zak. 'We're just two people who've been thrown together for some strange reason.' He glared at Maia, who scowled back at him.

Cassia glanced from one to the other. 'Come on. Let's go for a walk around the garden, while it's still light.' She put an arm through one of Maia's and began walking her towards one of the small paths that led into the formal garden. 'I've always wanted a friend of my own age and gender, Maia. And I can already tell you and I are going to be very good friends. Zak,' she added, looking back over her shoulder, 'you can keep Dexter company, and talk about ... well, whatever it is that boys talk about.'

While Cassia and Maia walked off, arm in arm, Zak looked at Dexter and tried to smile at him, but the boy continued to avoid eye contact. Though the slave boy already made him feel a little uncomfortable, Zak felt compelled to make conversation.

'Thank you, Dexter,' he said, as they followed the two girls into the garden. 'For helping us get away from those men in the street.'

'You're welcome.' His tone was polite, but flat, devoid of any feeling.

'Do you have any idea who they were?'

'No, I'm afraid I don't.'

'Do you think they were soldiers?'

Dexter shrugged. 'I don't know.'

Zak smiled wryly to himself. The conversation was going nowhere, so he decided to change the subject. 'So what do you think of Cassia?'

'Think?' Dexter replied, finally glancing at Zak. 'I'm a slave. I'm not allowed to think.'

The bitterness in his voice made Zak swallow nervously. 'Sorry,' he said eventually. 'It's just ... we don't have slaves where I come from. Slavery was abolished a long time ago.'

'Sounds like paradise.'

Zak chuckled. 'It's not bad, I suppose. But it's far from paradise. So what's Cassia like? Is she cruel or nice to you?'

'Forgive me, but it is not my place to speak of my mistress.'

Stopping abruptly, Zak touched Dexter lightly on the arm to halt him, too. He then glanced down the garden, where Cassia was chatting away with Maia several paces in front of them. They were partially hidden behind the gnarled branches of an olive tree.

'Look, Dexter,' he whispered. 'I don't know Cassia at all. I've never met her before today. I don't know whether I can trust her yet. So I'm certainly not going to tell her anything you tell me now, am I?'

Finally, Dexter looked down at Zak. He was only two years older than Zak, but his height made him look much older. 'All right. She has been kind to me so far, compared to my previous owner, who beat me repeatedly. But if you want to know what I think of her ... she is a rather arrogant, spoilt little girl, who has no idea just how privileged she is. Mainly because her evil father keeps her locked away in this house. She calls it her prison. But a luxurious house this size could only be called a prison by someone who has only ever known obscene wealth. There, I've said it now. I will probably get a good lashing when she hears what I've said. But it felt good to say it.' The flicker of a smile twitched across his face.

Zak grinned. 'That's more like it. And don't worry: she won't hear it from me.'

'And what are you two talking about?' said a voice behind Zak.

When he spun round, he saw Cassia and Maia gliding elegantly towards them in their long dresses. 'Oh, just boy stuff,' he replied with a smirk.

'Well, I insist you both stay for dinner tonight,' said Cassia. 'And I'll have two rooms made up for you. You must stay the night. Then, in the morning, we can think what to do next.'

Having just heard Dexter describe Cassia's father as evil, Zak quickly asked: 'What about your parents? They won't want strangers staying in their house, surely.'

Cassia's innocent smile dropped to a frown. 'Oh, don't worry about them. My father's in Rome, away on business. And my stepmother always goes with him. It's just me and the household slaves here at the moment.'

'They didn't want to take you with them?' asked Maia.

'I didn't want to go,' she replied. Then when she saw Maia and Zak's puzzled looks, she added: 'Don't worry. They won't be missing me. And I certainly don't miss them. But I won't bore you with that now. Dexter, go and ask cook to prepare dinner. I for one am starving.'

After the evening meal, Zak and Maia retired to their respective rooms. Although the meal had been filling and at times quite tasty, Zak had been too afraid to ask what they were eating. Judging by Maia's expression, she too had decided it was best not to know what was on their plates. Zak was certain one of the meat dishes was a mouse in sauce, and another course had been some sort of small bird. However, after such a tiring and stressful day, he had decided it was best to just eat up and then go to bed.

As he lay on the bed, lost in thought, his eyes wandered around the small room. The oil lamp by the side of his bed cast flickering shadows across the brightly coloured walls. There were large rectangles of red, blue and yellow. And in the middle of some of those rectangles were small paintings of figures, animals or trees. It was all expertly painted, but just so alien to what he was used to.

He felt a stiffness in his bandaged hand, so he carefully unwound the cloth to look at his wound. To his astonishment, his hand was clean. There were no marks, no scars, no sign of injury at all. He began to wonder whether he had imagined it. But no, he remembered the gash on his palm, with blood dripping all over his hand. He tossed the bandage across the room. None of this made any sense.

He fished out the watch from his pocket and stared at it. The guttering light from the lamp danced across its surface, making the casing look like liquid bronze.

Once again, he played with the settings, calling up maps and calendars and other mysterious sets of numbers. He could read it easily enough, and so could Maia apparently. But Arjun had said he could only see gibberish. And now it seemed he could speak and understand Latin.

He sighed and stared at the object in his hands. What on earth was it? How had it managed to transport him and Maia to here of all places? And why had that old man given it to him and not to some other stranger? He now wished he had refused to take it or had just thrown it away in the gutter.

And then there was Maia. What was her part in all this?

His head hurt, a headache born of confusion, stress and fear. He needed to rest. So he put out the lamp, closed his eyes and drifted off to sleep. A sleep full of dreams where strange, faceless men in hooded capes chased him wherever he went.

Chapter VI

The Head of Janus

The next morning, Zak awoke with a start from yet another disturbing dream. For several minutes, he lay curled up in his bed not daring to open his eyes. The more the memories of the previous day came flooding back, the more he just wanted to stay there, hiding under the blanket.

Maybe it had all been a weird dream, and the moment he opened his eyes he would see his familiar bedroom once again. His desk would be there, with his laptop and the new *Ultimate Rally* game he had received for his birthday. He would then go to school, see Arjun and tell him about the most amazing dream he had just had. They would both laugh about it, and then life would just carry on as before.

But, then again, what if he opened his eyes and everything had frozen once more? What if those men in their hooded capes were standing over his bed?

A knock at the door made him instinctively open his eyes. He was still in the brightly painted bedroom, which briefly made his heart drop; but at least he could hear soothing birdsong drifting in through the small window. If the birds were singing, he thought, then the world had not frozen.

A slave girl opened the door and placed a tray on the floor containing a bowl of water and a towel. 'My Lady Cassia invites you to breakfast, my lord,' she said without looking at him. She looked no more than fifteen.

'Thank you,' he replied. 'And please call me Zak.'

The girl gave him a brief, nervous smile before disappearing behind the door.

He washed his face in the water, got dressed and headed outside. His room opened out into the covered walkway, which encircled the enclosed garden, half of which was already bathed in sunshine. In the centre of the garden, obscured by a shrub, he could hear the pleasant sound of the fountain. Amongst all the colourful, autumnal trees and immaculately trimmed shrubs were several statues of varying sizes, most of which were painted with bright colours so they looked like miniature people frozen on their pedestals. A slave was bent over a broom, sweeping up leaves. Zak found himself troubled by the idea that several slaves worked for endless hours just to maintain such a pristine garden. And if they made a mistake, were they punished for it?

'Morning, sleepy head.'

He turned around and saw Maia approaching, a wry, rather guarded smile on her face. He smiled briefly back at her. He was still not sure he trusted her, but perhaps he had been a little tough on her the day before. As they walked through the colonnade towards the dining room, they exchanged rather frosty small talk about their bedrooms and how they had slept.

The dining room, in which they met Cassia, was another richly decorated room. The walls were so skilfully painted with frescoes of rolling hills, trees and pillars in the foreground that it appeared, at times, as if they were sitting in a gazebo in the middle of a garden. And on the floor, the animals depicted in the mosaic glistened as the light caught the thousands of tiny pieces of stone and glass.

'Chairs again,' said Zak as they walked into the room. 'I thought you Romans lay on couches while slaves dropped grapes into your mouths.'

Cassia laughed. 'That's only formal dining, such as when my parents are entertaining. Personally, I don't like all that nonsense. Reclining on a couch gave me indigestion when I tried it.'

She then proceeded to talk incessantly during the meal. At first, Zak felt sorry for her, recognising that she was obviously starved of contact with people of her own age. And now that she had a small audience, she was clearly going to make the most of it. But as time wore on, her constant chatting about trivial matters began to irritate him until he wished she would just shut up.

But then a pang of regret swelled up inside him. In just a few days' time, he remembered, this house and the whole city around them was going to be buried in metres of ash. And maybe Cassia and Dexter, who was standing dutifully in the background, would be killed when Vesuvius erupted.

'You look like you've just seen a ghost,' said Maia, looking at Zak.

He stared back at her uneasily. 'Just thinking about what might happen over the next few days,' he replied, stressing the last few words until he could see in her face that she knew what he meant.

'I think we should go out this morning,' said Cassia brightly, glancing between the two of them. 'Let's go shopping. As you have only just arrived, I can show you all the best parts of Pompeii. It's not a bad little city, really.'

'I'm not sure that's a good idea,' said Zak.

'Nonsense,' smiled Cassia. 'We'll be fine. Felix can come with us. No one will dare touch us with him looking after us.' She then stood up. 'I'll meet you in the atrium in a short while.'

As Zak and Maia headed back to their rooms, Zak sighed.

'I think we should go out,' said Maia. 'Explore the town.'

'We can't just go wandering about,' countered Zak. 'What if time freezes again and those guys come back? Big old Felix isn't going to be much use to us if he's frozen solid, is he?'

'Maybe. But I have a feeling that won't happen again. And before you say anything, I only think that because I reckon, if they were going to use their trick of freezing time, they would have done it by now. They know where we are, so why didn't they just do it again last night when we were asleep? And besides, we can't just stay here, imprisoned in this house. If we want to find a way back home, we have to work out why we're here. And maybe we'll find some clues in the town somewhere.'

Zak knew she was right. It would be a risk. But what choice

did they have?

The middle of October it might have been, but to Zak it felt like a warm summer's day, with the sun shining down from a cloudless blue sky. An autumnal day in England this most definitely was not. Yet as pleasant as the weather was, Zak found he was just too much on edge to enjoy it. As they strolled around the city, he kept looking over his shoulder, glancing into people's faces and peering at men's forearms, looking for that tattoo of a hammer he had seen the day before. And every time a man in a cape came into view he would stare in fright, half expecting the person to start chasing him.

With a wry smile to himself, he realised there were probably thousands of people back home who would have given anything to be walking the streets of Pompeii just days before it was due to be buried. However, no matter how hard he tried, he found he just could not relax enough to take in the sights as an excited tourist might have done.

'And this,' declared Cassia grandly, as they turned a corner, 'is the Forum.'

They were standing at the edge of a long, rectangular piazza, paved with large, smooth flagstones. Along the two long sides of the piazza there were various large buildings, each with a row of stone pillars at the front, while at the end was an impressive temple standing at the top of a flight of wide stone steps.

Looming over the temple in the background was the massive cone of Vesuvius, thin wisps of cloud clinging to its hazy, distant summit. Although he had recently seen photos of the volcano in class, seeing it with his own eyes made him stand and stare. It was truly enormous and must have dominated the land for miles around. After gawping at the mountain for a while, a shiver ran down his spine. Knowing it was due to erupt in only four days' time terrified him.

He quickly turned his attention back to the Forum. What

struck him immediately about the place was the amount of scaffolding erected around nearly all the buildings, some of which had whole sections of roof missing. Everywhere he looked there were men crawling all over the building site, striking their hammers, painting facades, working on the roofs and pillars. For all the many pedestrians walking around the piazza, or selling their wares at temporary wooden stalls, there seemed to be at least as many workmen repairing the buildings, some of which were clearly a long way from being completed.

'What on earth happened here?' asked Zak, gazing around.

'Oh, that was the Great Earthquake of seventeen years ago,' replied Cassia. 'A lot of the city was left in ruins. For several years, the city was virtually abandoned. But slowly, people started coming back and have been rebuilding ever since. The recent earthquakes haven't helped, but we'll get there eventually. Anyway,' she added with a grin, 'let's go and look around the shops. They have some amazing jewellery on sale here.'

Zak glanced at Dexter and rolled his eyes, while the slave gave a brief wry smile in return. As Cassia and Maia wandered off under the watchful gaze of the broad-shouldered Felix, Zak turned to Dexter. 'So if girls can go shopping, what fun things do boys get to do in Pompeii?'

Dexter stared at him for a moment, then chuckled. 'You really aren't used to slaves, are you? My time is not my own. If I go somewhere, it's because Cassia wants to go there. If she wants something doing, I do it.'

Zak slowly shook his head. 'How can you live like that?'

'I don't have any choice. But what keeps me going is the thought that one day I could be freed. If I serve well and am lucky to serve a decent master or mistress they will free me, eventually. But that won't be for, who knows, twenty years.'

'Wow!' said Zak. 'I wish there was something I could do to help you.'

'Why are you so interested in me?' asked Dexter. 'Most people don't even look at me.'

'I'm just trying to be friendly, really. Friends are what I need right now. I haven't got any here.'

'What about Maia? I thought she was your friend.'

Zak snorted. 'This time yesterday I didn't even know who she was.'

'Look what I've just bought,' said Cassia, rushing back towards the two boys. 'Do you like them?' She was pointing to her ears, from which a pair of earrings were now swinging. They were triangular in shape, with the point attached close to the ear, whilst three tiny strings of precious stones dangled from the base of the triangle. She was clearly very pleased with them and seemed to be expecting Zak to share her enthusiasm.

'They look heavy,' said Zak.

Cassia laughed and then handed her shopping bags to Dexter. 'Carry those, Dexter. Now then, off we go.'

As they began walking out of the Forum, Maia stopped suddenly. 'Just a minute,' she said, and darted into the shade of the colonnade at the front of one of the long buildings.

The others followed her and found her staring at a pair of large wooden doors, one of which was ajar. A builder wearing a belt full of tools came out of the doorway, but barely glanced at the five of them before marching off.

'Who's that?' asked Maia, pointing at the metal door knocker. It was as large as a balled fist and shaped like the head of a man, but with two bearded faces, one looking right, the other facing left.

'Oh, that's Janus,' said Cassia. 'You know, the god Janus.' She eyed their puzzled faces with surprise. 'You don't have Janus in Britannia, then? He's our god of doorways and keys and various other pretty useless things, really. Some say he lived in this area many years ago. Anyway, not that exciting.'

She, Dexter and Felix then began moving away again.

'What is it?' asked Zak when he noticed that Maia was still

staring at the door knocker.

'I've seen this somewhere before, recently,' she said, screwing her face up. 'But I can't remember where.'

'Did you hear what Cassia said about the Great Earthquake?' asked Zak, glancing over his shoulder to make sure the others were out of earshot.

'Yes, I did. Seventeen years ago. And that man said to me yesterday they'd been hunting me for seventeen years.'

Zak sighed heavily. 'Maia,' he said in as calm and conciliatory a tone as he could muster, 'please tell me what is going on? You must know something.'

She turned and looked at him and swallowed hard. 'Oh, Zak. I don't know anything, I promise you,' she said, her voice barely a whisper.

'But you must know something. You turn up at school out of the blue, and then, before we know it, you and I end up here.'

He could see tears welling up in her eyes. 'Please, Zak. All I want is for you to believe that I know nothing.'

'Why do you care what I think?'

'Because I'm scared,' she replied. 'I don't know what's going on. But what I do know is that you are the only person here from home. And it really hurts that you don't believe me, you don't trust me. You're right, I must have something to do with this, but I don't know what. But you must have something to do with all of this as well. You were given that watch, then you and I were the only ones not frozen in the classroom, and the only ones who came here. So you tell me what's going on, because I don't know. I don't want to stay here, either. I just want to go home, like you. And the only way I can think of doing that is if you and I work together to find a way.'

She sniffed and wiped away a tear.

Zak did not know what to say, did not know what to think. But, for the first time since he had met her, he was beginning to think she was telling the truth.

Chapter VII

Caius Philippus

Under the warm midday sun, the three children strolled back through the bustling streets of Pompeii, Dexter and Felix trailing behind them with bags of Cassia's shopping in each hand. Once again, Zak's eyes were flitting about in all directions, looking for signs of danger.

Progress along the arrow-straight road, where Zak and Maia had first arrived the day before, was painfully slow. Not only was the street thronged with shoppers and merchants, but Cassia insisted on stopping at almost every shop along the way, or so it seemed to Zak. One minute she was examining ornate vases, the next, more jewellery. Then it was clothing, followed by edible delicacies. Zak began to wonder whether this was the first time she had been allowed out of the house in ages. But whatever the reason, in light of their experiences the previous day on that street, he just wanted to get back to the relative safety of the house as quickly as possible.

'Look!' whispered Maia suddenly, and pointed down the road ahead. 'That man has a red hood.'

Zak's wide and anxious eyes shot in the same direction. Sure enough, a short distance in front of them, partly obscured by some young children playing around a large stone fountain, was a man dressed in a crimson cape with the hood drawn up. With his back to them, he was walking briskly away, moving his head from side to side as though scouting for something or someone.

Zak found his heart was pounding already, his breathing getting faster and faster. 'Come on,' he said. 'Let's follow him.' Although he was scared beyond measure, his desire to find out what was going on, to find a way to get home, began rapidly to override his fear.

'Where are you going?' asked Cassia.

But Zak and Maia had already begun striding down the street, weaving in and out of other pedestrians. The man in the cape was less than ten metres away. Then he jumped off the high curb into the dirty road in order to skirt around a dawdling mother and child, before leaping back up onto the path. He moved with the ease and grace of a trained athlete.

Zak was trying to keep at least one person between himself and the hooded figure, in case the man should turn around and recognise him. But when Zak dodged around the same mother and child, there was suddenly nothing between him and the man, just an open stretch of pavement. He felt horribly exposed.

'He's following someone,' said Maia, as she drew up beside him.

Zak had noticed it too. Up ahead, a boy, a little older than them perhaps, was scurrying along the pavement. When the boy cast a furtive look behind him, he seemed to notice the hooded figure pursuing him. A look of horror burst across his face, and he turned and ran. No sooner had he sped off, than the man began bounding after him.

Zak and Maia were now also running, trying to keep up. The boy looked terrified every time he looked over his shoulder, but no matter how fast he tried to run, he seemed unable to increase the distance between him and his pursuer.

The boy looked around once too often and collided with a man carrying a large basket out of a shop. He tumbled to the ground, nearly fell off the curb into the road. The hooded man was almost on top of him.

'Hey, you!' cried out Zak. By now anger had replaced his fear. Whoever he was, the boy needed their help.

The man spun round and, for a brief moment, he showed Zak his fierce, snarling face, before turning back to face the boy. But by this time, the boy had managed to scramble back onto his feet and was stumbling towards a side street, arms waving wildly in a desperate attempt to keep his balance. A moment later, he disappeared into the shadows, followed closely by the man in the crimson cape.

Not stopping to think what he was going to do when he caught up with them, Zak hurtled along the pavement and darted down the same side street. Up ahead in the deserted, narrow road, the man's footsteps echoed loudly as he closed in on his terrified quarry. In a heartbeat, the man had seized one of the boy's flailing arms, had dragged him down to the ground, despite the boy's croaking protests.

'Hey!' shouted Zak again, coming to an abrupt halt just a few metres away. 'Leave him alone.'

Without letting go of his prey, the man spun round and glowered at Zak. 'Keep out of this, boy,' he snarled through bared teeth. 'It does not concern you.'

'What do you want with him?' demanded Zak.

The man's expression suddenly changed. His eyes narrowed. 'Wait a moment. Don't I know you?'

Zak's heart skipped a beat. He felt his blood run cold. Terror flooded his body, drowning his anger in an instant. What on earth was he thinking, chasing one of the very men who, the day before, had been chasing him?

The man had lost interest in the boy, had released his arm, leaving him to scuttle away in ungainly fashion. The man's piercing eyes held Zak's, until a faint smile spread across his face. Zak heard the sound of a sword being drawn from its scabbard. By this time, Maia had joined him and, upon seeing the man's steel weapon appear with a flourish, let out a horrified gasp.

Zak was about to turn and run when he heard a booming voice. 'Put that down if you know what's good for you.' He spun round in time to see the massive figure of Felix standing at the end of the road, his own sword glinting in one hand. At his right shoulder stood the tall, brooding figure of Dexter.

As the pair marched down the road towards him, Zak glanced

back at the hooded man, who stood for a moment, poised to fight, or so it seemed. But then his eyes flitted between Zak and the approaching slaves. He then stared at Zak and Maia and pointed the tip of his sword at them. 'We're coming for you,' he spat with obvious glee. 'Best you sleep with one eye open. Because, rest assured, we will come for you. Sooner or later.'

With a flourish of his cape, he turned and sprinted away. Zak watched him disappear into the shadows at the other end of the street, his heart pumping so fast it seemed ready to burst.

'Are you all right?' asked Felix in his deep, accented voice, as he and Dexter joined them.

'Yeah, I'm fine,' said Zak, and then moved towards the boy who was sitting on the curb, breathing heavily and still looking frightened. His clothes were now dirty and ripped in several places. 'Hi. Are you hurt?' he asked.

Now that Zak was close to him, he could see that he was more young man than a boy, perhaps fifteen or sixteen. He had close-cropped hair and large, wild eyes, which seemed to be expecting danger from every corner.

'Thank you,' he gasped. 'Thank you. I think you have just saved my life.'

'Have I missed all the fun?' asked a smiling Cassia, as she swept into the group. 'By Juno!' she said, looking back and forth between the boy sitting forlornly on the ground, his hair and clothes all awry, and Felix's drawn sword. 'What has been going on here?'

'My name is Caius Philippus,' said the boy, in answer to Zak's question.

They were sitting once more in Cassia's garden around the small, low table, drinking cups of water. In the background, the fountain was tinkling its calming tune.

'Who was that man?' asked Maia. 'And why was he chasing you?'

Caius was breathing hard and still looked anxious. 'I ... I don't know,' he replied, averting his gaze. 'But he had a tattoo on his forearm.'

Zak's heart leapt. 'Was it a tattoo of a hammer?'

'Yes. The hammer of Vulcanus.'

Zak looked at Maia. 'One of those men who chased us had a tattoo of a hammer on his forearm. It was a different guy. But they must be connected.'

Caius was kneading his fingers round and round, while sweat was beading on his forehead. His fearful eyes never seemed to stay still.

By now, Zak could feel his own pulse racing. Whatever Caius' story was, it clearly had something to do with him and Maia being in Pompeii. There were so many questions to ask, he hardly knew where to start.

'Where are you from, Caius?' he asked.

'Pompeii. I've lived here all my life. I was born here sixteen years ago.'

'And you've never seen those men in hooded capes before?' asked Maia.

His eyes flitted back and forth between her and Zak. 'Well ... I ...' He swallowed hard.

'Look, Caius,' began Zak. 'About five of those men, dressed like that with tattoos, chased us yesterday. We only just got away, thanks to Cassia and Dexter here. You can trust us.'

'We don't know why they were chasing us, either,' added Maia. 'So if you know anything that could help us find out why they want us, please tell us.'

Caius' wild eyes studied each of them in turn. After a pause he said: 'They are called Vulcani.'

'They're called what?' asked Cassia, who hitherto had shown little interest in the conversation. In fact, Zak had the impression she was slightly annoyed that she was no longer the centre of attention.

'Vulcani,' continued Caius. 'Followers of the god Vulcanus. They all have a tattoo of Vulcanus' hammer, to show their loyalty.'

'And what are they trying to do?' asked Zak.

'I—I don't really know.' He buried his face in his hands. 'It has something to do with my father, but I don't know what.'

Although the wait was agonising, Zak decided to keep quiet and wait for Caius to volunteer his story in his own time, rather than bombard the poor boy with too many questions.

Caius swallowed hard and composed himself. 'My father was imprisoned by the Vulcani before I was even born.'

'Imprisoned?' asked Cassia. 'Why? What did he do?'

'That's just it: I don't know. I'm able to secretly visit him, but even he won't tell me what's going on. He says it's for my own good, to protect me.'

'Then why was that man chasing you?' pressed Maia.

'I don't know,' snapped Caius. 'I don't know anything.' He glowered, then looked away. 'I'm sorry,' he said eventually, looking at Maia. 'Look, I've seen them around the city and guarding my father, but they've never chased me before. Perhaps they saw me visiting my father the other day.'

'Where is your father?' asked Zak.

Caius went to speak, but then closed his mouth and looked away. 'I can't say.'

After a brief pause, Dexter, who was standing behind Cassia, said: 'If your enemies have imprisoned your father, it hardly matters if you tell us, surely.'

'Dexter!' snapped Cassia. 'You will hold your tongue. Speak when spoken to.'

'Oh, leave him alone, Cassia,' said Zak. 'Treat Dexter the same way you'd like others to treat you.'

'May I remind you, Zak, you are guests in my house ...'

'And we are very grateful,' cut in Maia, putting a hand on Zak's arm. 'Aren't we, Zak? We apologise. It's been another stressful day.'

Zak wanted to say more, to put Cassia in her place. The way she treated Dexter was wrong. But just before he was about to let out his bubbling anger, he managed to stop himself and bit his tongue instead. Maia was right: emotions were running high.

'This is my fault,' said Caius rising to his feet. 'I should go home.'

'Do you have a slave to escort you?' asked Cassia.

'No,' he replied. 'That Vulcani stabbed him.'

The others gasped.

'You must report this,' said Cassia. 'My uncle is in the *ordo*, the city council.'

'No!' said Caius quickly. 'Don't, please. I don't know whom I can trust. The Vulcani have infiltrated the *ordo*. And they have spies everywhere. You must say nothing.'

'Then you shall stay here for the night,' said Cassia. 'We can decide what to do in the morning.'

Reluctantly, Caius agreed.

'Perhaps tomorrow you could take us to see your father,' suggested Zak.

'I don't know if that is a good idea,' replied Caius.

'We need to work together, Caius,' insisted Zak. 'Those Vulcani are after both us and you, for some reason. If we can find out why, perhaps we can solve this mystery ... and then we can all hopefully get our lives back.'

Chapter VIII

The Man in the Mysterious Cage

The next day dawned another sunny October morning. Perfect for a walk in the countryside, Cassia had declared over breakfast. And so, by mid-morning, Zak, Maia, Cassia, Dexter and Caius were travelling away from Pompeii inside a covered wooden carriage. One of Cassia's household slaves was sitting outside at the front, directing the two horses. The plan was to travel some of the way in the carriage and then complete their journey to see Caius' father on foot. It would have been too far to walk all the way, Caius had said.

As the carriage trundled along the bumpy coastal road, Cassia talked incessantly, pointing out sights of interest left and right, like an over-zealous tour guide. To Zak's left he could see the Bay of Naples, sparkling under a bright sun. Dozens of boats were bobbing gently over the waves: small fishing boats, pleasure craft enjoying the weather and further out, much larger cargo vessels seemed to move along the horizon at a snail's pace.

Zak turned to his right and looked out across the vast expanse of fields between Pompeii and Vesuvius. With large vineyards to one side and farms to the other, all basking under the warm sun, it all looked a sleepy and idyllic landscape. That was until Zak heard the crack of a whip. Then he looked more closely and could see groups of poorly dressed slaves, some of them chained together, moving forlornly under the menacing gaze of men wielding whips or thick wooden sticks.

When Caius suggested they stop and walk the rest of the way, Zak stepped out and stood staring across the fields for a while. In a nearby vineyard, several slaves trudged from one part to another, heads and shoulders bowed, while a fierce-looking man barked incessant orders at them.

Dexter moved beside him. 'You all right?'

'I've read about slavery in Roman times,' he said quietly, 'but I never really realised just how awful it was till now.'

Dexter nodded gently but said nothing.

'Where do you come from, Dexter?' asked Zak.

'Italy. I was born somewhere around here. I don't know where exactly. I was taken away from my parents, who were slaves, when I was a baby. I was brought up by a very kind woman, also a slave, until I was sold on. Then last year, Cassia's father bought me.'

Zak wanted to say he would help Dexter to escape this life of slavery, but he knew they would just be empty words. What could he, an insignificant thirteen-year-old boy from the future, possibly do to help him?

'Anyway, what did you mean — in Roman times?' asked Dexter. 'These are Roman times.'

Zak laughed at his slip of the tongue. 'I'll tell you another time.'

Caius led them off the main road and onto a much smaller dirt track, which snaked off into the distance towards Vesuvius. Now that they were much closer to the volcano, Zak stared up at it in awe. Shaped like an enormous cone, it rose impossibly high into the sky, its summit so hazy and distant it looked like it would have taken a week to climb. And its forested slopes reached almost to the very top. Since it was covered in such lush vegetation, it was clear it had not erupted in a very long time.

The five teenagers moved along the track, having left the slave behind to look after the carriage and horses. Caius had also said it would be better if as few people as possible knew exactly where they were heading. Of all of them, Caius at sixteen was the eldest, yet he was by far the most nervous. He constantly moved his head left and right as though expecting someone to jump out from behind every tree at any moment. Though he tried not to show it, Zak too felt nervous. He was beginning to wish they had brought Felix along with them.

After half an hour, the ground began to rise up more steeply, and they entered the forest at the base of Vesuvius. As vast as the volcano was, Zak was surprised how gentle the incline was at first. It was just like climbing up a wooded hill he and Arjun used to play on back home, except that it just seemed to go on for ever.

Every so often, the path would open out into a sunny glade, with a babbling stream tumbling over rocks through the trees. In one such clearing, they all sat down for a drink and a rest, while Caius went off to scout ahead.

'A beautiful spot for a picnic,' said Maia, leaning in and speaking quietly to Zak.

'Yeah,' he replied, glancing at his watch, which he kept hidden in the pouch on his belt. 'It's the twenty-first today. We've got three days left before this thing explodes.'

'Assuming all those historians have got the date right.'

'What do you mean?'

'They used to say Vesuvius erupted in August,' continued Maia. 'But now they reckon it was October.'

'I guess we'll find out soon enough,' said Zak, pulling a face. 'If we can't find our way back home.'

Caius reappeared and beckoned to them to follow him. He now led them down a narrow, winding path through the trees and bushes. Proceeding in single file, they had to negotiate gnarled tree roots and numerous boulders, until they arrived at the entrance to a cave.

'Wait here,' said Caius, looking even more nervous and fidgety than before. 'I'll check it's safe to go in.' Ducking his head down, he then disappeared into the black hole.

'Are we sure about this?' asked Cassia. 'I mean, we don't really know this boy at all, do we?'

'If he was going to trick us,' said Maia, 'I think he would have done it by now.'

'I hope you're right,' said Cassia, who seemed to have lost her normal joyful composure.

Caius reappeared and waved his hand, urging them to silently follow him. The cave was narrow and dark, with moisture dripping off the roof. Yet, to Zak's surprise, the tunnel was warm, and a faint, unpleasant smell of sulphur wafted through the air. Then again, he soon realised, he should not have been surprised — after all, they were climbing into an active volcano, days before it was due to erupt.

After only a minute or so, he could see a faint glow up ahead, and before long the tunnel opened out into a large cavern. As they filed into the underground chamber, they all gasped at the sight before them. What should have been a dark and foreboding place was full of shimmering light and colour. A large structure filled most of the cavern, looking like a temple, surrounded by dozens and dozens of thin pillars, which glowed like vertical rods of fire, casting reds and oranges and yellows against the glistening walls of rock around it.

As Zak moved closer, he realised he was looking at some sort of vast cage, the bars of which were made of some unknown, glimmering material which hummed like it was charged with electricity. Inside the cage, there stood a small, single-storey house. The brightness radiating from the bars prevented Zak from seeing the house clearly, but he could make out tiny windows, a door and a flat roof.

'Father, it's me!' said Caius in a loud whisper. He was standing close to the shimmering bars of the cage, peering through towards the house.

A figure emerged from the door and shuffled slowly towards the bars.

'Father,' continued Caius, 'these are the people I told you about. My new friends. They saved my life.'

The man moved closer and stopped a short distance from his son. The pair were now so close they could have reached out and touched one another at arm's length through the bars, but, Zak presumed, the cage would have prevented such contact. The man was tall and well muscled, but his powerful-looking shoulders seemed to be hunched forwards in despair. Behind a thick beard and long, greying hair, which cascaded down onto the shoulders of his simple red tunic, his lined face looked gaunt and weary.

'You should not have come,' he said in a deep and gravelly voice.

Caius looked up at the man with wide-eyed eagerness, much as a small child might look into the eyes of the father he worshipped. 'But I think these people could help us,' he insisted.

'If they catch you here ...' The man's voice trailed away and his large, troubled eyes looked down at the ground. 'You should go, before the guards come back.'

'I *will* get you out of here,' said Caius. 'I promise you, father.'

'I know you will, son. Now go, please.'

With tears in his eyes, Caius watched as his father turned around and plodded wearily back towards the house. 'Come,' he said to the others. 'My father was right: we should go now.'

The five of them traipsed back down the side of the volcano in near silence, the shock of what they had just seen making speech virtually impossible.

When they finally emerged from the forest at the foot of Vesuvius, Zak moved next to Maia. 'What did you make of that?' he asked.

Maia puffed out her cheeks. 'I don't know, but that clearly wasn't Roman technology, was it? It's far too advanced for them. I'm not sure we're any nearer knowing what's going on.'

Just when Zak was beginning to worry once more that time was fast running out for him and Maia, the ground began to tremble. At first, it was only gentle compared to some tremors they had felt recently, but disconcerting, nonetheless. Individual small rocks and stones skittered down the slope and rolled out of the forest and onto the ground around them. Then, almost as soon as the tremor had begun, it stopped.

A strong stench of sulphur floated past them, before dispersing in the wind.

As they hurried away from the mountain, Zak trotted forward to join Caius. 'Do you have any idea how to get your father out of there?' he asked.

'None whatsoever,' he sighed, his eyes cast down. 'I've spent the last few years trying to figure out what to do. It's all I ever think about.'

'Sounds like you need the Key of Portunus,' said Cassia with a brief laugh.

'The what?' asked Zak.

'Oh, it's just a silly story told to children,' continued Cassia. 'The god Portunus - the god of keys and locks - was said to have been tasked by the other gods to build prisons for their enemies. The prisons were to have locks that could never be opened by anyone. But, against the wishes of the gods, he made a secret key, a key that could open any door or any lock just in case these prisoners were ever pardoned and could therefore be released. But as soon as he had made this key, he realised that if it ever got into the hands of the wrong people, they could release any prisoner they wanted to. So he hid the key where only someone worthy would ever find it again. But it's a daft children's story, nothing more.'

Zak and Dexter looked at one another and rolled their eyes. How were fairy tales ever going to help them free Caius' father?

'Well,' said Caius, 'I've looked into everything, including the Key of Portunus, and maybe it's not just a silly children's story, after all. Come with me. Let me show you something.'

He led them along another narrow dirt track, which snaked away from Vesuvius. After half an hour or so, they came to a much wider track, which led to a villa in the distance. As they approached the isolated building, it became apparent that no one lived there, or indeed, had lived there for quite some time. Trees and bushes were smothering it from all sides, while creepers were slowly but surely obscuring the white walls and the red roof tiles. The windows had long since lost their glass and, in at least two places, sizeable sections of the roof had collapsed. A pair of startled birds fluttered noisily away as they drew near.

Since the main entrance seemed to be still barred by a massive wooden door, Caius led them round the side of the building and in through a narrow opening in the crumbling wall. Once inside, Zak was surprised to see just how vast the place was. The creeping vegetation outside had completely obscured the size of the building, which seemed to spread endlessly from one large room to another. Bright shafts of sunlight filled the villa, both through man-made openings and through the collapsed sections of roof. The lavishly painted walls were still largely intact, although here and there thick cracks zigzagged across the frescoes on the walls.

Caius took them through what once must have been a long and impressive ornamental garden, but where weeds and bushes had grown out of control over all the many statues and ponds, which now lay lifeless and stagnant. He finally stopped once he had brought them inside a building so large it contained more of a hall than a room. High above them, the ceiling was covered with ornate pictures and carvings. Just below the ceiling, a line of small windows, so high that one could see nothing more than the sky through them, let shafts of golden sunlight into the vast room.

'What is this place?' asked Zak, gazing around at the brightly painted walls.

'No one has lived here since the Great Earthquake seventeen years ago,' replied Caius. 'But it used to belong to a man named Portunus, who died some years ago.'

'Portunus?' laughed Cassia. 'Well, it can't be *the* Portunus, because the gods are supposed to be immortal.'

'That may be so,' continued Caius, 'but I found a note in his things, which seems to relate to this mosaic.'

It was only then that Zak looked down and opened his eyes wide. Narrow shafts of sunlight were angled down from the small windows above, illuminating parts of a vast mosaic on the floor. He had seen pictures of some impressive mosaics in books and on the internet, and also some good ones in Cassia's house, but nothing to compare with this one. It must have been as big as two tennis courts, end to end, and even under a thin layer of dust and dirt the colours were still vibrant. They all walked to the side of the room in order to take in the whole of the enormous picture.

'I think it's meant to show Julius Caesar,' said Caius. 'After he defeated Vercingetorix at the battle of Alesia. That's him sitting there, and this is the defeated Vercingetorix surrendering to Caesar.'

The many figures in the mosaic were at least twice the size of a real person.

'Very nice,' said Dexter, rather indifferently. 'But what does this have to do with setting your father free?'

Zak noticed that Cassia looked like she was going to explode with fury at her slave speaking out of turn. But when she caught Zak's eye, she seemed to think better of saying anything.

'I found this when I was searching the villa,' replied Caius, and produced a small scroll from the folds of his tunic. 'It reads:

> If the gods do deem thee worthy,
> So shalt thou find my hidden key,
> Then upon lowering to one knee,
> Shall mighty Caesar say to thee,
> Veni, vidi, vici.

I've no idea what it means,' continued Caius. 'But I'm certain it relates to this mosaic because of those words under your feet.'

He pointed to the floor.

Zak stepped to one side and noticed at the bottom of the mosaic was written in letters half a metre high: VENI VIDI VICI.

'I came, I saw, I conquered,' said Caius. 'Caesar's famous line from his book on the wars in Gaul.'

As Zak knelt down to take a closer look at the mosaic, a small lizard scurried across the surface, leaving a jagged trail in the dust. Zak brushed away some of the dirt to examine the tiny stones that made up the picture. There must have been thousands of them, hundreds of thousands, all not much bigger than a thumbnail. He pressed one or two, but they were firmly set in cement.

'I think "lowering to one knee" means get down to look at the mosaic,' continued Caius. 'But, believe me, I've spent hours in here trying to work it out, and I've come up with nothing. Maybe I'm just chasing shadows, but I'm sure this must have something to do with my father.'

For the next few minutes, they all wandered up and down the room, going over the riddle and trying to interpret its meaning, until finally hunger and thirst drove them out of the villa.

'Don't worry,' said Cassia to Caius, as they all walked away from the house. 'I'm sure together we can solve it.'

'I do hope so,' sighed Caius.

Behind them, Maia mumbled to Zak: 'I wish I had my phone with me. We could look up all sorts of stuff. And a map would be useful. I'm used to checking out my location all the time on my phone.'

'A map!' said Zak suddenly. 'Of course. There's a map on this watch.' He fished it out of his leather pouch and began fiddling with it just as he had in class two days previously, until the map reappeared, standing proud of the watch's surface. When he zoomed in, he could see a map of Pompeii and the surrounding area, with two or three little pulsing red dots. One of them was at the foot of Vesuvius, so he zoomed in further until he was certain it was showing him his current location.

'Of course. I've been so stupid,' he continued. 'Not only did I change the year to 79 AD, but I remember moving the map over Italy. Without really thinking, I must have selected Pompeii because Mrs Sullivan kept mentioning it.'

By now, Maia was bent over next to him, peering down at the watch as they walked along. 'So what happens if you move it back over our school?' she suggested. 'Then select the date that we left.'

Even as she spoke, he was changing the year and the date, and moving the map back over the UK. Once completed, he found the tiny button at the side and pressed it. Immediately, the red ring reappeared around the watch face and began pulsing as it had on the day they had arrived in Pompeii.

'This is what it did last time,' he said excitedly.

They stared at it a few moments.

'Now what happens?' asked Maia.

'I don't know. When I did this in class, you appeared. And then a while later ... well, you know what happened after that.'

'There must be something, some trigger, that caused us to come here. But what?'

'It happened when we went into Mrs Sullivan's office.'

'So ... what? She has a time machine in her office? She's an alien?'

'Well, maybe,' laughed Zak. 'Or perhaps she's really a Roman goddess in disguise as a history teacher.'

Maia laughed rather uncertainly. 'After what has happened over the last couple of days, nothing would surprise me.'

'What's that you've got there?' Caius had turned around and was looking at the watch.

As quickly but as casually as he could, Zak wrapped his fingers around the watch and put it back in his pouch. 'Oh, nothing,' he said with a smile. 'Just a miniature sundial. They're all the rage in Britain at the moment. Anyway, come on. Let's get back. I'm starving.'

After walking for a while through the countryside, they finally made it back to the carriage guarded by Cassia's slave. When they had climbed aboard, Dexter pulled out a basket from under their feet and handed out some much-needed food and drink, which they began devouring almost before the carriage had started moving.

As the countryside moved slowly by, Zak could feel his eyelids getting heavier and heavier. As he watched a small flock of birds flying in the distance, he was about to give in to the urge to fall asleep, when the birds froze in mid-flight. At the same moment, the gentle rocking of the carriage stopped abruptly.

For a second or two, he thought he must be dreaming. But then he heard Maia exclaim with anguish: 'No! Not again.'

Chapter IX

The Woman on the Wall

Everything had frozen once more. The birds in the sky, the boats on the sea, the horses on the road, even the wind. There was not a sound and nothing moved. Nothing except Zak and Maia.

His drowsiness gone in a flash, Zak looked frantically around the carriage. Dexter, Cassia and Caius were as still as statues, whilst Maia looked terrified, her eyes darting about, full of fear.

'Come on,' urged Zak. 'We can't stay in here.' He then clambered out of the carriage and onto the cobbled road. Maia joined him, their heads twisting in every direction, desperately praying they would not see anyone else moving.

A faint noise made Zak look back down the road they had just travelled along. There in the distance, something was moving along the road towards them, a drumming noise getting slowly louder.

'Horses!' said Zak. 'It must be them. We've got to move.'

'What about Caius and the others?' asked Maia, as they turned and fled down the road towards Pompeii.

'There's nothing we can do. There's no point all of us getting caught, is there? Anyway, something tells me those men are after us this time.'

After running for a short distance, they came to a fork in the road. To the right, the road went down to the port, which lay at the bottom of the hill, while to the left a road climbed the gentle slope towards the walls of the city. Zak hesitated for a moment, desperately trying to think where the best hiding place would be.

When he glanced back along the road, he could see the small group of about five horses approaching fast, the red capes of their riders billowing out behind them like the flames from a fire.

He quickly realised that the port was just too far away, whereas the cemetery, which lay just outside the walls of Pompeii, began only a short distance up the slope. Maybe in there they could find somewhere to hide.

'I knew wearing this stupid dress was a mistake,' hissed Maia, as she tried to run with a clump of material hitched up in each hand.

Running as fast as he could, Zak urged her up the hill. They weaved in and out of the many carts and horses and people on foot, all as still and lifeless as stone carvings. Amongst the scattered trees outside the city, large stone tombs began to emerge on both sides of the road, some so grand they looked like miniature temples and houses with pillars and archways and tiled roofs.

The sound of clattering hooves grew louder behind them. The gate to the city was still agonisingly far away. Zak knew then they were not going to make it.

On a sudden impulse, he pulled Maia off the road and almost dragged her between two large tombs, each one taller than an adult. They hunkered down in the shadows, gasping for breath, whilst desperately trying not to make a sound.

The horses drew near and pulled up close to where they were. One of the riders wheeled his horse around, snatched the hood away from his head and scanned the area.

'Spread out!' he ordered. 'They can't have gone far.'

Terrified, Zak watched with one eye peering out from behind the tomb. His heart was pounding fast. He had no idea what to do next.

But then, everything began moving again. Cartwheels turned, screeching on the flagstones, hooves clopped along the road, dozens and dozens of voices filled the air as though nothing had happened.

'Oh, what *is* going on?' gasped Maia.

'I don't know,' replied Zak. 'But we need to move.'

Crouching low to the ground, he eased out from between the two stone shrines. To his left, back down the hill, he could see that one of their pursuers was struggling to control his horse as it reared up, clearly spooked by all the sudden movement. So he quickly waved to Maia to follow him up the hill towards the city gate.

After no more than a minute, everything stopped once again, frozen like a giant photograph. Zak cursed under his breath, but just kept running. If they could just get into the city, he hoped they would be able to lose themselves in the crowds thronging the streets or in the warren of side roads and alleys.

He could hear the horses on the move again behind him. As he and Maia approached the large stone gateway to Pompeii, he looked up and saw someone moving along the battlements of the city walls. With long, wavy grey hair and a slight frame, it appeared to be a woman, someone else who was unaffected by the freezing of time. He glanced up at her several times and noticed she was pacing up and down with a staff in her hands. As the two of them raced under the arch of the gateway, she disappeared from view.

'I can see them!' yelled a man's voice behind them. 'This way!'

Without turning round to look, Zak pressed on into the city. He used to think he was fit, could run a long way without getting out of breath. But now he was struggling. His legs felt heavy and tired, his lungs ready to burst. Yet fear somehow kept him going.

He looked back up at the city wall behind him. The woman was standing, staring down at him with cold, menacing eyes in a stern face. Or was it barely contained rage etched into her features? Who was she, and what on earth had he or Maia done to attract her apparent scorn?

The city sprang back into life. The orchestra of noises was every bit as overwhelming as the eerie silence a moment earlier had been. But it would at least sow confusion in the streets, giving them some hope of escape.

They darted around a large cart drawn by a pair of mules, and then leapt down a narrow side street. Zak fell against the brick wall, gasping for air, while Maia bent over, hands on knees.

Zak was only just beginning to get his breath back when the ground began to shake. At first, it was just a tremor, but soon it grew and grew into something far greater than they had experienced hitherto.

'Oh, you have got to be kidding me,' said Zak.

The road was shaking so much he had to steady himself against the wall. A tile fell off a nearby roof and shattered on the cobblestones. People began to scream as more and more crashes and bangs filled the air. Was this it? thought Zak. Had historians got the date wrong? Was Vesuvius about to erupt and bury them all?

'Come on, Zak,' cried Maia. 'We can't stay here. We need to get out into the open. Let's head to the Forum. It's just up here, I think.'

They ran along as best they could, while everything around them trembled. Several frightened people ran past them in the opposite direction. As they hurtled unsteadily around a corner, they ran straight under the wooden scaffolding outside a two-storey house. In the blink of an eye, the crisscross of wooden timbers collapsed and came tumbling down towards them. In the split second that Zak had time to think, he just knew he was about to be crushed. Instinctively, he closed his eyes and raised his arms above his head, bracing himself for the impact.

Nothing happened.

He opened his eyes, realised the ground had stopped shaking, and noticed the mass of falling wooden planks was suspended above him, floating in mid-air. Everything, save for the pulse drumming in his ears, was silent.

'Quick!' cried Maia. 'Before it starts again.' She tugged at his arm until they were both clear of the frozen scaffolding.

'Phew! That was close,' he said, looking at her. They then both burst out laughing; laughing from sheer relief and laughing at the utter absurdity of it all.

Running footsteps echoed down the street behind them, drawing closer by the second. With nothing more than a brief look at one another, Zak and Maia turned and ran.

Zak no longer knew what to think. When would it end? How would it end? How on earth were they ever going to get out of this? The world had gone mad. Or was it him who was going mad, caught in some bizarre nightmare that refused to end?

The nearer they drew to the Forum, the more the streets became crowded with frozen people alongside their frozen carts and motionless horses. People's faces showed nothing but fear and anguish as their attempts to flee the dangers of the earthquake around them had, for the time being at least, been halted.

Zak chanced a look over his shoulder. Amongst the living statues in the road, he could make out at least three running figures, no longer on their horses and skipping nimbly around the obstacles in their way.

And then, with an abruptness that made Zak jump and almost lose his balance, the crowds began moving again, contributing their small parts to the great wall of noise caused by the earthquake. While the ground and the buildings resumed their shaking, people ran in all directions to the sound of falling scaffolding and tiles and masonry.

The moment Zak and Maia turned into the long, paved piazza that was the Forum, the earthquake ceased its assault on the city. Yet even when the tremors had stopped, the panic and destruction continued. A whole section of wooden scaffolding around the front of one of the large, pillared buildings in the Forum collapsed just metres away from Zak and Maia. A cloud of dust and splinters rose into the air, as tools, paint, plaster and cement crashed onto the flagstones.

The piazza was crowded with people. No doubt many had had

the same idea to seek somewhere in the open, away from collapsing buildings. Zak was still running, without really knowing where he was going. He weaved around people who all seemed to be heading in the opposite direction.

Slowly, he noticed that some people were beginning to regain some level of composure. The screams and the shouts began to subside. Many walked about nursing cuts and bruises and anguished faces.

Realising he would be hard to spot in such a crowd, Zak finally slowed to a walk. He spun round, looking for Maia, but she was nowhere to be seen. Only a day or two earlier and he would not have cared one jot if he had lost her. But now, whether she was the cause of all this chaos or not, they were in this together. She was clearly just as scared as him. He could not abandon her now.

With growing panic, he scanned the mass of faces around him, and began walking back the way he had come, using his arms to brush people aside. And then he saw her a short distance away. She was still struggling to move quickly, her hands holding her long dress up above her knees. She was running right beside the long row of pillars at the front of one of the two-storey buildings, where a narrow path had opened up in the crowd, as people tried to avoid the threat of falling objects. But in the open, it meant the Vulcani could see her. Two of them, hoods still over their heads, were closing fast.

He rushed towards her, not concerned with whom he upset as he barged past people to reach her. Ahead of him, between two of the pillars, he could see the open doorway they had stopped to look at the previous day. Maybe it would be madness to go in, but he could think of nothing else to do. If they stayed out in the open, racing against powerful, athletic men, he knew they would soon be caught.

They converged close to the doorway. Zak grabbed Maia by the arm and pulled her into the shade of the covered walkway. He glanced to his right and saw the two hooded men sprinting towards them, fewer than ten paces away. As he headed for the open door, he caught a glimpse of the strange woman with the staff, some fifty paces or so behind the men, staring intently at the chase unfolding before her.

Zak and Maia ran through the doorway.

There was a blinding flash of light, followed by a second or two of dizziness.

When Zak opened his eyes, he realised with astonishment that he and Maia were standing, panting heavily, in the corridor outside Mrs Sullivan's office.

'Oh, hi Zak,' said Arjun, who was walking along with several other pupils. 'Fancy seeing you here. And why are you wearing a dress?'

Chapter X

The Bronze Door Knocker

'It's not a dress — it's a tunic,' mumbled Zak. As well as feeling thoroughly disorientated, he also felt painfully self-conscious, just as if he were standing there with nothing on.

'If you say so,' said Arjun with a confused chuckle. 'But why are you and Maia dressed like that, anyway?'

'It's part of the topic on Pompeii, obviously,' cut in Maia.

'Right,' said Arjun slowly. 'And you two are suddenly friends now, are you?'

'Yes,' replied Zak, glancing at his watch. 'Listen, that doesn't matter right now. What day is it?'

Arjun screwed up his face as though Zak had just gone mad. 'What day is it? You've become a teenager and suddenly it's made you act all weird.'

'Just tell me what the date is, please.'

'It's still your birthday, Zak — the 19th of October. Are you feeling all right?'

'Yes, I'm fine,' said Zak, trying not to show his impatience. 'Look, were we missed this afternoon?'

'Why? Did you go somewhere?'

'Yes. No. I mean ... look, did anyone notice we were not in class?'

For a moment, Arjun stood with his mouth wide open, clearly lost for words. Then he slowly shook his head. 'No. Not that I'm aware of. Why? What have you been doing?'

'Oh, never mind. I'll explain it all sometime. Just not now.'

'Well, it's time to go home now. You could tell me on the way.'

'No. I'll catch you up. We need to see Mrs Sullivan.'

Arjun stood and stared at his friend for a moment. He then

shrugged and walked away down the corridor, shaking his head.

Zak turned to Maia and showed her the watch. 'Look. We've come back just an hour or two after we left — two days ago.'

'So it *is* the watch,' said Maia. 'It must be some sort of time machine. You can set the date and time, and then choose the location on the map.'

'Yeah. I know how to set it now. But I still don't understand how it works or what triggers it.'

Maia turned back to look at Mrs Sullivan's door, which stood closed behind them. 'Look!' she said suddenly, pointing at the door. 'I knew I'd seen that bronze door knocker somewhere before.'

'What do you mean?' asked Zak.

'It's the same door knocker we saw in Pompeii with the twin heads of Janus on it.'

Zak looked more closely and saw, amongst the jumble of small pictures and badges spread across the teacher's door, a knocker, the size of a clenched fist, with two bearded faces on the same head, facing in opposite directions.

'I reckon,' continued Maia, her face full of excitement, 'if you set your watch to Pompeii in AD 79, and we walk through that door, we'll go back there.'

'Maybe,' said Zak, looking down at the watch again. 'But I'm not sure I want to.'

Maia was aghast. 'Zak, we have to.'

'No, we don't. We were being chased by madmen in a city that's going to be destroyed in a couple of days. Why go back to that? We might not be able to get back here next time.'

Some more children ambled past in the corridor, eyeing Zak and Maia with growing smirks on their faces. Maia pulled Zak in close in order to whisper to him. 'The Vulcani came here, remember — chasing me. We're no safer here than we were back there. Something tells me they are not going to stop until they get me. We need to find out why, so we can stop them. Or at least *I* do, even if you're not bothered.'

Zak sighed. It had been a draining few days. He just had no idea what to do.

'And our friends, Zak,' continued Maia. 'I've grown to quite like Cassia, for all her faults. And I've seen you chatting with Dexter a lot. They've become our friends, haven't they? We can't just leave them to die when Vesuvius erupts.'

'It has already erupted,' said Zak. 'Two thousand years ago.'

'Yes, but we have the power to warn them, to save them, maybe.'

'We don't even know for sure they die in the eruption. Perhaps they escape.'

Maia gave him a withering frown.

'What on earth are you two doing dressed like that?'

Zak turned around and saw Mrs Sullivan standing before them, a large pile of books and papers clutched to her chest, and a thoroughly bemused expression on her face.

'Oh, hi, Mrs Sullivan,' said Maia. 'We ... um ... were inspired by your lesson on Pompeii. So we ... er ... thought we'd dress up as Romans.'

'I see,' said the teacher, though she still looked rather perplexed.

'Yeah, and we wanted to ask you some questions about Pompeii,' added Zak. 'If you have the time.'

Mrs Sullivan's face broke into a smile. 'Well, of course. Come in.'

Zak and Maia followed her into the office, closed the door behind them and sat down in front of her small, cluttered desk.

'That strange door knocker on your door, the one with two faces,' said Maia, before the teacher had even sat down. 'What is it?'

Mrs Sullivan dumped her pile of papers on top of an even larger pile on her desk and sat down. 'Oh, that's the head of the Roman god Janus. He was the god of doors and gates, beginnings and endings, time, that sort of thing.'

At the casual mention of time, Zak threw a quick glance at Maia.

'And where did you get it?' asked Maia.

'It was found during an excavation in London. I was part of an archaeological dig one summer and they found that. Because it was found in the ruins of a Roman building, some argued it had to be Roman. But it's made of bronze, which usually turns green over time, and that is in such perfect condition that eventually the experts said it had to be a much later copy of an original Roman one. So, after they said it was worthless, I kept it and just put it on my door as a souvenir.'

From her reaction and the innocent expression on her face, Zak was already beginning to feel she had absolutely no idea about the time machine.

'Anyway, I am so pleased Pompeii has inspired you,' continued the teacher. 'It is such an amazing place. So what was it you wanted to know?'

Maia and Zak looked at one another, before Zak said: 'Well, it's mostly about the eruption, really.'

'Ah, yes. It usually is with the boys,' she said with a playful roll of the eyes.

'Would the Romans have seen any signs that Vesuvius was going to erupt?'

'Well, there would have been more and more earth tremors in the weeks and months leading up to the eruption. And we have evidence that the water supply failed a few days beforehand as well. The constant tremors would have badly damaged the aqueduct that carried water into the city from the hills. But these things would have happened before in that region. And at that time, Vesuvius had not erupted for hundreds of years. So the locals would have had no idea it was about to erupt.'

'Did any of them leave before it erupted?' asked Zak.

'Oh, yes. They reckon there were at least ten thousand people living in the city. But they have never found anywhere near that number of bodies. So the theory is that many left during the period of earth tremors beforehand. But it is also possible that many were killed outside the city as they fled and we just haven't found their bodies yet.'

Zak felt his heart sink. Until recently, he would have followed this account with a rather morbid, detached interest. But now, he personally knew some of these people who were going to die: Cassia, Dexter, Caius, Felix and the other household slaves.

'So how did it happen?' asked Maia. Zak noticed she too looked decidedly unsettled. 'The eruption, I mean.'

'Ah, well, I've got a short video somewhere I can show you,' said Mrs Sullivan, brushing aside numerous papers on her desk, until she revealed a laptop. Once she had found what she was looking for, she turned the laptop around so that all three of them could see the screen.

'Around midday on the 24th of October AD 79, Vesuvius erupted,' the teacher continued.

Zak and Maia stared intently at the screen, where a very life-like animation was now playing, showing the top of the volcano exploding into the air.

'Before long, a huge cloud of ash and pumice was thrown into the air, which the wind then blew towards Pompeii. At first, tiny pieces of pumice began to rain down on the city. This phase would have lasted a few hours and would probably not have killed that many people because they would simply have sought shelter in their homes. We think a lot of people would have started to leave the city during this time.'

The animation showed the streets of Pompeii getting darker and darker as the cloud of ash blotted out the sun.

'As the layer of ash and pumice got deeper and deeper,' the teacher continued, 'the weight would have begun to cause roofs to collapse. During the initial stages of the eruption, it would actually have been collapsing buildings that killed most people, rather than falling pumice.

'But as the day wore on, larger pieces of pumice would have begun to fall, which would have caused considerable damage to buildings and to anyone out in the open, trying to flee the city.

'The eruption continued into the night. But then there comes a point in an eruption like this when the volume of ash and pumice in the air becomes just too heavy. So the enormous cloud began to collapse in several waves down the side of the volcano like avalanches. These are called pyroclastic surges and travel at over one hundred miles an hour and are incredibly hot. The first couple of surges failed to reach Pompeii, which is five miles away from Vesuvius.'

Zak watched the animation as a massive dirty grey cloud raced towards the by now half-buried city.

'But then, in the early hours of the morning, one of them finally did. It is this cloud of super-hot ash that would have instantly killed all those many people who were still alive in the city at the time.'

When the fast-moving cloud hit the city, Zak shivered, as though he were watching live footage of his own house being destroyed. For several seconds, he sat staring at the screen, where the image had frozen at the end of the animation. He felt as shocked, as numb as he would have done if Mrs Sullivan had just shown him a video of his own town being buried.

'Gosh!' said the teacher. 'You two look as white as ghosts. I'm sorry if that was a bit shocking.'

'It's just,' began Maia, swallowing hard, 'I think we can imagine what it must have been like for those left in the city.'

'I know,' continued Mrs Sullivan. 'It must have been awful. But at least those who were killed by the cloud of ash would have died instantly.' Her fingers then rippled across the keyboard, and she began calling up the images of the bodies she had shown them in the lesson earlier. They were largely featureless statues of plaster, but the poses they struck were undeniably those of real people, frozen at the moment of their deaths.

'Wait!' said Zak, as various images continued to flash across the screen. 'Go back. There. What is that one showing?' His blood ran cold. There on the screen was an image of an earring. It was triangular in shape, with three tiny strands of jewels hanging down from the base.

Mrs Sullivan's face lit up. 'Oh, that is an exquisite piece of jewellery, in amazing condition. It has only recently been unearthed in the northeast of the city, near a particularly well-preserved fountain of Neptune, which—'

'Was it found with anyone?' Maia cut in sharply.

Mrs Sullivan's face turned grave. 'Well, yes. It's quite sad really. A group of seven or eight bodies was found inside a collapsed building.' She flicked through the images on her laptop until a picture appeared of several white figures huddled together. 'The earring was found on one of them. They believe she was a girl of about thirteen or fourteen.'

Still wearing their Roman clothes, Zak and Maia walked away from the school in silence, utterly oblivious to the curious looks they were still drawing, as well as to the gathering chill in the air.

'I thought you were going to activate the time machine when we went into her office,' said Maia at last.

'I couldn't, could I?' snapped Zak. 'It would have looked a bit strange if we had just disappeared in front of her.' Maia flinched slightly at Zak's aggressive response. He glanced at her as they walked. 'Sorry. It's just ...' His voice caught in his throat.

'I know,' said Maia. 'That was one of Cassia's earrings, wasn't it?'

Zak did not reply straightaway, but just stared ahead. After a while he said: 'Maybe they're common, those earrings. Perhaps everyone in Pompeii is wearing them. Or was wearing them.'

Maia puffed out her cheeks. 'No,' she said emphatically. 'Cassia knows her jewellery. She bought them because they are beautiful and because they are unique.' She then stopped walking abruptly and grabbed Zak's arm to halt him. 'We have to go back. We have to warn them.'

'We can't. They won't listen. They won't understand.'

'We have to at least try,' insisted Maia. Then, when she saw the indecision on Zak's face, she held out her hand: 'Give it to me, then. Give me the watch. I'll go back on my own. You can walk away from all this if you want to. But I'm not.'

She held his eyes with a piercing, intimidating stare, until he looked away. He was just too tired to argue, to even think. He just wanted to curl up and go to sleep.

'All right,' he sighed, rubbing his tight forehead. It was absurd. He could have just given her the watch and walked away. But something, some little voice in his head told him not to. He was, somehow, as much a part of all this as she was. 'Let's go back.'

She gave him a wan smile. It was nothing to get excited about, but they both knew it was what they had to do.

'We should hang around till we see Mrs Sullivan leave,' said Maia. 'Then try to sneak back in.'

'We're going to look a bit conspicuous wearing these,' said Zak, tugging gently at his tunic.

'You're right. I know. Our coats should still be hanging up. Let's go and get them, then if anyone asks why we're going back into school, we can say we forgot them.'

'Good idea,' said Zak, as they strode quickly back towards the school. Then he chuckled. 'I've just thought. Our school uniforms are still in Cassia's house, and our blazers are now owned by a pair of Romans. Imagine if some archaeologist uncovers pieces of a twenty-first century English school uniform buried in Pompeii.'

Maia laughed. 'That would cause quite a stir, wouldn't it? Although I guess if our clothes had been found, they would have been dug up long ago, even though we only left there two days ago.'

It was Zak's turn to laugh. 'This time travel thing hurts my head.'

Presently, they arrived back at school, then found and put on their coats. They then spent the next few minutes prowling around the school, trying to avoid the teachers and the cleaners, whilst at the same time keeping an eye on the car park to see when Mrs Sullivan left. As luck would have it, they saw her leave only a short while later.

'Now what?' said Maia, as they stood in front of the teacher's closed door once more, the bronze twin heads of Janus on the door knocker glinting in the light.

Zak took out the watch and began fiddling with all the settings he was by now beginning to know off by heart. 'I've set it to five in the afternoon on the day we left and moved the map to the Forum in Pompeii.' The red ring around the face of the watch was once again pulsing. He tried the door handle. 'It's locked.'

'Maybe the door doesn't have to be open,' suggested Maia. 'Perhaps we just have to walk towards it.'

'Okay. Let's give it a try. Hold my hand,' said Zak. He braced himself and then lunged towards the door. 'Ow!' he said as his face hit the solid wood. He rubbed his nose. 'Well, I guess that doesn't work.'

'Maybe we have to walk past it, or something,' said Maia, scratching her head.

'In that case, we'll have to come back tomorrow. It won't matter because we can just programme the watch to whatever date we want.'

'No!' said Maia, glowering. 'What if the Vulcani return?'

'Oh. I forgot about them.'

'Yeah. Easy for you to forget,' grumbled Maia. 'They're not after you, are they?'

'We'll have to take it off, then,' said Zak. 'Put it on another door.' He looked closely and saw it was held on with two screws. He stopped to think for a minute, then realised he could use the metal buckle on the watch to unscrew the door knocker. Working as fast as he could, Zak loosened the screws, then ripped it off the door. Without even checking to see if they had been spotted, they then dashed out of the school grounds.

They headed for a nearby park and sat down on a bench, staring at the strange knocker between them. Zak moved the watch close to it till the two items touched. Nothing happened. He moved the watch around in circles, brought it closer then further away from the door knocker, but still there was no change. His watch continued to pulse silently. It was clearly primed and ready to go, but he just had no idea what triggered it to work.

'Hang on,' said Maia at length. 'Janus was the god of doors and doorways, wasn't he?'

'Er, yeah, I think so.'

'Then what if this thing has to be attached to a door or a door frame, and we then have to pass through that door?'

'Right,' said Zak slowly. 'So we need to attach it to a door, that is hidden out of sight so people don't see us coming and going. And we have to conceal the door knocker itself, in case someone sees it and decides to steal it. That won't be easy.'

Maia thought for a moment. 'I think I know just the place.'

Having told Zak where she lived, Maia hurriedly led him towards her house. Her back garden backed onto some woodland, she said, accessed through an overgrown gate. It would be the perfect place to attach and hide the door knocker. And what was more, she considered it unlikely anyone would ever see them disappearing and reappearing.

As they rushed along the streets, Zak asked: 'Where do you come from, Maia? Where were you born?'

She eyed him suspiciously, as though expecting him to start accusing her of holding something back from him.

'Sorry,' he added quickly. 'I'm just trying to make sense of all this. Why you? And why me?'

'I don't know where I was born,' she said finally, averting her gaze. 'I'm adopted. Apparently, I was abandoned as a baby and left outside a hospital. My parents, or who I call mum and dad, adopted me when I was still a baby. So I have no idea where I come from. But I'm just beginning to think it has something to do with all this.'

Glancing across at her forlorn face, Zak thought it best not to pry any further.

At last, they arrived at Maia's house. They went straight up the side and into the garden, which, although not very wide, extended a long way into an overgrown area of trees and bushes at the bottom. She led him along a narrow path, which ended in a wooden gate. The gate itself was almost entirely covered in ivy and other creeping plants. She pulled back some of the leaves to reveal a padlock with a combination lock.

'If we attach it here,' she said, 'then cover it with ivy, no one should see it. Me and my parents haven't used this gate in years.'

Using the screws he had ripped from Mrs Sullivan's door, Zak attached the bronze head of Janus as securely as he could to the wooden frame around the gate.

'I feel bad about stealing this from Mrs Sullivan,' said Maia, as Zak worked. 'She is such a nice teacher.'

'We're only borrowing it,' said Zak. 'We'll take it back one day. Perhaps then we can tell her all about this adventure.'

'Not that she would believe us,' added Maia.

'Maybe not. Anyway — you ready? Let's try this.'

Maia undid the padlock and eased open the gate, just enough for them to pass through into the dark woods beyond. They held hands and stepped forward.

There was a brief, dazzling explosion of light. Then the two of them vanished into thin air.

Chapter XI

Maximus the Gladiator

'Oh, thank Juno!' exclaimed Cassia. She leapt up and rushed towards Maia and Zak. She had been reclining on a divan like a haughty princess when they had entered the room, but the moment she saw who it was, she had lost all her composure and nearly tripped over the folds of her long dress in her haste to reach them.

'Where have you been?' she demanded, flinging her arms around Maia, then giving Zak a mighty hug, too. 'You just disappeared from the carriage. And then when the earthquake struck, we feared the worst.'

As Cassia pulled away from Zak, still chatting incessantly as was her wont, he noticed under the curls of her blonde hair, the triangular earrings swaying gently. Immediately, he winced at the recollection of the pictures he had just seen on Mrs Sullivan's laptop.

'Let them tell us what happened,' interrupted Caius with a smile, as he too rose to greet them.

'Before we do, are you all okay?' asked Maia, removing her dark, twenty-first century coat and laying it on an empty couch. 'That earthquake was pretty bad.'

'We're fine,' said Cassia. 'A little damage to the house, but nothing serious. This is a well-built villa compared to some.'

'That's good,' said Maia. Then her face darkened. 'We were chased again by the Vulcani on the way back from that villa. We managed to get away, but they're just not going to give up.'

'What do they want with you?' asked Caius.

'We still don't know,' said Maia. 'If they didn't look so threatening, we'd stop and ask them.' She turned and looked at Zak, clearly expecting him to speak next.

He paused. On the walk from the Forum to Cassia's house, they had been planning what to say. He had intended to tell them that he and Maia had travelled back from the future and that they knew Vesuvius was going to erupt and bury Pompeii. He was going to insist they all leave the city immediately, before it was too late. But now that he stood in front of the three of them, he found he could not. He would sound ridiculous. And besides, he did not want to leave the city just yet. There were still so many answers he was desperate to find.

'Yeah,' he said. 'We need your help more than ever to find out what they want from us.'

Maia frowned at him but said nothing.

'If only we could free my father,' said Caius, 'then perhaps he could help us solve all this.'

'Anyway, sit down, both of you,' said Cassia, waving her arms towards a table at one end of the room. 'Dexter, fetch us some more bread.'

Zak glanced at the slave, who looked as impassive as ever. As Dexter was about to leave, Zak quickly said: 'No, stay. There's enough food here already. Join us, Dexter. I'm sure Cassia won't mind.' He glared at Cassia, defying her to say no.

With a thin smile, she offered Dexter a seat at the table. After a moment's hesitation, he sat down.

For the next few hours, they sat around chatting, trying to solve the riddle found in Portunus' villa. Cassia found her copy of The Gallic Wars, Julius Caesar's book, from which the quotation "VENI, VIDI, VICI" was taken. They pored over the relevant passages hunting for clues. They reversed the letters, assigned them numbers, translated them into other languages. In short, they tried everything they could think of, until, no further forward, they eventually retired to their bedrooms.

'Why didn't you say anything?' mumbled Maia, as she and Zak headed along the colonnade towards their rooms. 'About where we come from and about Vesuvius?'

'Why didn't you?'

'I thought we'd agreed we would tell them everything,' huffed Maia.

'You really think they'll believe a single word we say? They'll think we've gone mad. They might even just throw us out on the street. We have to think of a different way to tell them.'

'Well, we have to tell them soon. We're running out of time.'

'I know!' he snapped. Then he mumbled 'Good night' under his breath and shut himself in his small room. Maia really was insufferable at times, he thought, as he lay down on his bed. His life would have been so much simpler if he had never met her.

The next morning, Zak woke with a start. It was unusually quiet outside his room. He feared that once again the Vulcani had frozen time, but then he heard a noisy bird chirping away in the garden and sighed with exaggerated relief.

He dressed quickly and went outside. The sun was still low in the sky, so the garden was largely in shade. A slave was hurrying away from the fountain in the middle of the garden. Of course, that was it. He had already grown so used to the constant and soothing plashing of the fountain, but now it was silent. He rushed over to take a closer look.

'It seems we have lost our water supply.'

He spun round and saw Dexter walking towards him.

'How will Cassia cope?' Dexter added with a smirk.

Zak grinned, but then his heart sank. He remembered Mrs Sullivan telling them that Pompeii's water supply seemed to have failed shortly before the eruption. It was now the 22nd of October. Two days to go. He felt the urge to tell Dexter there and then, to tell him to just run as far away as he could.

'Good morning, Zak,' said a bright and cheery voice. Cassia was approaching with Caius close behind. 'I trust you slept well. You see our water has failed. Never mind. I'm sure it's only temporary. I have our steward looking into it. But it's not all bad news. The city council have agreed to proceed with the games today, despite yesterday's earthquake. I suppose they want to try to raise all our spirits.'

'I've heard Maximus is going to fight today,' said Caius with a glint in his eye. 'I bet you're a Maximus fan, Cassia.'

'Absolutely not,' said Cassia, screwing up her nose. 'I like the sporting events and I love all the parades at the beginning of the games. But I cannot abide watching men try to hack great lumps out of one another. It's barbaric.'

Dexter stood behind Cassia, straining not to laugh at her pompous tone. This in turn made Zak have to look away to stop himself from smirking.

'Who's Maximus?' asked Maia, as she approached the group standing around the dry fountain.

'Who's Maximus?' said Caius incredulously. 'He's only the most famous gladiator in Pompeii. And probably in this whole area, that's who. All the girls love him. And all the men wish they were him.'

'Not *all* the girls,' said Cassia, rolling her eyes. She then did a double take, when she saw Maia was wearing a simple dress, which came to just below her knees, like a man's tunic. 'You can't wear that, Maia. You'll look like ... like some sort of slave. Or a boy.'

'But at least I'll be able to run,' said Maia. 'I had to do a lot of running yesterday in that ridiculously long dress. And I am not doing that again.'

All the boys laughed.

'If you're going to be hanging around with us, Cassia,' continued Maia, 'I suggest you change out of your long dress, too. Because sooner or later, you might have to run for your life as well.'

Cassia looked horrified, and for once, she was lost for words, as though Maia had just suggested she walk through the city stark naked.

Later that morning, they walked along the streets towards the east of the city, where the amphitheatre was situated. As they jostled their way along the busy main road near to Cassia's house, Zak noticed a large cart piled high with boxes and furniture, travelling in the opposite direction. Two young children sat on top next to a well-dressed woman, while two men directed the mules through the busy street. A short distance later, another fully laden cart creaked past them, heading in the same direction.

Dexter leaned in closer to Zak. 'Looks like some people have had enough of all the earthquakes.'

'Yeah,' said Zak. 'Very sensible. I think we should leave tomorrow as well.'

Dexter smiled. 'Good luck trying to persuade Cassia to do that.'

Zak pulled a face but said nothing more. One way or another, he was going to have to get her and her household to leave the city, even if he had to drag her by the feet.

A little further down the road and Cassia stopped abruptly under the wide awning of a shop, declaring the spot to be perfect to watch the forthcoming procession. In no time at all, the pavements on either side of the road were thronged with people, teetering on the edge of the high curb stones.

A short while later, the road in front of them was suddenly empty of all traffic. Trumpets sounded in the distance, then the beating of drums rose above the chatter of the crowds.

Before long, the procession could be seen advancing down the street from the direction of the Forum where it had begun. Men on horseback trotted past, followed by bright and colourful carnival floats pulled along by mules or slaves, each one carrying musicians, dancers or acrobats. There were also men dressed in pristine white togas, solemnly carrying a collection of small statues, brightly painted boxes and other unfamiliar items. In response to Zak's puzzled look, Dexter leant close to his ear and explained that these were the city's most important politicians, who were preparing to make offerings to the gods.

The bright river of colour, the rousing wall of noise were so similar to what Zak had seen many times back home during carnivals, that he could not fail to become caught up in the excitement of the spectacle.

A temporary hush then fell over the crowds, followed shortly afterwards by a crescendo of excited cheering. The gladiators were coming. With an obvious swagger, two dozen men marched powerfully down the road, their large muscles glistening with oil and sweat. They wore only minimal pieces of armour, all of it highly polished and glinting in the sun. Some wore a helmet, while others had armour along just one arm. Some waved a sword in the air, others a trident or a spear. All seemed to be enjoying the adulation, beaming broadly and waving to the adoring crowds.

Zak's eyes briefly caught those of one of the gladiators, and his heart almost leapt out from his chest. The man was in his late thirties or early forties, with short black hair and had a piercing stare. As he waved his gleaming short sword in the air, Zak caught sight of a tattoo on his forearm. The tattoo of a hammer.

It was the man he had seen on the day he and Maia had been chased through the school. He was one of the Vulcani.

Zak tried to shout to Maia, who was standing transfixed a few paces along from him. But the din was too great. He gesticulated more and more urgently as the gladiator slowly marched away down the street, until at last Maia turned towards him. He kept tapping his forearm and pointing at the back of the man. Caius, who was standing between them, looked puzzled. But then Maia seemed to realise what he was trying to say, her eyes widening with a mixture of surprise and horror.

Zak wanted to leap out and run after the gladiator, but he was hopelessly hemmed in by the crowd.

As the procession slowly receded into the distance, the crowds began to surge after it down the road towards the amphitheatre. At last, Zak managed to barge his way next to Maia.

'We should follow him,' he shouted above the noise of the jostling crowd.

Maia looked horrified. 'Is that wise?'

'If we can find where they go, we might get some idea what they're up to.'

Caius came up beside them. 'What's the matter?' he asked.

'That gladiator, with the black hair and the short sword,' replied Zak. 'He had the hammer tattoo. He's a Vulcani.'

'What? Are you sure?' Caius' jaw dropped. 'That was Maximus.'

A great roar erupted in the amphitheatre. Twenty thousand people were crammed onto the benches around the oval-shaped arena below. If Zak had closed his eyes, he could have believed he was at a football or rugby match. People were chanting, singing, screaming, clapping. Every now and then the crowd would roar as one.

It had all begun like a circus. There had been acrobats and gymnasts performing astonishing aerial feats. But then wild, half-starved animals had been released into the arena and Zak had had to look away, while a mixture of skilled hunters and defenceless criminals were thrown in with them. Though he had not actually watched any of it, he gathered from the noise of the crowd that more animals than humans had survived the ordeal.

And now it was the turn of the gladiators. Caius, who was clearly relishing the spectacle more than Cassia, explained that they were highly trained slaves who could eventually earn their freedom if they survived long enough.

'Oh, don't worry,' said Caius, clearly enjoying Zak's obvious squeamishness, 'only a small number of gladiators actually die in the games. It costs far too much money to train them to then have them die in their first fight.'

'Oh, that's all right, then,' said Zak with a grimace. He was at least grateful that, as children, they had to sit right near the top of the stadium. From up there it was not always easy to make out exactly what was going on down below on the sand of the arena.

Another roar, greater than any hitherto, erupted.

'Here he comes,' shouted Caius excitedly. 'It's Maximus.'

Together with several other gladiators, Maximus entered the arena, his short sword raised above his head. The crowd were stamping their feet and chanting his name while he saluted a group of men in togas, who were sitting in a prime spot close to the edge of the arena.

Zak looked along the bench he was sitting on and saw that Maia and Cassia were watching with the same pained expression, the same trepidation that he himself was no doubt displaying. Dexter, meanwhile, was looking down into the arena with that look of indifference he always seemed to wear.

When the fighting began, Zak forced himself to watch. He wanted to see this Maximus in action, see what he was capable of. Even from a distance, his skill was immediately obvious. He fought with such speed, such nimbleness that he could easily fight two opponents at once. His sword seemed to move faster than was humanly possible, scything through the air, creating nothing more than a series of blurred streaks. Both his opponents reeled under the onslaught, frantically blocking blow after blow with their swords and shields. Mesmerised by the swordplay, Zak stared open-mouthed, unable to take his eyes from the action.

Several times, Maximus knocked one or other of his adversaries to the ground, had him at his mercy, but then backed away to focus on the remaining gladiator. The crowd roared its approval over and over again. Zak began to realise that the man could probably have finished off his opponents in no time at all, but was instead, intentionally prolonging the spectacle for the enjoyment of the crowd.

During a brief lull in the fighting, Zak happened to look up and across to the other side of the arena. In the shadow of the great awning which encircled the entire top of the stadium, affording the upper sections of the crowd at least some shelter from the blazing sun, he saw a tall, slender figure. It was walking slowly along the top walkway, just above the highest rows of benches. Although it was impossible from that distance to tell who it was, there was something familiar about the long, flowing gown the person was wearing. Then Zak noticed the figure was walking with a long staff. It was the woman he had seen on top of the city walls the day before, he was sure of it.

Instantly losing interest in the ongoing clash of swords below, he jumped to his feet and shuffled along to Maia.

'Look. It's her again,' he shouted into her ear above the roar of the crowd. 'The woman we saw yesterday. I'm going to follow her.'

'I'll come with you,' she replied.

'No. You stay here. Keep an eye on Maximus. And I can move faster if I'm on my own.'

Maia looked like she was about to protest, but Zak gave her a quick reassuring squeeze of the shoulder and then darted away. He reached one of the many flights of steps used to access the rows of benches. Leaping up the steps two at a time, he arrived at the upper walkway below the large awning.

He peered across to the other side of the oval pathway and noticed the woman was still there, apparently unaware of his presence. Luckily for him, several other people were milling about in the shade of the walkway, chatting in small groups whilst watching the action below, so he was unlikely to stand out. He quickly decided he should try to get nearer to her from behind, so he hurried along the path in the opposite direction to the woman.

Another mighty cheer reverberated around the stadium, so loud it seemed to shake the stone amphitheatre. Everyone's attention was focused on the arena below. Even the woman, who was still some distance away from Zak, was apparently engrossed by the combat down on the sand.

He dodged around a small knot of men, keeping the woman in sight, drawing ever closer. When he glanced back, he picked out Maia and Cassia still sitting in the crowd, their concerned eyes following his progress around the rim of the stadium.

He was close now. A good throw of a stone would have hit her on the back of the head. Her long, wavy grey hair was clearly visible, cascading over her cloak. Still she was moving gracefully away from him.

But then she ducked through one of the many small archways around the top of the amphitheatre and disappeared from view. Zak turned into an identical archway nearer to him, knowing that they all opened out onto another walkway that ran around the outside of the amphitheatre.

Trumpets blared from inside the stadium, making Zak jump. Moments later, more trumpets sounded. The fighting in the arena must have been brought to a close, he realised, and something else was apparently about to begin. He was glad he was no longer watching; he had seen enough gore for one day.

For a few seconds, he remained in the shadow of the small passageway, listening intently, before peering cautiously out. The graceful figure of the tall woman was descending one of the flights of steps built onto the outside of the giant building, her staff tap-tapping on the stone as she went.

As soon as she had moved out of sight, Zak eased out of his hiding place and crept towards the steps. When he reached the top, the woman was already at the bottom and was turning back towards the base of the amphitheatre. Zak followed her to the sound of more cheering and applauding.

Once at the bottom, Zak hugged the side of the building as he moved along, just keeping her in sight around the curve of the stadium. She then disappeared into the blackness of one of the huge archways that were built into the entire perimeter of the amphitheatre.

Zak crept up to the edge and peered round the corner. The woman was walking away from him down a dark tunnel, at the end of which a vast archway of daylight opened out onto the arena beyond. A large, silhouetted figure was approaching her from the direction of the arena, his footfalls silent beneath the ongoing roars from the teeming crowd.

Zak knew at once it was the gladiator Maximus.

The powerfully built man stopped a pace or two in front of the woman and bowed his head respectfully. The two then began talking in hushed tones.

'I might have guessed,' muttered Zak under his breath. She and the gladiator were clearly in league with one another. If he could just follow one or both of them, what might he find out? Or better still, if he could only hear what they were saying ...

He crept into the tunnel, inching along the cold stone wall, trying to keep out of sight.

Maximus and the woman were now in heated conversation. The gladiator was whispering harshly, gesticulating with his arms. But above the roar of noise from the amphitheatre, Zak could still not make out a single word they were uttering.

'Hey! Who's there?' shouted Maximus, turning his shadowy face sharply to look straight at Zak.

Zak's blood ran cold. Without a second thought, he turned and ran, back towards the glaring daylight. Behind him, he could clearly make out the echoing clatter of hobnailed shoes sprinting after him through the tunnel.

Chapter XII

A Futile Attempt

Panic, sheer, uncontrollable panic, seemed to surge through every part of Zak's being. He had just witnessed what Maximus was capable of, had seen that most fearsome fighting machine in action in the arena, and now that man was after him.

Once back out in the sunshine, his terrified eyes scanned the scene ahead, desperately searching for somewhere to hide. In front of him, there was a mass of carriages and slaves milling around beside them, waiting to transport their masters home after the games. Sprinting as fast as he could, Zak headed for a small gap between two such carriages. Some of the slaves turned to stare at him with a disinterested air. He leapt over the protruding, horizontal poles used to carry one of the carriages and continued running, not daring to look back.

Ahead of him, the place was almost deserted. There were no crowds to hide in, no narrow alleyways to escape down, just an open patch of ground and a long, straight wall approaching fast.

As the noise from the amphitheatre began to recede behind him, he could clearly hear the gladiator's bounding footsteps drawing ever closer over his shoulder. He expected to be seized from behind and to be dragged to the ground at any moment.

He shot through an arched opening in the wall in front of him. Beyond the wall, there was a large open space, bigger than a football pitch, with patches of lawn, some trees dotted about and a large open-air swimming pool in the middle. Immediately, his panic levels increased, for the whole space was enclosed by a long colonnade running along three sides. Unless he found another way out, he would be trapped.

One or two men were exercising in the open, but otherwise

the place was quiet. There was nowhere to hide.

Believing sudden changes of direction might just buy him some precious seconds, Zak darted to his left straight for the colonnade. As he sprinted along in the shade of the covered walkway, he kept looking for another way out.

To his left, a short distance away, a man emerged from a doorway. Zak had to swerve past him at the last second, missing the thickset man by what felt like millimetres, and nearly losing his balance in the process. Ignoring the man's indignant cries, Zak glanced past him into the doorway, hoping to see a way out of the enclosure. But there was nothing inside but public toilets. So he sprinted on.

He finally felt compelled to look behind and saw Maximus hurtling towards him like a charging bull, his powerful limbs pumping and his face red and contorted into a snarl.

As he continued to run, Zak's eyes flitted about in wild panic. He spotted a large wooden trolley carrying a bucket of water, a mop and other items for cleaning. He sprinted towards it and just as the gladiator drew near, he grabbed the trolley and swung it in the way of his pursuer. With a loud clatter, he heard Maximus collide with the trolley. The gladiator let out a curse.

Not waiting to see what state the man was in, Zak burst back out into the sunshine from under the colonnade and sprinted across the lawn. As he skirted around the swimming pool, he finally chanced another look over his shoulder. Maximus was still there, once again closing fast.

Zak's legs felt like lead. His lungs and his heart seemed on the point of bursting, and panic was constricting his throat. What on earth was he going to do?

He headed back towards one of the openings in the wall, behind which the bulk of the amphitheatre rose up like a cliff face. Despite his desperation, he was slowing down, he could feel it. He felt dizzy, felt sick.

As he passed through the archway in the wall, he collapsed

and fell. Whether because he had stumbled over something or just from sheer exhaustion, he could not tell. But there he lay, winded and unable to move.

'Maximus!' said a girl's excited, high-pitched voice. 'Look! It's the gladiator Maximus. Look, everyone. Over here. It's Maximus.'

Zak looked up and saw Cassia standing over him. Maia, Dexter and Caius were with her, together with a rapidly growing number of onlookers, anxious to catch a glimpse of the famous gladiator at close quarters.

Zak looked round, and just a few paces away from him, Maximus was slowing down, as a dozen or more people surrounded him with eager faces. Breathing heavily, the man glared down at Zak, murder in his eyes, but moved no further forward.

'Thanks, Cassia,' gasped Zak, still lying on the ground. 'You just saved my life.'

'Listen, we have something to tell you all.' Maia and Zak exchanged an anxious look.

They were back at Cassia's house, standing in front of a seated Cassia, Dexter and Caius, who eyed both of them with a mixture of confusion and suspicion.

Before resuming, Zak looked around the room, checking that no one else was in earshot.

'What we're going to tell you is going to sound absurd,' he began solemnly. 'You'll probably think we're mad. But here goes, anyway.' Three pairs of eyes were studying him intently, and even with Maia standing beside him, he suddenly felt a little nervous. With a deep breath, he began. 'The day after tomorrow, Vesuvius is going to erupt. And when it does, it will completely bury Pompeii and several other towns along the coast. A lot of people are going to die.'

His small audience stared up at him, their expressions frozen.

'You have to believe us,' said Maia. 'We have to leave the city, all of us, and go far away from here.'

'And how exactly do you know this?' asked Caius. 'I mean, how can you be so sure?'

Again Maia and Zak exchanged an uncertain glance.

'We ... um,' began Zak. How on earth was he going to phrase this? 'We have, somehow, travelled here from the future. We do come from Britain. But two thousand years in the future. We learn about Pompeii at school, and the destruction caused by Vesuvius.'

Dexter's frown turned to a brief chuckle. 'If that were true, how in the name of all the gods did you get here, then?'

'A stranger gave me this the other day,' continued Zak, showing them the watch. 'Somehow, it sent us back in time to here.'

'We guess it has something to do with the Vulcani,' added Maia. 'And why they keep chasing us. And maybe even to do with Caius' father.'

Cassia screwed her face up as though in pain. 'I'm not sure I understand. You're saying you came here from the future? But the future hasn't happened yet?'

'Look, I know it must be very confusing for you,' continued Zak. 'It's confusing for us, too. But for now, what matters the most is that Vesuvius is going to erupt. So we have to leave Pompeii. If nothing else, you have to believe that.'

'Where would we go?' asked Caius.

Zak was tired and frustrated. 'I don't care where we go — we just have to get out of this area. Anyone who stays in the city will die. It's as simple as that.' Horrified, the three of them stared at him. He had not intended to sound quite so blunt, but then again, maybe that was exactly what they needed to hear.

Of the shocked and sceptical faces before him, Zak found it was Dexter's that hurt him the most. He felt they were slowly becoming friends, that a level of trust was building up. But now he looked at Zak as though he were mad, or worse still, that Zak was somehow telling the most outrageous lie and had thereby betrayed that growing trust.

'Are we honestly expected to believe this?' said Dexter. Almost imperceptibly, his head was shaking from side to side, as if he were saying to himself, he should have known Zak was like this, that he was no different to anyone else.

'I promise you, it's the truth,' insisted Maia in a quiet, weary voice.

An uncomfortable silence flooded the room for what, to Zak at least, seemed an age.

'Well,' said Cassia at length, her beaming smile suddenly lighting up the room, as it so often did. 'The way I see it — Maia and Zak have become my friends — our friends. So I think we should believe them. We have no reason not to.'

'Thank you, Cassia,' said Maia.

'If the city really is in danger,' continued Cassia, 'we should go and see my uncle Marcus. He is one of the *duoviri* who control the city council this year. He will know what to do.'

'I thought Caius said the city council had been infiltrated by the Vulcani,' said Zak.

'Oh, not Uncle Marcus,' grinned Cassia. 'He's the most honest man I know. He's nothing like my parents.'

'You will let me see the *duumvir* now,' demanded Cassia.

'Sorry, love,' said the man with a smirk. 'He's busy. Come back another day.'

They were standing in a small entrance lobby glaring at one another across a marble desk. Zak, Maia and Dexter stood rather sheepishly behind Cassia.

'Do you know who I am?' said Cassia, thrusting her nose into the air.

The man behind the desk shrugged his indifference.

'I am the *duumvir*'s niece. Yes, that's right. His sister is my mother. And if you do not take us to see him right now, then by all the gods, I will ensure he makes your life a complete misery. I hear they are looking for more criminals to feed to the wild animals in the amphitheatre. Perhaps you would like to join them?' Cassia folded her arms and glared at the man.

Finally, a look of doubt began to creep into the man's face. 'Fine!' he muttered through clenched teeth. 'Follow me.'

As they were led down a corridor, Zak smiled to himself. He was beginning to like Cassia. And there were definitely times when her snooty arrogance came in handy.

The man knocked on a door, opened it and stepped in. Talking fast, he began to apologise profusely for disturbing the politician, blaming the intrusion on Cassia. But the moment he saw his niece walk into the room, the *duumvir* totally ignored the man's ramblings and dismissed him.

'Cassia! What a pleasant surprise. Come in. How are you?'

He was a plump, middle-aged man with thin, greying hair and a warm smile.

'Did you enjoy the games today?' he asked, offering them all a seat in front of his large desk. 'We put on quite a show, didn't we?'

'Sorry, Uncle Marcus,' replied Cassia. 'But you know the games are not really my thing. Too much blood.'

'No, they're not really mine either, truth be told. But the people like them. Or most of them, anyway. But who have you brought with you?' he added, peering at the others with a glint in his eye.

'You know Dexter, of course. And these are my friends Zak and Maia from ... Britannia. They have some disturbing news, Uncle, which I think you need to hear.'

His eyes widened with exaggerated surprise, and he began staring directly at Zak, clearly expecting him to speak.

'Tell him, Zak,' said Cassia.

Feeling even more nervous than when he had told the others,

Zak cleared his throat. 'Um. Well, we know that Vesuvius is going to erupt the day after tomorrow. When it does, it will completely destroy Pompeii.'

Uncle Marcus' face froze and he blinked several times, as if Zak had just spoken an incomprehensible foreign language. 'What in Jupiter's name do you mean?'

'Vesuvius is a volcano. All these tremors and earthquakes you've been getting recently mean it's going to erupt ... very soon.'

'Well, young man, there was a far worse earthquake seventeen years ago. But Vesuvius didn't erupt then. It has not erupted for hundreds of years. So long ago in fact that there are no records of when it last did. Volcanoes are like mount Etna on the island of Sicily. Every few years they erupt, eject a mass of spectacular but slow-moving lava and then go still again. I understand your concerns over Vesuvius. But I assure you, they are unfounded.'

Zak could feel his frustration growing again. 'And I assure you, sir, Vesuvius is going to erupt and kill a great many people, unless you evacuate the city.'

Zak's tone made Uncle Marcus' smile vanish. His eyes narrowed. 'And just how do you know this, young man?'

Zak was struggling to know what to say. If he told the truth, he would just be dismissed as a fool. 'I ... we just do. You have to trust us.'

'Oh, I do, do I? I'm just going to evacuate the entire city based on ... well, what exactly? Have you had a premonition? Have you visited an oracle? Have the gods spoken to you in some way?'

'Well, yes, sort of,' lied Zak. He had no idea what else to say, how else he could convince the man he was telling the truth.

The man's smile returned. 'Some of us, these days, don't believe in the gods anymore. Or at least, we don't believe they interfere in the affairs of men. There is no evidence to suggest they do. I suspect you have just had a bad, and I'm sure a very lifelike, dream; nothing more.'

'Uncle,' said Cassia leaning forward. 'What if he is telling the truth? Should we at least all go to your house in the hills for a few days?'

'No, no, no! Your mother would crucify me if I took you away from the city and your betrothed. Besides, I have far too much work to do.' He paused and looked at their despondent faces. 'Look. I tell you what: I will make sure that an extra sacrifice is made to Vulcanus, the god of all volcanoes, just in case. Hopefully, that will be enough to appease him.'

When they walked back outside, Zak looked up into the blue sky and sighed. What more could he have done?

'I'm sorry he didn't listen,' said Cassia.

Zak looked at her and smiled. She still had *those* earrings on. 'Never mind,' he said. 'At least *we* can all leave town.'

'No, Zak,' she replied. 'I can't.'

He stopped and stared at her. 'You have to, Cassia. Please!'

'If my uncle had ordered the evacuation of the city, I could have left. But if I just leave now, my parents will go mad. They will be livid as it is when they find out I left the house. I'm meant to stay there the whole time and never go out. If you knew my parents you'd understand.' A tear rolled down her cheek, and then she stormed off, Dexter following in her wake.

Maia moved next to Zak and put a gentle hand on his shoulder. 'We tried, Zak.'

'Yeah. Maybe it's for the best.'

'What do you mean?'

'Well, imagine what would have happened if we'd persuaded Marcus to evacuate Pompeii. Suddenly, back in our time there would no longer be all those bodies in the city. And what if we saved someone who should have died, like Maximus, for example? What if that person then went on to become emperor? History would have changed completely. Who knows what our time would have been like when we finally got back there?'

'I guess so. But what are we going to do, Zak?'

'We could just go home.'

Maia looked at him askance. 'You know I'm not going to do that, don't you?'

'I know. Me neither,' said Zak, although deep down he had been briefly tempted by the idea of just running away and leaving them all to it. 'We'll just have to wait for the eruption, and then hope we can get our friends away in time.'

Zak closed his eyes and sighed. When he reopened them, he looked around at the bustling Forum. Workmen had already begun repairing the scaffolding that had collapsed the day before, and shoppers were once again out in force, moving between the many temporary market stalls.

As his eyes scanned the scene, trying not to imagine the whole place buried under metres of ash, he saw a sign over one of the stalls. From where he was standing, he could not see what was being sold. But the sign said one hundred and one sesterces a piece. In Roman numerals CI. His mind began racing, thoughts tumbling over one another in quick succession.

And then his heart leapt. 'Maia. I think I might have cracked the riddle.'

Chapter XIII

The Key of Portunus

That night, Zak hardly slept at all. By the time they had got back to Cassia's house, the sun had already begun setting. To have gone out at dusk to look at the giant mosaic in the derelict villa and try to solve the riddle would not, they all acknowledged, have been wise. So Zak had had to go to bed with his mind full of jumbled thoughts.

One minute, he would think about Vesuvius and the destruction it was about to cause. The next, his mind would wander to the riddle Caius had told them. Then it would flit to the Vulcani and Maximus and his mysterious female accomplice.

By the time the sky began to lighten in the early hours of the morning, Zak's eyes were heavy and tired. He finally gave up trying to sleep, swung his legs off the side of the bed and sat up, looking at his watch. In the pale light of dawn, he fiddled with all the buttons and settings that he could find, discovering new features all the time. He called up the map, moving the location back and forth across Europe, looking at the collection of tiny red dots. As he did so, something occurred to him.

'Of course!' he muttered triumphantly, and resolved to tell the others of his discovery over breakfast.

An hour or two later, the first rays of the morning sun burst into the garden, signalling the end of Zak's interminable night. Apart from one or two of the household slaves, he was the first one up and dressed. While he waited for his friends to appear, he paced up and down the garden, occasionally looking at the fountain, which had now been without water for over a day, and which, he realised with some sadness, would never spout water again.

'You're up early,' said Maia from the colonnade at the edge of the garden. Like him, she was wearing a woollen cape over her shoulders against the cool morning air.

'Maia,' replied Zak, rushing towards her. 'I've realised something. Look,' he added, thrusting the watch under her nose. 'The tiny red dots on the map are showing the location of those bronze door knockers. There's the one in England. It's in London instead of where we live. But remember, Mrs Sullivan said she found it on a dig in London. So that's its current location.'

Maia looked uncertainly from the watch to Zak and back again.

'Then, when I move the map south,' continued Zak excitedly, 'there's one in Rome, then two here in Pompeii.'

'Two?' said Maia.

'Yes. We've used the one in the Forum the last couple of times. But then I remembered: the day we arrived in Pompeii, we appeared on the main street. It was so busy I never thought to look behind us, but there must be an image of Janus in that doorway. There's a red dot on the map right where I think we arrived.' He felt so exhilarated at his discovery that he was speaking more and more quickly.

However, Maia's puzzled frown indicated she did not share his excitement. 'So, we have more than one way of getting home,' she said, rather flatly. 'That's useful, I guess.'

'No, but Maia. Don't you see?' He paused waiting for her to react. But she still looked just as confused. 'If I set the date and time, then yes, we can use those points to travel through time. But if I keep the date and time the same, then we just travel instantly from one point to the other.'

Finally, realisation dawned across her face. 'Oh, I see what you're saying. But again, how is that going to be useful to us?'

'Look. There's another dot on the map, just north-west of here close to Vesuvius. Near to where that villa is. The villa of Portunus. And since I think I might have cracked the riddle, we can get there in a flash without spending hours travelling on the road.'

'And when are you going to tell us how you solved the riddle?' said a voice behind him.

Zak turned round and saw Caius and Cassia coming towards them, with Dexter a respectful distance behind.

Zak grinned. 'Not just yet. I'll show you when we're in front of the giant mosaic. It's more dramatic that way.'

'Oh, come on, Zak,' urged Caius, with a playful punch to Zak's shoulder. 'Don't keep us waiting like this.' He was smiling broadly and seemed a long way from the quavering boy they had rescued a few days earlier.

'Let's have breakfast first,' laughed Zak. 'Then we'll go straight there.'

'You little tease,' giggled Cassia. She then looped an arm through one of Caius' arms. The couple turned and wandered off, sharing a joke.

When he watched them walk away towards the house with Maia, Zak felt his mood drop.

'Jealous?' asked Dexter, who had moved silently next to him.

'No!' snapped Zak, and immediately realised he had reacted far too quickly.

Dexter chuckled briefly. 'I'm sure my mistress will soon realise he is not the one for her.'

'You don't trust him with Cassia, then?'

Dexter smiled again. 'He's a Roman, Zak. I don't trust any Romans.'

'I thought *you* were Roman. You were born in Italy.'

'I was born here. But that doesn't make me a Roman. I have to be granted my freedom and citizenship to be classed a Roman. At the moment, I'm nothing more than a lowly slave.'

'Oh, I see,' said Zak. When Cassia, Caius and Maia had disappeared into the house, Zak turned to look up at the taller Dexter. 'What about me, Dexter? Do you trust me?'

The slave smiled at Zak, a warm but wry smile. 'You turn up here out of the blue, claiming to have travelled here from the future. Yet you speak perfect Latin. And then you expect me to trust you?'

'Fair point,' conceded Zak. 'Look, I don't pretend to understand any of this stuff, or why me and Maia are here. But I promise I will do everything I can to help you before I return home.'

Dexter's face dropped and he snorted. 'I'm sure you will.'

Zak could read in the boy's face that he had perhaps heard such empty words before. 'If you hate it here so much, why not just run away? Try to find your family in Africa, or wherever they might be.'

Dexter's face had hardened further. 'Do you have any idea what they do to runaway slaves who are caught? No? A good flogging if you're lucky. Crucifixion if you're unlucky. Besides, where would I go? This is my home. This is all I have ever known.'

Zak opened his mouth to speak but realised there was nothing he could say to make it any better. Dexter lived in an impossibly harsh world, and there was little or nothing he, a mere schoolboy from the future, could do to change that.

'Right. This is it,' declared Zak. He was standing with the others in a wide doorway which looked onto the main street in Pompeii. On the door before them was a bronze door knocker with the twin heads of the god Janus upon it. The door was unlocked and stood ajar.

Zak activated the watch so that the thin circle of red pulsed around the rim. He then centred the map over the red dot close to the villa of Portunus. Now all they had to do was wait for a lull in the stream of pedestrians filing past. If the five teenagers vanished into thin air, watched on by crowds of passing shoppers, they would draw unwanted attention.

When the moment came, Maia made sure they were all holding onto one another, before, as a group, they lurched forwards through the doorway.

After the usual dizzying flash of light, they found themselves standing inside a room, the total silence contrasting harshly with the bustle of the street they had just left behind. The cooing of a dove broke the quiet.

Cassia started and let out an audible gasp, as though someone had just crept up behind her and made her jump. She put a trembling hand over her mouth.

Apparently unable to speak, Caius looked like he had just seen a ghost.

'What just happened?' asked Dexter. His usual composure having vanished, he stood stock-still and looked terrified.

Zak looked at him with a faint smile. He patted him on the arm and said: 'You've just travelled about five miles in the blink of an eye. Don't worry: you'll get used to it.'

'Not sure that's true,' mumbled Maia.

'Where are we?' asked Cassia, still looking startled.

'I don't know,' replied Zak. He and Maia moved cautiously forwards, leaving the other three rooted to the spot behind them.

They were in a room, the size of which was almost impossible to gauge since the signs of destruction were everywhere. Large parts of the roof had caved in, leaving several wooden beams angling down to the ground. Some areas of the floor were buried under piles of broken tiles and planks of wood. The morning sun was bursting through gaps in the roof like spotlights on a stage.

He turned around and saw that they had just passed through a large frame that stood towards one corner of the room where a section of the roof remained intact. It looked like a solid doorframe with no door, and had a tangle of cables running from both vertical struts. Even with his limited knowledge of the ancient world, Zak immediately knew he was looking at something that was clearly not Roman.

'Looks like this place was destroyed in the Great Earthquake,' said Caius.

'Yes,' agreed Maia. 'And hasn't been lived in since.'

Zak picked his way carefully over the rubble towards a table that stood against one wall. He ran an arm across the surface, clearing away dust and small pieces of plaster and brick, which pattered onto the floor.

'What is it?' asked Maia, who had moved beside him.

Peering down, Zak said: 'To me that looks like a touch screen and maybe a computer terminal. There's no power here, but I reckon this is some sort of laboratory.'

'Did you notice there is no door knocker on that frame back there?'

Zak looked back at the rectangular frame standing in the corner of the room. 'You're right. There isn't. If I had to guess, I'd say we've found the lab of the person who built this whole time machine thing. There are bits of technology all around this room that are just far too advanced for Romans.'

'To be honest, some of it looks far too advanced for our time, as well,' said Maia. 'If only we knew who made all this stuff.'

'I know,' said Zak, lost in thought. 'Anyway, come on. Let's go to the other villa,' he added, turning to the other three, who were by now wandering gingerly around the place.

When they had finally managed to clamber their way through the ruined villa, and were standing outside, they realised they were right at the base of the great mountain of Vesuvius. A twisting and overgrown track led down a gentle slope through the colourful, autumnal trees towards the villa of Portunus in the distance.

'I'll meet you in the villa,' said Caius. 'You go on.'

'Where are you going?' asked Cassia.

'While we're here, I might as well visit my father.'

'I'll come with you,' offered Cassia.

'No. It'll be safer on my own,' insisted Caius, who, after a quick wave, strode off towards the forested slopes of the volcano.

As the others were threading their way through the small trees growing between the two villas, Dexter suddenly held up a hand. 'Ssh! I can hear footsteps.'

The others froze, straining their ears. It was a few seconds later before Zak heard the sound of a horse whinnying. The four of them rushed behind a line of bushes close to the leaf-strewn path, and peered out through the foliage, their hearts already beating fast.

Presently, three horsemen in crimson cloaks appeared, their hoods pulled over their heads. In single file, the horses ambled past, the faces of their riders almost invisible, save for a protruding nose or a chin. The jingling of tack and swords was loud and strangely menacing in the otherwise silent surroundings.

Moments later, the riders had moved away and out of sight.

'There are more of them over there,' whispered Dexter in Zak's ear, pointing in the opposite direction.

'They don't seem in much of a hurry,' said Zak. 'They must just be patrolling.'

'But why here?' asked Cassia.

'I have no idea,' replied Zak. 'Come on. Let's go down to the villa.'

Walking in silence, the four of them tiptoed down the path, their eyes scanning the countryside on both sides. Through the thinning trees, Zak caught sight of at least four clusters of red capes, patrolling in twos and threes. The place seemed to be crawling with Vulcani. Twice more they had to duck down and hide from passing riders. But eventually, they clambered through a gap in the perimeter wall and into the grounds of the villa.

Once more, they found themselves standing in the high-vaulted hall with the enormous mosaic at their feet. Shafts of sunlight lit up sections of the impressive picture. Zak positioned himself near the large lettering at the bottom and studied the mosaic.

'So, come on, Zak,' said Cassia, her eyes wide with anticipation. 'We're all waiting to be amazed by your brilliance.'

Now that he was standing in front of the picture, Zak suddenly began to doubt himself. Back in his bedroom, the answer had seemed obvious, but what if he were wrong? He would look a fool, and he would have brought them here for nothing.

'Well,' he began. 'I wondered whether the VIDI and VICI parts were not words at all, but numbers. So VIDI is six, VI and five hundred and one, DI. And VICI is six, and one hundred and one, CI.'

'Brilliant!' said Cassia. But then her face dropped. 'But how does that help us, exactly?'

'I'm not really sure,' replied Zak, rubbing his chin. 'But if we start at VENI, which isn't a number, and then count the pieces of the mosaic, the tesserae, and see what happens.'

Maia and Cassia looked doubtful.

'Whatever you're going to try, you need to get a move on,' said Dexter quietly. He was standing apart from the group, looking through the door out into the garden beyond. 'I can see more Vulcani patrolling the grounds of the villa.'

Zak got down on his knees and began counting the tiny squares. He began with six sideways followed by five hundred and one up. The final stone and those immediately around it revealed nothing. He began to worry he had miscounted. But undaunted, he then counted six tesserae up and five hundred and one across.

When he pressed the last stone, he felt a sudden surge of elation. He let out a quick 'Yes!'

'What is it?' asked Maia, moving in for a closer look.

'It moves!' said Zak. He pushed it down repeatedly, like the key on a computer keyboard. None of the other stones around it moved at all.

His initial excitement, however, began to quickly fade. He had expected something to happen, but nothing did. So he quickly counted out the VICI part of the code: six up from the moveable stone, followed by one hundred and one along.

The tiny tessera moved. Once more, he felt the initial thrill at having found a moveable stone, followed by the disappointment that still nothing dramatic was happening.

'Hurry up!' urged Dexter in a harsh whisper.

'Quick, Maia,' said Zak. 'Stay here and get ready to press this stone. I'll go back to the other one.'

Once he had located the first moving tessera, he nodded to Maia, and then they depressed their respective stones simultaneously.

An agonising wait of a few seconds followed, during which nothing happened. But then, the round shield of one of the figures in the centre of the mosaic began to rise up with a gentle grinding sound. They rushed over to watch the circle, which was about a metre across, move upwards a few centimetres, before it then began to split in half. The two semicircles slowly spread apart until a hole had appeared in the middle of the mosaic.

Nervously, Zak peered over the edge and saw a shallow recess just below the level of the floor. At the bottom was a simple metal container the size of a shoebox. He reached out and lifted the lid. Colour burst out from inside, reds and oranges and yellows. The colours of fire, the colours of the cage containing Caius' father.

'The Key of Portunus,' gasped Cassia.

When Zak's eyes had adjusted to the glare, he could see what looked like a large key, thick and larger than his hand, lying in the metal box.

'Let's pick it up and get out of here,' suggested Cassia.

Zak hesitated. 'It looks kind of ... hot.'

Cassia huffed and rolled her eyes. She then bent down and tried to pick up the object. After straining for a few seconds, she huffed once more. 'It's stuck,' she said. 'It seems to be bolted to the floor or something.' She let go and pulled a disappointed face.

'Let me try,' said Maia, and reached in a hand.

With no effort at all, she lifted up the key and held it in front of the other two.

'What?' said Cassia, her jaw dropping. 'How did you ...?'

'Why am I not surprised you can lift it?' smirked Zak.

Maia did not look amused at his comment. She was about to speak when Dexter came rushing over. 'They're coming.'

'We need to close this if we can,' said Zak, 'to cover our tracks.'

'There's no time,' said Dexter, running past them. 'We have to move — now!'

He ran to the opposite end of the hall, where another door stood ajar. Stopping briefly to peer around the doorframe, he beckoned urgently to the others to follow him out of the room.

As they raced through the villa, they could hear voices behind them. What began as talking, very quickly turned to shouting. Barked orders echoed through the building; hobnailed boots began running across the stone floors. They must have seen the hole in the mosaic, Zak realised.

No longer trying to keep their footfalls quiet, the four of them ran as fast as they could, rushing through the ruins of the villa, dodging pieces of fallen masonry and wood. They burst through a side door out into the bright sunshine, the narrow, winding path back up to the other villa in front of them.

The building lay only a short distance up the gentle slope through the trees and bushes, and yet the safety of the portal back to Pompeii seemed impossibly far away.

As they sprinted through the trees, the urgent voices behind them drew ever nearer. And then Zak realised they were never going to make it, especially with Cassia trailing behind in her long dress. The villa was still not even in sight. Only Dexter, swerving through the trees up ahead, looked like he might make it away in time. The rest of them, he realised, were going to be caught by the Vulcani in a matter of seconds.

Chapter XIV

The Vulcani

Knowing he had to do something different, Zak stopped, glanced back, saw that their pursuers had temporarily disappeared behind a bend in the path. Dexter, up ahead, turned just in time to see Zak stop and wave at him frantically, telling him to hide with Maia. Then Zak grabbed Cassia and pulled her off the path and into the bushes.

She looked at him with wild, frightened eyes as they lay panting on the ground. Moments later, they saw three tall figures running up the path, their crimson hoods keeping their faces in shadow. With their muscular arms and legs pumping and their capes flowing behind them, they looked terrifying, like something from another world. The thought that one of them might be Maximus made Zak go cold.

As the men approached their hiding place, Zak put an arm around Cassia's shoulders, and then lowered himself and her, face down into the dry and dusty soil. He closed his eyes, praying they would not be seen.

He heard the three men run past, then stop a short distance away. Cautiously, Zak lifted his head. He saw the men pull back their hoods to reveal their close-cropped heads, and watched as their eyes scoured the area. That Maximus was not among them was a small crumb of comfort.

'Did you actually see someone?' hissed one of the men.

'No. But I heard footsteps,' replied the other. 'And someone has clearly been playing with that mosaic.'

'Come on. Let's go back. We need to report what's happened. If someone has been in there and found something, Caeculus will crucify us.'

The three Vulcani sauntered back, grumbling about whose

fault it was that someone had gained access to the villa when they were meant to be guarding it.

Once the voices had trailed away, Cassia sat up and dusted herself off. Some of her blond curls had come unhooked and lay across her face, which, like her once pristine dress, was now covered in patches of dirt. 'Look at me,' she said harshly. 'I'm a complete mess.' Her long, triangular earrings swayed from side to side as she shook her head with disgust.

'You're welcome,' replied Zak, standing up and then pulling her to her feet. He picked up her fallen shawl and wrapped it haphazardly around her shoulders.

She frowned at him. 'I suppose I should thank you,' she mumbled.

'Well, only if it's not too much trouble.'

They stared at one another for a moment, then both burst out laughing.

'When you two have stopped rolling around in the mud,' said Maia, coming back down the path to join them, 'we should be getting back, before they return.'

They marched swiftly back up the hill to the villa, the whole time looking anxiously about for more Vulcani.

Just as they reached the front door, a trumpet sounded nearby, shrill and menacing. A group of three or four birds flapped noisily into the air and hurriedly flew away as if they knew what dangers were coming.

The drumming of horses' hooves and more barking voices seemed to come from every direction all at once.

Not waiting to see what was happening, the four friends were already hurrying through the crumbling villa. Along the dark hallway from the front door they ran, through the atrium with its many statues and where at least half of a once impressive mosaic was now obscured by a collapsed roof, and into the room where the strange portal stood in the corner.

While he had been running, Zak had been programming the

watch on his wrist, setting the location to Pompeii. Now that it was primed, he looked up. Maia was heading to the rectangular frame at the far end of the room.

But Dexter and Cassia had stopped abruptly. They stood as still as the painted statues he had seen in the atrium, their expressions frozen on their faces.

'Oh, give me a break,' muttered Zak.

Perhaps sensing that the others had stopped running, Maia spun sharply round, and her face dropped the moment she saw Zak staring forlornly at their two motionless friends.

'No!' she gasped, and rushed back to join Zak. 'Not now!'

Zak put a hand on his head and closed his eyes. He had no idea what to do.

'Can we lift them?' suggested Maia, her voice cracking with panic. 'Or drag them?' She seized one of Cassia's arms and tugged, but it only moved slowly and with much effort.

Zak was breathing heavily, trying to think. Footsteps and voices filled the villa, closing in with every second.

'We can't just leave them,' said Maia.

'I know,' was all Zak could say. Then he looked up at Maia. 'Quick! Over here. Turn and face the wall. Pretend we're also frozen. They might just ignore us. Only Maximus and one or two others know what we look like.'

'That's ridiculous,' whispered Maia, her eyes wide with fear. 'They'll catch us.'

'Do you have a better idea?' snapped Zak, tugging her across the room. 'It's either that or we leave those two behind.'

Maia looked like she wanted to speak but could not find the words.

'The moment they unfreeze,' continued Zak, taking up position facing the wall, 'we make a dash for that gateway.'

He braced himself just as footsteps clattered ever more loudly behind him.

'Hey!' barked a voice. 'There are people in here. Kids, by the look of it.'

The running steps slowed to a walk. Zak could hear their hobnailed boots crunching on the layer of debris on the floor. His heart was pounding so fast he was sure the noise was going to betray him. He tried to breathe through his nostrils, slowly in and out, desperate to calm himself, even as his whole body seemed to be yelling at him to run.

His eyes flashed the briefest of glances across at Maia, who stood nearby as still as him, save for her chest rising and falling in slight, shallow movements.

'These two are frozen solid over here,' said one of the men. Zak guessed he meant Cassia and Dexter. 'Don't know about those two over there, though. Go and check them out.'

Zak could hear one of the Vulcani approaching gingerly across the floor. He swallowed hard, his pulse now so fast he could not have counted it even if he had tried. The tiny shallow intakes of air through his nose were just not enough. He just wanted to open his mouth and swallow a huge breath. Waves of panic kept rising up inside him, frantically trying to burst out.

A bead of sweat crawled down the side of his face, like an annoying insect.

The footsteps were drawing ever closer. At any moment, he expected to feel a hand land on his shoulder. Then he thought he could feel the man's hot breath on his neck.

'No. It's not them, is it?' said one of the men. 'They wouldn't be frozen if it were, would they?'

'No, suppose you're right,' replied another. 'Must just be kids larking about in here. Come on. Let's check another room.'

As the footsteps receded, Zak closed his eyes, forcing himself to wait and then wait some more before he dared look.

Finally, he turned around and saw that the men had gone. Immediately, he began taking in great lungfuls of air, as though he had just been holding his breath under water. Maia beside him was doing likewise.

They tiptoed back towards their motionless friends, desperately willing the world to start moving again.

'Come on, come on, come on!' Zak kept muttering impatiently to himself.

They stood in silence staring at one another, praying for the spell to be broken as it always seemed to be in the end.

In the blink of an eye, Cassia and Dexter were breathing hard, were jogging across the floor. Zak and Maia wasted no time, dashing towards the frame in the corner of the room.

Behind them, a man roared with anger. 'Ah! Not again! How do they keep blocking our signal?' There was a brief pause while someone else spoke, before the man bellowed again. 'Well, find out. Or, by Jupiter, you'll all be spending the rest of your pathetic lives in the lead mines.'

As Zak and the others held hands and then passed through the frame to the safety of Pompeii, he could not help thinking that the voice sounded vaguely familiar.

The relief at having so narrowly escaped the Vulcani, and at having obtained the Key of Portunus, was very quickly tempered by the realisation that Caius had been left behind. Their friend was no doubt being pursued by the Vulcani just as much as they had been. But this time, they had had to abandon him on Vesuvius with no easy way for him to get back.

'What are we going to do about him?' asked Cassia, as she slumped down onto a divan back in her villa. 'We can't just leave him there.'

No one felt as guilty at that moment as Zak. 'We'll have to try to go back later,' he suggested. 'And hope the Vulcani have gone.'

'If they have half a brain between them,' said Dexter, 'they'll have already worked out how we got in and out of there. They'll be guarding it like the Temple of Saturn in Rome.'

'Oh, that's it then, is it?' snapped Cassia. 'We just leave him there, do we? Who was he anyway? Just some poor boy from

Pompeii. Plenty more where he came from.' She jumped to her feet and flounced away. 'I need a bath.'

Zak puffed out his cheeks. He felt so helpless. 'What's the Temple of Saturn, anyway?' he asked at length.

'It's the state treasury,' said Dexter, absently. 'Where the Emperor keeps all his gold.'

'Oh, I see,' replied Zak, barely registering Dexter's reply. 'Maybe I should go back to the villa,' he added. 'On my own this time.'

'No,' sighed Maia. 'We don't have a clue where on earth he is. Where would you even start looking?'

'She's right, Zak,' said Dexter. 'Listen, I'll go and get us all some refreshments. Perhaps that will help you think of something.'

Dexter left the room, leaving just Zak and Maia, as exhausted, despondent and bereft of ideas as one another.

Maia wearily lowered herself onto a couch. She then felt for the Key of Portunus in her pocket and took out the bulky, glowing object. She stared at it blankly in the palm of her hand, as though it were somehow hypnotising her.

Zak looked across at the bizarre, shimmering object in her hand. 'How come you could pick that up when Cassia couldn't?' he asked.

'I'm just stronger than she is.' They looked at one another and smiled. 'I honestly don't know, Zak. I've just about given up trying to work out how any of this stuff works.'

Zak gazed into space. He was so tired he could barely think. Slowly, one single thought crept into his mind, pushing out all others. It grew and grew until there was nothing else in his head. It made him go ice cold.

Tomorrow was the 24th of October. The day Vesuvius was going to erupt.

The next morning, Zak woke with a start. The realisation of what day it was, hit him like a blow to the stomach. The evening before, he had been worried that he was going to have yet another sleepless night. But in the end, sheer, overwhelming, paralysing exhaustion had taken hold and plunged him into a deep, dreamless sleep.

But the moment his consciousness had returned, his eyes had shot open. He swung out of bed and opened his door. The cool, grey light of dawn still hung in the garden. Other than birds singing in the trees, a pleasant silence hung in the air. He let out a huge sigh of relief, closed the door and collapsed back onto the bed.

Now that he was awake, he knew there was no chance at all of falling back to sleep. Thoughts were swirling around in his head like tiny boats caught in a whirlpool. He had hoped that a good night's sleep would have cleared his head, and then filled it with fresh, inspired ideas. But still he had no idea what to do about Caius.

After hearing faint voices outside, he hurriedly got dressed and met the others in the atrium. A slave had lit a brazier in the corner of the room to drive the morning chill from the air.

'Any news of Caius?' asked Zak hopefully, when he saw Cassia and Dexter.

The concerned look on Cassia's face gave him an instant answer. She shook her head. 'Nothing. Nothing at all.' She slumped her shoulders and collapsed onto her divan. 'What are we going to do?' Her eyes were red, and stared at Zak, pleading.

Zak felt a knot in his stomach. He felt sick. Turning to Maia, he asked: 'What time does it erupt?'

'Mrs Sullivan said it was around midday.'

'But how do they know exactly?'

'There was a writer called Pliny who lived along the coast. He saw the whole thing and wrote it all down. I just hope he got his timings right.'

'Are you still convinced Vesuvius is going to erupt?' asked

Dexter, looking dubious.

Zak nodded, unable to speak for a moment.

'Well, I guess we'll find out soon if you're right,' the slave added.

Lost in their own thoughts, the four of them fell silent. As Zak's mind was racing, he became aware of a commotion outside. A small group of household slaves were chatting excitedly outside the room.

'What is the meaning of this?' demanded Cassia, jumping to her feet. She strode to the open doorway and stood regally, glaring at the slaves.

The large frame of Felix appeared before her. 'I think you should come and see this, my lady. The whole city has stopped to watch.'

They all followed him upstairs and into one of the richly decorated rooms, which had a large, open window overlooking the red roofs of the nearby single storey buildings below. In the distance, the window framed a stunning view of the countryside beyond the walls of the city and the massive bulk of Vesuvius beyond that.

All looked as beautiful, as serene as the day Zak and Maia had arrived.

Except that now an enormous plume of white smoke was rising silently into the blue sky from the summit of the volcano. As it rose up and up towards the heavens, the wind was catching it and blowing it slowly, inexorably towards Pompeii.

Chapter XV

Vesuvius

Zak stared at one of his own hands. It was trembling uncontrollably. Or perhaps it was just another earth tremor, he could not be sure. Either way, he felt sick with nerves.

'I thought it erupted at midday,' he said. His throat was so dry he could hardly speak.

'I don't think this is the main eruption,' said Maia. 'This is just the beginning. If what the historians say is accurate, we still have a few hours.'

'And what if they're wrong?' he snapped.

Maia glowered at him. Immediately regretting his harsh tone, he mumbled an apology. His nerves were fraught.

The other three looked at him. They were in the garden once more, just as the first rays of sunshine were bursting over the roofline. Like him, Maia and Cassia had begun pacing up and down. Only Dexter stood calmly to one side, as though merely waiting for the next command to fetch something.

'I'll go,' said Zak. 'I'll go on my own. If Caius has not been captured, he must be with or near his father, particularly now that Vesuvius is smoking.'

'Don't be daft,' said Maia. 'You can't just go on your own.'

'If I can't find Caius quickly, I'll go to his father with the key and see if I can free him myself. Then perhaps his father will know where to find him.'

'No, Zak,' insisted Maia. 'What if you get caught? How can we all get to safety without the watch?'

Running a hand through his hair, Zak said: 'I'll take you back to England now. I'll take all of you, in fact. You can wait—'

'No way!' snapped Maia.

'Certainly not!' added Cassia. 'He's a friend to all of us. We should all go and look for him.'

He was glad of their support but knew he could probably move more quickly without them. If only Dexter would speak up. The two of them could rush about the foot of the mountain looking for Caius. But the slave seemed to be indifferent to the fate of their friend.

Felix walked swiftly to join them. 'A message for you, my lady,' he said, holding out a small piece of paper.

'Oh, not now, Felix,' said Cassia, barely looking at the proffered message.

'The man said it was extremely important,' insisted Felix. 'He came from your uncle.'

Cassia flashed him a fierce look, before snatching the paper from his hand. Her eyes flickered across the writing. 'By Castor!' she said, lowering the paper and looking at the others. 'It is indeed from my Uncle. He says we must leave the house without delay and meet him in the vineyard by the amphitheatre. He says it is extremely urgent, and we are to make sure we are not seen.'

'Could be a trap,' suggested Zak.

Cassia shook her head. 'No, I don't think so. He has used the family seal on his ring. Anyone but family would expect him to use his official seal, not the family one.'

'Right,' said Maia suddenly. 'That settles it. You and Dexter go to your uncle. Me and Zak will go and look for Caius.'

A short while later, the four of them spilled out onto the side street next to Cassia's house. Dressed in dark capes against the morning cold, they hurried along the narrow, grey street, towards the pool of sunlight at the end, coming from the main road.

'Now, when we go through to the villa,' Zak was saying to Maia, 'if we see any Vulcani—'

Dexter, who was just stepping into the sunlight in front of him, thrust out an arm in a flash, stopping Zak dead in his tracks.

'What—?'

'Vulcani,' whispered Dexter, easing back into the shadows of the side street.

Zak peered round the corner to look up and down the street. Just down the road, he could see hooded Vulcani standing guard outside a doorway. He quickly ducked back to face the others.

'There are two guards right outside the door,' he said. 'The door with the head of Janus on it.'

'What in Juno's name are they doing there?' asked Cassia.

Maia rolled her eyes and sighed. 'If I had to guess, I'd say they now know exactly how we travelled to and from the villa.'

'There's still the doorway in the Forum,' said Zak, refusing to give up just yet.

'Don't be daft,' said Maia. 'If they have guards here, they'll have more at that one, too. Besides, I bet they'll have guards at the other end, in the villa, as well.'

Zak closed his eyes and slumped his shoulders. Was there really going to be no way to save Caius and his father before Vesuvius exploded?

Cassia put a hand on his arm and gave him a weak smile. 'No one wants to look for Caius more than me,' she said, as if reading his thoughts. 'But let's go and see my uncle for now. Perhaps we'll think of something else on the way.'

Zak knew she was right. Yet even so, he found he was unable to move, longing for a sudden spark of inspiration to ignite in his mind.

'We should stick to the back roads,' suggested Dexter. 'They'll easily spot us if we go that way,' he added, pointing to the main street.

Dragging himself away from the glare of the busy road, Zak turned and followed the others back down the side street.

Trying to avoid the main thoroughfares by crisscrossing the city's back streets seemed to take an age. However, it soon became evident that their caution was well founded, for, on two separate occasions, a small group of mounted Vulcani clattered down a road, causing them to dive for cover in a shadowy doorway.

'Wait till my uncle hears about this,' huffed Cassia, as they emerged for the second time from such a hiding place. 'These brutes have no authority in this city.'

Nervously, Zak watched as the horsemen ploughed down the middle of the road, forcing aside anything that got in their way. Where once they had been skulking about the city, lurking in the shadows, now they were strutting about with brazen menace.

Eventually, the four friends arrived at the wall surrounding the large vineyard, which lay within the city walls near the amphitheatre. Avoiding the main entrance, Cassia took them down a side road and up to a small door in the high stone wall. Just as they approached, the door opened a fraction and a face appeared. With nothing more than an impatient, waving hand, someone beckoned them in.

Hunched over as he moved, a small man led them along the edge of the vineyard, keeping them in the narrow gap between the wall and the vines. In the early morning sunshine, the leaves of the vines glowed red and gold, like a field of fire. After a short distance, the man took them under the angular branches of a large tree which stood close to the wall.

'Uncle Marcus!' yelped Cassia, leaping forward.

'Hush, my dear,' wheezed the middle-aged man. He was sitting rather awkwardly against the trunk of the tree, facing the wall, looking thoroughly exhausted.

Cassia knelt down and flung her arms around his neck. He winced as she did so. Zak noticed there was a large bruise around one eye.

'What has happened?' demanded Cassia, her voice trembling.

Her uncle's large body heaved a couple of laboured breaths, and he gave her a weary grimace. 'Someone has taken over the city. Someone calling himself Caeculus.' He stopped to breathe deeply again, as though coming up for air from a strenuous swim. 'His men are everywhere.'

'Wearing red hooded capes,' muttered Zak.

'So, you've seen them already, then,' Marcus sighed. 'They are not letting anyone in or out of the city.'

'What do they want?' asked Cassia.

'They came to my house, roughed me up a little.' He ran a hand through his tousled grey hair.

'Are you all right, uncle?'

'Oh, I'll live. Ditus here has been tending to me,' he replied, nodding to his servant who stood impassively to one side.

'But why did they do this to you?' pressed Cassia.

'I told them in no uncertain terms that this is my city, that the people have elected me to represent them and that they should get out. They didn't take kindly to that. As I lay on the floor being beaten, I overheard two of them saying they were looking for four children. Two boys and two girls. I heard them mention you, Cass. So, as soon as they had gone, I sent you that message.'

Cassia's wide, frightened eyes glanced around at her friends.

'Why in the name of all the gods are they after you?' asked Marcus. 'What exactly have you done?'

'They've been after Maia and Zak,' replied Cassia, 'and Caius here for several days now. But we still don't really know why.'

With considerable effort and the help of Cassia and his slave, uncle Marcus clawed his hands up the tree trunk until he stood unsteadily on his feet.

'Where do you think you're going?' demanded his niece.

'I need to go back, to contact the other members of the council, see if we can't regain control of the city.'

'Are there any soldiers in Pompeii?' asked Zak.

'No, young man. This is supposed to be a peaceful area. There are no soldiers around here. Our one hope is to try to send a distress signal to the admiral up the coast in the port of Misenum. He has plenty of marines up there.'

'We'll come with you,' said Cassia.

'No, my dear,' said Marcus, patting her wearily on the shoulder. 'You and your friends need to keep your heads down. Perhaps go back to your house and barricade yourselves in. That's a sturdy house your father has there. It'll take some breaking into.' He turned to his slave. 'Come now, Ditus. Let's go to the theatre. I've heard some people are gathering there.'

'May the gods protect you, uncle.'

'And you, my child. And you.'

After watching Uncle Marcus shuffle away back into the city, the four friends decided to head off in the opposite direction. Since the city's eastern gate was only a short distance away from the vineyard, they decided to go and check if there was a way out of the city. But sure enough, as Marcus had informed them, there were several Vulcani standing in front of the stone tower, their swords drawn. Behind them, the wooden gates had been shut, while in front of them a small crowd of people had gathered with their horses or their carts. Some brave souls were even arguing with the guards, demanding to be allowed through the gate. One of the Vulcani pointed his sword at a man who stepped too close, and then pointed his sword to one side, where an upturned cart lay in the middle of its spilt and broken contents. The cart's owner sat on the ground, nursing a bloody gash to the head. The warning was all too clear: if anyone came too close, they should expect the same fate.

Realising there was no way out of the city, Zak and his friends turned around and headed back. As they walked along, Zak looked up at the enormous, forbidding volcano in the distance. The white smoke continued to pour from its summit, draining the blue from the sky. As the vast cloud crept towards Pompeii, it had turned the sun into a hazy and pale disc.

As Zak looked at the sun, he realised it must be approaching its zenith. Time was passing at a frightening pace, midday approaching fast. They were trapped in the city, and time was running out.

For the time being, they could think of nothing else to do but return to Cassia's house as her uncle had suggested. Perhaps when Vesuvius erupted, reasoned Zak, they could use the confusion to escape through one of the city's gates or even through one of the two portals.

The walk back to Cassia's house again took longer than usual as they sought to hide from the frequent patrols of mounted Vulcani. While they were still some distance away, the ground began to shake. At first, it was a mild tremor, barely perceptible. But this time, it refused to fade away. Instead, the thrum of shaking buildings and rattling roof tiles grew and grew. Walking became harder and harder as the ground rocked under their feet.

And then it came: the most enormous, ear-splitting explosion Zak had ever heard. He felt as if his head were going to split apart. The eruption sent a sound wave tearing through the streets like a sudden, mighty gust of wind. The wall of sound punched its way across the city, ripping countless tiles from roofs, knocking people to the ground and causing trees to sway and bend, as though an invisible giant were striking them as he ran through the city.

After the wave had blown through, Zak, like so many others, found himself lying on the ground, a painful ringing in his ears, which had replaced all other sound. Slowly, groggily, he managed to stand up again and helped his friends return to their feet, too.

When he looked up, he saw that Vesuvius had changed. It had cast off any pretence at being a benign, dormant volcano. Where once there had been a brooding mountain breathing out harmless puffs of white smoke, there now stood something alive and terrible. Great clouds of grey smoke billowed into the sky, up and up, miles and miles into the heavens. When it could reach no higher, the cloud began to spread out, until the whole thing resembled a giant mushroom.

Remembering the account that Mrs Sullivan had given him and Maia, Zak spun round to face his friends. 'We need to get back to the house — quickly.'

Dexter was staring dumbfounded at the volcano. 'By Jupiter, you were right,' he mumbled.

Zak grabbed his arm. 'Yes, we were. But we can discuss that another time. We have to go. We need to find shelter.'

With the ground still vibrating, they hurried along the cobbled streets, no longer caring whether any Vulcani saw them or not. Many other people were dashing about, apparently in blind panic. Some were screaming, while others just stood, transfixed by the sight of Vesuvius spewing forth unimaginable amounts of smoke and ash and rock into the sky.

As they ran, small pieces of pumice began to fall. Both light in colour and weight, they did little damage at first, drifting down like a sporadic scattering of marble-sized hailstones, filling the air with a constant tapping sound. As they hit the ground, they began to bounce like exploding popcorn.

The moment they turned into the road leading to Cassia's house, they knew something was wrong. The large wooden door in the long, featureless wall stood ajar.

Cassia gasped. 'Felix never leaves the door open.'

They rushed towards the doorway and entered the house. Almost immediately, they saw the slave's thick-set frame lying face down in a pool of blood. Cassia let out a shriek.

Dexter dropped to his haunches and felt his neck. 'He's dead.'

The four of them crept forward out of the short hallway and into the large atrium. Above them, they could hear the rain of pumice clattering on the roof. A constant smattering of pieces was falling through the square opening in the atrium roof and plopping into the small pool of water below.

All around them were the signs of a struggle. One of the statues had been toppled from its pedestal and lay in several pieces across the mosaic floor. Splintered pieces of a wooden table lay scattered about.

'Are they still here?' asked Cassia, her voice barely above a terrified whisper.

Without asking, Zak knew she meant the Vulcani. 'We need to check,' he said, his head darting this way and that. 'Let's split up. But go carefully.'

To the constant sound of the falling pumice, the four of them crept off in different directions.

Peering cautiously around corners, Zak moved slowly into the covered walkway around the garden. Aside from the rattling tiles, the place was eerily quiet. And it was growing steadily darker outside in the garden. A peculiar grey light was descending over the city as the murky cloud above blotted out any remaining signs of what had been a pleasant autumnal day only a short while previously. And that same cloud was depositing an ever-growing layer of dirty-looking pumice and ash over the garden, as if someone had sprayed the place with dry cement.

Satisfied there was no one in the garden, he returned to the atrium just as the others were also returning.

'There's nobody here,' said Cassia. 'And no sign of the slaves. I hope they managed to get away.' For once, Zak thought her concern sounded sincere.

A noise from the hallway made them all start. It sounded like footsteps.

'Did someone close the front door?' asked Maia.

'I thought it best not to,' said Cassia. 'In case we needed to run back out.'

Before they could utter another word, a slender figure appeared in the doorway. It wore a hooded cape and held a staff in one hand. As they stood watching in shock, the figure pulled back the hood to reveal a head of long wavy, silver hair and a pair of piercing grey eyes. It was the woman Zak and Maia had seen on the city walls, and whom Zak had seen talking to the gladiator Maximus.

Chapter XVI

Minerva

'I would speak with the girl called Maia,' said the woman. She spoke with a deep and haughty voice, like an overbearing teacher, and in the failing light, her harsh, creased features appeared even more menacing than before.

Zak's first thought had been to run away once more, but when he glanced down the gloomy hallway behind her, it was clear she was alone.

'That's me. But I guess you know that already.' Maia was trying to sound confident, thought Zak, but he could tell she was feeling anxious.

Without apparently moving a muscle, the woman's eyes studied them each in turn, before a faint smile seemed to crease one corner of her mouth.

'Is there somewhere we can talk?' she asked. Then, seeing their obvious hesitation, she added: 'I mean you no harm. You have my word.'

Zak snorted more loudly than he had intended. 'And just why in Jupiter's name should we trust you?'

She gave him a thin smile. 'A good question. But I'm certain you are intrigued enough to listen to what I have to say. Now, somewhere to sit, if you please. I am old and very tired.'

After a brief pause, Cassia sparked into life. 'Come, Dexter. Help me light the lamps in here. We can sit overlooking the garden.'

As they moved into an adjacent room, Zak caught Maia sniggering next to him. 'What's up with you?'

'Back there, you said "in Jupiter's name".'

'No, I didn't ... did I? Crikey, I think I've been in this place far too long.'

Moving gracefully, head proudly in the air like a monarch, the elderly woman glided along, while Cassia and Dexter busied themselves with lighting a lamp in each of the four corners of the room. The lamps flared into life, casting an orange glow over the vibrant, almost lurid blocks of colour on the three walls. Several luxurious couches lay in the middle, angled towards the far side of the room, which opened directly onto the colonnade around the garden. Zak guessed the room was used for entertaining important guests, although with a grey and now lifeless garden in front of them, the view was not as impressive as it would normally have been.

'Now, what is it you have come here to say to my friends?' demanded Cassia. She, too, was trying to look and sound self-assured, like the lady of the house, but Zak knew she was just as nervous as the rest of them.

The woman opened her mouth to speak, but almost immediately, the sound of clattering boots filled the atrium behind her. She spun round just as a slim figure darkened the doorway. The man pulled back his hood and looked around the room.

'Caius!' yelped Cassia, and took a step forward.

But Zak was next to her and held out an arm to check her. Something was not right, he could tell instantly.

Without paying them much attention, Caius glared at the woman. 'Minerva,' he said through clenched teeth. 'I should have known it was you.' Although it was clearly Caius, his voice, cold and menacing, seemed to belong to someone else.

The next moment, five other men poured into the room behind him. They were all wearing crimson, hooded capes, their features as obscured as ever. Vulcani.

'Wh—what's going?' demanded Cassia.

'This concerns you and me, Caeculus,' said the woman called Minerva. 'Let these children go. They have no part in it.'

An ugly sneer crept onto Caius' face. 'Oh, but they are not just children, are they? We both know that. And besides, they are in possession of two objects that I need.'

Cassia was shaking next to Zak. 'But—but the Vulcani were after you,' she said, her voice incredulous.

'Oh, you stupid little girl,' said Caius, throwing a disdainful glance towards her. 'You saw what I wanted you to see.'

By this time, Zak's eyes were flitting around the room, looking at everyone in turn, trying to make sense of what was happening. Minerva stared impassively at Caius with those cold eyes of hers. He returned her look with a thoroughly unpleasant leer. And the five Vulcani began to slowly fan out into the room, each one with a hand permanently on the hilt of the sword dangling from his waist.

All the while, Zak was inching slowly backwards, desperately trying to coax Maia, Cassia and Dexter with him. He sensed something was about to happen, and the further away they were, the better.

'You killed Felix, didn't you?' said Dexter suddenly. Then, without waiting for a response, he leapt towards Caius, a growl rising from his throat. But before he reached him, one of the Vulcani darted between them and struck Dexter a blow to the head with the pommel of his sword, sending him instantly to the floor.

It was Zak's turn to take a step forward before Maia grabbed his arm to restrain him. He looked from Dexter's crumpled body on the floor to the look of utter contempt on Caius' face and felt numb with shock. A horrible churning feeling twisted inside his stomach. Caius, if that was even his name, had deceived them, had betrayed them.

'Enough of this!' shouted Caius. 'Take them all.'

The events of the next few heartbeats seemed to take an age to unfold, as though viewed in slow motion. Zak watched, mesmerised, paralysed.

Swords were being drawn. Caius drew back the loose folds of

his cape to reveal some device on his bare wrist. Minerva spread her feet, bracing herself as if ready to fight. Then one of the Vulcani threw back his drooping hood, drew his sword in one swift, fluid motion and turned on his colleagues. It was Maximus.

Swords were flying through the air, nothing more than blurs of glinting steel. It was four against one, but the one was winning, pushing his opponents back and back. One of them fell backwards through the open doorway and out of sight. His three colleagues retreated after him, yielding before the relentless onslaught from the gladiator, amid showers of sparks that flew like fireflies in the gloom, as swords clashed again and again.

In no time at all, they had left the room, the endless crashing of swordplay echoing in the atrium beyond, receding with every second.

Caius seemed momentarily stunned by what he had just witnessed. But the moment he regained his composure, he extended his right arm and pointed his fist at Minerva. She was stepping slowly backwards, her right hand, which held the staff, facing Caius. A small flaming dart flew at great speed from the device on Caius' wrist straight towards the woman. It was just like the one Zak had seen striking the old man in the playground. Yet somehow before it struck her squarely in the chest, it deflected off something blue that was there for a split second before vanishing again. The flash of colour was so brief that Zak was not even sure he had seen anything at all.

Another small bolt of fire shot from Caius, then another. But each time they veered off course abruptly. One of them tore into the ceiling above Minerva, removing a piece of plaster the size of a dinner plate, sending it crashing to the floor. Minerva seemed able to deflect the missiles away using the staff in her hand.

More blurs of fire shot towards her. And with each one, Zak could see the faint outline of a blue shield in front of Minerva, transparent and only visible for the fraction of a second when the fire bolt struck and rebounded away.

'It's over,' snarled Caius, as he continued firing at his opponent. 'Your time has come to an end. Soon my father will rule this world.'

'Not while I still have a single breath left inside me, he won't,' retorted Minerva, her face grim and determined.

While she slowly retreated towards the colonnade behind her, Caius continued his onslaught. The strange bullets of fire flew from his weapon, struck the blue shield more and more frequently. Away they flew to every corner of the room, exploding on the ceiling, the walls, flying low over the heads of Zak, Maia and Cassia, who by now were sheltering behind the couches in the middle of the room.

'What on earth is going on?' asked Maia, turning her anguished face towards Zak and then ducking her head as another fiery dart tore into the wall nearby.

'I have no idea,' replied Zak. 'But I reckon we want her to win now, don't we?'

Just as Minerva seemed on the point of stepping backwards under the colonnade, she took a sudden step forwards, thrusting her staff and near-invisible shield towards Caius. His next two shots hit the shield squarely in the middle and flew straight back at him. One of the bullets grazed his arm, while the other narrowly missed his head, slamming into the wall behind. He collapsed in ungainly fashion onto the floor, clutching his arm with a cry of pain.

With a grimace on his face, he aimed his fist at Minerva once again and fired off another salvo of bolts. As she held her staff up in front of her face, he rolled over and sprang back to his feet.

'I need to get Dexter,' mumbled Zak. 'He's in the firing line.'

'I'm coming with you,' said Maia.

'Be careful,' whispered Cassia, who looked scared out of her wits.

With streaks of fire crisscrossing the room like fast-moving birds, Zak and Maia crawled on all fours towards the door to the atrium, where Dexter lay on his back, groaning as he returned to consciousness.

Another piece of plaster from the ceiling exploded onto the mosaic floor between them, sending dusty fragments into the air like a cloud of smoke. Moments later, a section of the painted wall, the size of a door, fractured and fell to the floor.

Glancing over his shoulder, Zak could see that Minerva was now almost out of the room, ducking around one of the many pillars of the colonnade, as more shots flew over her head and disappeared into the grey garden behind her.

He jumped up and ran towards Dexter, his feet crunching on the many pieces of plaster now strewn across the mosaic. With Maia's help, he pulled the slave to his feet and then tugged him back towards Cassia, just as more of the ceiling came crashing down around them.

With the firefight now raging outside, the four of them rushed out of the room, crouching low as they went, and ducked for cover behind a pillar in the covered walkway. Minerva was retreating along the other side of the colonnade, her tall, elegant figure slowly blurring behind the rain of pumice that continued to fall over the garden.

Cassia was crouching over Dexter, concern written across her face. 'Are you all right, Dexter?' she asked.

'I'll be fine,' he replied, rubbing his head. 'But your father's going to go mad when he sees what you've done to the house.'

For a couple of seconds, they stared at one another in silence, before suddenly both bursting into laughter. Cassia then threw her arms around her slave. 'Oh, Dexter. I don't know what I would do if I lost you.'

'It's over, Minerva!' boomed Caius.

Zak's head shot round. A short distance away, Minerva was on one knee, holding her staff before her. Her stony-cold composure was cracking. There was something like fear seeping into her eyes. Caius was firing at her, bolt after fiery bolt, more than one every second. As he did so, he moved his outstretched arm about, constantly changing the angle of attack. Her shield was now being struck so frequently it was almost permanently visible as a large blue disc.

Then she was hit in the foot. She cried out, lost her balance, rolled onto one side, still holding her shield in front of her.

'We need to help her,' cried Maia.

'I know,' said Zak, who was already rushing along the colonnade. He had no idea what he was going to do, but he felt such a surge of anger, such hatred towards Caius that nothing else seemed to matter.

As he turned the sharp corner to face the back of Caius, he saw Minerva hit once more, this time in the shoulder, he thought. As she tossed her head back and yelled, another bullet tore into her body.

A sudden rush of wind flew past Zak, barging him to the stone floor. He looked up and saw a crimson cape flying towards Caius. The young man was knocked off his feet, flew against the side wall and fell in a crumpled heap on the ground.

Zak instantly recognised the broad shoulders of Maximus. The gladiator bent down ripped the wrist band off Caius' arm and tossed it away. In the next moment, he was kneeling over the stricken Minerva.

'My lady,' he gasped, as Zak crept up behind him. 'You are hurt.'

Minerva coughed, before a faint smile played at the corners of her mouth. 'Maximus, my faithful friend,' she said, her voice rasping. 'I am indeed hit, but I can still breathe. Now watch out for that cur over there. He is stirring already.'

Springing to his feet like a wild animal, Maximus then pounced on Caius and yanked him up as if he were no more than a rag doll.

Maia rushed past Zak and helped to prop up Minerva against a pillar, whilst Cassia stood before Caius, a seething anger in her eyes.

'Who are you ... Caius?' she demanded.

Maximus stood behind him, a head taller than the young man, twisting his arm behind his back. As he lifted his head to look up, a trickle of blood ran down the side of his grubby face, which he tried desperately to turn towards Maximus. 'Let me go!' he roared, defiance flooding into his face. 'I order you to let—'

'I don't take orders from little boys,' growled the gladiator.

'I am not a boy ... I am nineteen.'

'I thought you were sixteen,' said Cassia.

'Ha! You little children! A five-year-old could have deceived you lot.'

'I felt sorry for you, Caius,' spat Cassia.

'My name is not Caius, you silly little girl,' he roared. 'My name is ... Caeculus.' He paused, looking from one face to the next.

'Are we supposed to know who that is?' asked Maia.

'You know, Caeculus. The son of the god Vulcanus.'

Zak looked at Maia, then back at the young man and shrugged.

'Does my name mean nothing to you?' he bellowed.

'Er, well, no actually,' said Zak. He moved closer and looked up into the young man's face. 'Well, that was kind of awkward, wasn't it?'

'I liked you,' continued Cassia, looking like she was about to explode. 'We nearly risked our lives trying to save you.'

He opened his mouth to speak, but before another insult could be uttered, Cassia slapped him hard across the face.

While the prisoner's reddened face hung in silent shame, Maximus turned to Minerva. 'What shall we do with him, my lady?'

Still slumped against the pillar, the woman was looking pale and weak. 'We should take him with us,' she replied.

Before anything else was said or done, the earth began to shake, growing and growing in ferocity, till the whole house seemed to have come alive. All around them, the sounds of destruction rose above the relentless clatter of pumice stones on tiles. The cries of frightened people rang out over the city, amid what sounded like the crash of collapsing walls and roofs in neighbouring houses.

A shower of roof tiles cascaded down into the garden with a terrifying crunch. Then a section of the roof over the colonnade collapsed in a cloud of billowing dust. Zak lost his balance and tumbled to the floor, landing painfully on his hands.

When the dust began to clear, he rolled gingerly onto his back, coughing loudly. Something hard dug into his hip. When he moved to see what it was, he saw Caius' weapon lying on the ground and picked it up. It was similar in design to the wristwatch that had transported him and Maia through time, except it had no face and the piece worn on the top of the wrist was a little thicker.

After only a short while, the earth was no longer shaking quite so violently, and the noise of falling pumice resumed its incessant tapping all round them.

'Where's he gone?' cried Cassia. 'Caius has gone.'

Still on all fours, Zak looked around through the grim light. Covered in ash and dust, Cassia, Maia, Dexter and Maximus were all getting stiffly back to their feet. The gladiator then darted back into the house and returned a few moments later.

'He's gone,' he said. 'We need to get out of here before he returns with more Vulcani.'

Chapter XVII

The Daughter of Janus

Maximus picked up the long, thin frame of Minerva as though she were as light as a small child. Holding her carefully, respectfully, in both arms, he carried her out of Cassia's house, while the others followed behind.

Out in the street, the light was fading, while the steady hail of pumice continued unabated. There was now a thick layer of pumice and ash over the road and path, several centimetres deep, looking like a covering of dirty snow.

As they moved along in single file, they hugged the side of buildings, trying to keep under the overhanging roofs to avoid the falling stones as best they could. When they reached the main road up ahead, they could see many other people were also on the move, no doubt trying to escape the city. Several carts loaded with household possessions were crunching along at a snail's pace, as the men and mules that tried to pull them struggled through the growing layer of volcanic debris.

'You knew all along, didn't you?' said Zak to Dexter, as they took momentary shelter under the awning outside a shop. 'About Caius, I mean?'

'Well, yes, I did suspect he wasn't all he seemed. There was just something not quite right about him.'

'Why on earth didn't you say something?' asked Zak.

Dexter shrugged. 'I'm just a slave. It's not my place to offer opinions.'

'You might be Cassia's slave. But you're not mine,' he said rather crossly. 'As long as I'm around, you can say anything you like to me.'

Dexter gave him an enigmatic smile but said nothing.

'Why don't we go through the doorway, back to our time?'

suggested Maia. 'Look, the Vulcani have gone.'

Zak looked at where she was pointing and sure enough, the two men, who had been guarding the door with the bronze head of Janus on its front, had gone.

By now, Maximus had picked up Minerva once more and was trudging through the layer of pumice again. He was heading off down the main street, away from the doorway.

'I think we should stick with them for now,' said Zak. 'Maybe Minerva can tell us what we want to know. We can always come back here later.'

Reluctantly, Maia agreed, and they all set off after Maximus. As they walked along, Zak looked down a side street at where the massive shape of Vesuvius should have been. But now, all he could see in the gloom was a huge billowing cloud of blacks and greys, swirling from the horizon up to the heavens.

The longer they trudged through the ever-thickening layer of pumice, the more tired Zak's legs became. His mouth was parched and his eyes and lungs full of dust. He longed for fresh air and a cup of cold water.

At last, Maximus took them down a narrow street and halted before a large wooden door. Holding Minerva in one arm, he rummaged in a pouch around his waist and took out a key which he used to unlock the door. After a quick glance in either direction, he ushered them all into the dark house.

After slamming the door behind him, he carried Minerva into a gloomy, windowless room and laid her on a couch. He then hurriedly rushed around the room, lighting candles and oil lamps, filling the room with a pale, orange glow.

'Are you all right?' asked Maia, kneeling down beside Minerva.

She smiled weakly, coughed then spoke. 'My time is nearly done. But before I go, I must explain. I promised your father I would, if ever such events as these should occur.'

Maia glanced round at Zak, wide-eyed, before leaning in closer to the woman.

Maximus, who had momentarily left the room, returned with water and a pillow, which he put under Minerva's head to prop her up slightly. He then wiped her face and gave her a drink, before pouring cups for the others.

'You know who my father is?' asked Maia, staring intently at Minerva.

Zak moved near to Maia and sat on the couch opposite.

Minerva nodded gently. 'You are the daughter of Janus,' she said simply.

Cassia gasped. 'You mean, the god Janus?'

Minerva smiled, then chuckled, which immediately made her cough. 'We are not gods. Not any of us. Though some among us would see themselves as gods.'

'But—' began Cassia.

Minerva raised a weary hand to check her. 'I'm sure you have many questions, all of you. I will try to answer them. Let me explain.

'My ancestors were travellers, explorers from another world, far, far away from here. They had no supernatural powers, only the science and technology they brought with them. Of course, over the years some of the primitive people who lived on this planet witnessed some of this technology in use and considered it to be magic, thinking us to be gods. Much of what the humans have seen us do over the years has been exaggerated, embellished, distorted, such that the truth behind many of these stories has been lost for ever.

'You see, each of us has particular skills, knowledge passed down through our families. Mine include medicine and healing. But it is nothing more than science, not magic.

'When the first explorers arrived in Greece and Italy and elsewhere, they quickly fell in love with the beauty of your world. What is more, they discovered that they could live here for hundreds of years, many more than is possible back on our home planet. So most of them decided to stay.

'In the beginning all was harmonious. But as time went by, two factions began to emerge: those led by the Jupiter family, who said we should share our knowledge with the people here, and those led by the family of Vulcanus, who said we should not. At first, it was just endless, vigorous debating. But then one day, the bickering turned into fighting.

'It all began many years ago when your father, Janus, began working on time travel. He became obsessed with it, encouraged by his great friend Jupiter. If they could unlock the secrets of travelling through time, they reasoned, they could end all suffering, by going back and altering any unpleasant event.

'But then Vulcanus got to hear about this work and became convinced that they were holding back information from the others. Before long, arguments erupted into skirmishes, which in turn led to a terrible battle in the mountains of Greece.

'Using all our technology, my people fought one another in this great, bloody battle. Many, many of my kind were killed. But eventually, Vulcanus and his supporters were defeated. While many of his followers fled, he was captured and put on trial. Needless to say, he was found guilty of using violence against his own kind and of endangering the lives of innocent people on this planet with his selfish actions.

'Many wanted him to be executed for his crimes. But that is not our way. His punishment was to be imprisoned underground for the rest of his days. They thought it somehow fitting that the ancestor of the original Vulcanus, from whose name the Romans had derived their word for volcano due to his ability to manipulate fire, should be entombed under a volcano.'

'You stuck him under Vesuvius, an active volcano?' said Zak, incredulous.

'Yes. It was the easiest place to find a chamber big enough for his cell. And besides, many thought that if Vesuvius erupted that would be a just punishment for him.'

'But what has this to do with me and Janus?' asked Maia,

quietly.

Minerva took a sip of water. By now, her breathing was becoming increasingly laboured. 'I said that many died in the battle to defeat Vulcanus. One of them was Tiberinus, your brother, who died many years before you were even born. Janus was distraught. Over the next few years, he was driven as never before to unlock the secrets of time travel so that he could go back and save his beloved son.

'Then, one day, all his hard work paid off when he finally developed a time machine. He immediately travelled back through time and saved his son. But in so doing, he changed history. When he got back to his then present time, he found that other events had changed for the worse. So he went back again and again, trying to restore things to the way they were whilst at the same time trying to save his son's life. But each time he travelled back and made alterations, he returned to find that some other terrible event had occurred as a result of his actions. The more he went back to change the past, the more the present had unravelled when he returned, until he came back one day to find his son still dead and Vulcanus more powerful than before.

'You see, he had spent so many long years working to solve the problem of time travel, that he had never stopped to consider the implications of his work. He was a great man, a great scientist with a big heart, but his pursuit of knowledge had blinded him to the dangers.

'So he went back through time one final time to ensure that Vulcanus was still in prison under Vesuvius, and then he left his time machine to gather dust, while he mourned the loss of his son.

'But all this time, unbeknownst to us all, the remaining supporters of Vulcanus were plotting his escape. Seventeen years ago the attempt to free him was made. Humans believe there was a great earthquake at the time, but it was in fact caused by the last great battle between our people. So many of my race were killed that day, including our great leader Jupiter himself, until not many of us remained. But Hercules, our greatest warrior, was still alive — the one person Vulcanus truly fears. While he and I set off with our few remaining friends to ensure Vulcanus could not escape, Janus activated his machine one last time and told his servant Primus to take you, a mere baby, to safety, not into the past this time, but into the future. Your safety was all he cared about, even above his own life.'

Zak looked across at Maia. Tears were running down her cheeks, leaving streaks on her dust-covered face.

'What happened to my father?' she asked.

'When we got back to his villa, we found him dead in the rubble. We assume Bellona, Vulcanus' sister, had killed him.'

Maia buried her dirty face in her hands. Zak put a comforting hand on her shoulder, while Cassia gave her a hug.

'So what is going on now, exactly?' asked Zak.

'We have known for a long time that Caeculus has been planning to free his father by causing Vesuvius to erupt. Maximus here has been my spy in the Vulcani for several years. He has told me they have been laying explosives under the volcano for many months. It would seem they have succeeded.'

'But surely the eruption will kill Vulcanus?' said Zak.

Minerva smiled weakly once more. 'We are not humans. We are not easily killed. The blood in our veins is called Ichor and can protect us against most things. For example, it is very hard for a human to kill one of us. Only our own technologies can cause us any serious harm. So Vulcanus will be battered and bruised when his prison is ejected from the volcano, but he will not die. Nor will the cell designed by Portunus, his jailer, be damaged. But if the cell is buried for long enough, he will suffocate. We need air to breathe as much as humans do.'

'So without the Key of Portunus he can't escape the prison?' continued Zak.

'Correct. I understand you managed to remove it from the

villa. Well done on solving the riddle, but that was not wise. Caeculus must never get his hands on that key. If Vulcanus is ever freed, he will take over the planet. There are so few of us left to stop him now.'

'What about Hercules?' asked Dexter. 'You said Vulcanus fears him.'

'After the battle seventeen years ago, Hercules returned to find his family dead. He went away in despair and has not been seen since.'

'But why did Caeculus not just steal the key from us?' asked Cassia. 'Why the need to make Vesuvius erupt?'

'Portunus believed he had designed the perfect prison. Only the key can unlock the cage, and the cage is holding up the roof of the cavern. So even if someone managed to find the key and unlock it, the cage would dissolve into nothing, the roof would collapse and Vulcanus would be buried alive. So their answer is to eject him from the volcano and hope they can find the key before he suffocates.'

Zak's head was spinning. It was all too much to take in. 'And where do I fit into all this?' he asked. 'An old man gave me this,' he added, holding out the watch, 'and said it was now mine.'

Minerva eyed it suspiciously. 'He gave you the *Temporum*?' She looked genuinely puzzled. 'That must have been Primus, Janus' loyal servant. But why he gave it to you instead of to Maia, I do not know.'

'It's called a *Temporum*?' said Zak, staring at the object.

'That was the name Janus gave it, yes,' replied Minerva.

'How come we can speak and understand Latin, when we've never learnt it?' asked Maia, regaining a degree of composure.

'You are one of us, Maia,' replied Minerva with a benevolent smile. 'You have Ichor in your veins. Speaking Latin is second nature to you, like breathing. You may not realise it, but when you are here, you are speaking Latin.'

'Then what about me?' asked Zak. 'How come I can

understand it, too?'

Minerva's forehead creased into a frown. She sighed. 'I do not know that either. But I suspect it has something to do with your wearing that time machine built by Janus.'

Zak was still struggling to make sense of it all. And there were still so many questions he wanted to ask. 'I still don't understand,' he said. 'If Maia was sent to the future for safety, how did the Vulcani track her down?'

'I do not know. You need to tell me exactly what happened.'

'Well, as I said, this old man gave me what I thought was just a watch on my birthday. I took it to school, fiddled with it and then suddenly Maia appears out of thin air in the classroom. A while later, everything freezes, except Maia and me, and then the Vulcani start chasing us.'

Minerva closed her eyes and was silent for a while, so long in fact that Zak began to wonder if she had fallen asleep or had even died. But eventually, she opened her eyes again. 'It would seem you must have inadvertently activated the *Temporum*. In so doing, you summoned Maia to you. Janus would have wanted to keep her away from the device, at least in the beginning, to keep her out of harm's way. But then, knowing him, he would have programmed it such that if the device were activated, it would instantly summon Maia from wherever she was, so that she could use it to escape from the Vulcani. But this would also have alerted the Vulcani to the whereabouts of the time machine. They cannot travel through time to a point of their choosing, but they can track the device when it is activated. That much Maximus has been able to learn.'

'If the time machine summoned me to Zak's classroom,' began Maia, 'then where was I before that?'

'You would have lived a completely different reality, a different life up to that point. Then, when the device summoned you, reality would have changed for you. Your whole past would have changed, your memories, everything. That is what it can do.

That is why it must never be used lightly.'

Zak looked at Maia. 'That must be why I had never seen you before that day. Wearing the watch must have stopped *my* memories from being altered.'

Maia still looked confused. 'But if all these events took place seventeen years ago, why am I only thirteen?' she asked.

Minerva smiled, then gave a brief, weary chuckle. 'Ah, the endless mysteries of time travel. For those of us here, it was seventeen years ago. But in the future, Primus must have waited only thirteen years before giving Zak the watch. He could so easily have waited twelve or fourteen, or any number. When you are travelling back and forward through time, the actual numbers become irrelevant.'

'So the Vulcani have been chasing us because they want this *Temporum*, so they can travel through time,' said Maia, more statement than question.

'Precisely. To begin with, they were searching for you, Maia, believing you had the device. Caeculus and his father are desperate to get their hands on it. If ever they did, they would be unstoppable.'

'And why did time keep stopping whenever they were chasing us?' asked Zak.

'They have their own magical device,' said Maximus. It was the first time he had spoken, and his words came out in a humourless growl. 'They can slow down time to the pace of a snail crossing a path. Only those with Ichor in their veins or those who wear their special capes are immune.'

'Here take this,' said Minerva, fumbling with her hands until she had removed a large ring from her finger. The ring contained a large green stone in the centre. 'My time is nearly over. I can feel my life slipping away. Even with my knowledge of healing, there is nothing more I can do. So, Maia, take this and wear it at all times. It can block their attempts to slow down time. If time does slow again, just twist the stone in tiny increments, until you find a spot where everything returns to normal.'

Maia took the ring and stared blankly at it, before returning her gaze to the dying woman.

'What if we used the time machine to go back and stop Vulcanus?' Zak asked.

Minerva shot out a hand like a cobra and seized his arm. 'No!' she snapped. 'You must promise me, never to go back in time to try to undo something you have already done. It never works. Janus was a brilliant scientist, but even he could not find a way to change history for the better. All he ever succeeded in doing was making matters worse. Do you understand?'

She was gripping his arm so tightly it hurt. 'Yes. Okay. I understand,' he said, wincing.

She let go of his arm and slumped back on the couch, her strength ebbing away before their eyes. 'Maximus,' she said, her voice barely above a whisper. The gladiator moved closer to her. 'Look after them, my loyal friend. They will need your help in the coming days.'

'Of course, my lady.'

A few moments later, he bowed his head over Minerva, and stayed in that position for several minutes.

'Is she dead?' asked Cassia after a while.

Maximus gave a slight nod, before rising slowly to his feet. 'We must burn the body. Help me make a fire.'

He picked her up and carried her through to the small courtyard garden in the centre of the house. By now, the garden was completely buried under a mound of ash and pumice over knee-deep. With the help of the others, he broke apart several pieces of wooden furniture and constructed a makeshift pyre on top of the pile of pumice. He then placed Minerva's body on top and set fire to the wood.

As the flames quickly took hold and leapt into the air, Cassia said: 'This might set fire to the house.'

When Maximus did not respond, but instead knelt down and

seemed to be praying in front of the funeral pyre, Zak whispered to her: 'Trust me, it won't matter. In the next few hours, this whole town is going to be buried.'

When they left the house and headed out onto the streets, they found the rain of pumice was falling more heavily than ever. But before leaving the house, Maximus had given them each a round shield. So, holding them above their heads, they clambered up onto the layer of ash and pumice which was now approaching a metre in depth, and headed for the main street that ran the length of the city.

Zak had studied his map and determined that they were much closer to the time portal near Cassia's house than they were to the one in the Forum. So they had all agreed that the best plan to escape the slowly vanishing city was to pass through the doorway into present-day England. Once safely there, they could then consider what to do next.

However, progress was slow. Walking on top of a constantly moving, crumbling surface was hard going, made worse by the need to hold their shields above their heads, while small pieces of pumice continued to clatter down on top of them. Every few steps at least one of them would lose their footing and fall onto the dry, shifting layer of stones.

Behind them, to the West, the sun was sinking in the sky, and was just beginning to appear below the thick ash cloud. Sporadic shafts of a pale, eerie light swept across the city, like searchlights from a helicopter.

To their left, the cone of Vesuvius was now nothing more than a huge black mass of cloud, towering into the sky far higher than any mountain on the planet. Regular flashes of lightning erupted from the enormous column of blackness, momentarily lighting up parts of the bulging, angry cloud.

The sooner they could escape this hell on earth, the better, thought Zak.

While they were trudging along, wading through the stones, there was a sudden, loud creaking sound, followed by a deafening crunch. Once more, Zak fell to the ground and a cloud of dust enveloped him.

'Is everyone all right?' asked Dexter, appearing out of the gloom. He had been at the front of their small group and seemed to be the only one still standing. He quickly stumbled back to help his friends.

Still cowering under his shield, Zak rose gingerly to his feet. 'What happened?' he asked, trying to peer through the thinning cloud behind them.

'Part of that building just collapsed,' said Maximus, as he held his shield over Maia and helped her back up. 'From the weight of all these stones. Some of these buildings are weak after all the recent earthquakes. We need to get a move on.' And without another word, he marched forwards down the road, his knees rising up high with each step.

The others followed him, now so caked in grey dust and dirt they looked like a line of ghosts haunting the dying city. On and on they walked through the failing light, till their legs and arms ached and ached, and their throats became so dry it was hard to speak.

At last, Zak began to recognise some of the buildings around him. He knew they were approaching the doorway that would finally lead them back home. When he looked up ahead, he saw Maximus standing with his buckler over his head. He seemed to be staring at something, a puzzled frown growing across his face.

'Oh no!' said Maia.

Zak had seen it too, just at that same moment. The building had gone, collapsed into a pile of roof tiles, brick and timber, covered with a growing layer of volcanic stones and ash. Frantically, he fished out the *Temporum* and scanned the map.

'Is the door knocker still there?' asked Maia, peering over his shoulder.

Zak stared at the map of Pompeii, willing the red dot to appear. But nothing did. 'It's gone,' he said simply.

'Maybe we can dig it out and fix it to another door,' said Maia.

Zak looked across at the pile of rubble through the curtain of falling pumice. Stones continued to patter on the shield above him. His heart sank. 'That'll take too long in this,' he said, shaking his head. 'We'll have to head back to the Forum. At least that dot is still flashing.'

'But that will take for ever,' gasped Maia.

But all Zak could say was: 'I know.'

Chapter XVIII

The Earring

The noise was beyond deafening, the vibrations beyond any pain he had ever felt, almost beyond his ability to endure it. The roar in his ears, in his head, and the incessant quaking of every tiny molecule in his body made it feel like he was on the point of being torn into a thousand pieces. Even when he tried to hold onto something to steady himself, it made no difference.

Yet despite all the intense pain, Vulcanus had a faint smile on his lined face. He had waited years for this moment. Long, long, interminable years of incarceration, when even he had begun to wonder whether he would ever see daylight again. So now that he was on the point of freedom, no amount of pain and suffering could dampen the anticipation of his imminent release. Had he been a mere human, he would have already been dead. But he was not human, did not have one of their puny, fragile bodies. No, it would take more than an exploding volcano to kill him.

When the moment finally came, he nearly passed out. There was a huge explosion underneath him, which rocked his cage like never before. There was a sudden rush of air as his prison for so many years was launched upwards. Up and up it travelled, all the while the constant roar enveloping him like solid rock.

And then he was out, shooting high into the sky at such speed he felt gravity pulling savagely at his entire body. Finally, the pain caused him to black out momentarily. When consciousness floated back, he was falling, pressed against the roof of the cage. Beside him, the shattered remains of the pathetic house his captors had built for him inside the cage rattled about at great speed, like a building torn apart by a whirlwind. Over and over again, he was hit by flying pieces of wood and masonry, till it felt as though his whole body were covered in bloody gashes and stinging bruises.

The landing, when it came, was just as violent, just as abrupt. The glowing bars of the cage struck the ground with such force that the whole structure jumped back up into the air. Down it crashed again, then over and over it rolled, tossing its captive around like a tiny mouse caught in a tumbling barrel.

After what seemed like an age, his prison finally came to rest, leaning at a steep angle in the gloomy, desolate wasteland of pumice and ash, which now spread for miles around Vesuvius.

Vulcanus lay gasping on the floor. He wiped a streak of blood from his face, then watched as a deep gash on his arm began to close before his eyes. Slowly but surely, his wounds all began to heal themselves, his Ichor doing its job. His hearing, his eyesight returned to normal. He stood up stiffly and peered out over the landscape.

Apart from the distant smudge of a fiery sunset, everything was dark. Occasional streaks of lightning cracked across the billowing blackness above Vesuvius, while behind him there was a faint glow from what he guessed to be the dying embers of Pompeii.

He held onto the bars, gazing out across the dead landscape, and then let out a tremendous roar, a bellow of elation. At last, he was out. It was not the warm sunshine he had dreamed of for so many years, but at least he was outside.

Time ticked by. More and more pumice fell around his cage, until it began to creep through the bars. Slowly, that initial burst of joy began to evaporate. His cage was being buried, swallowed by the land around him. And there was nothing he could do to stop it. If he became entombed, not even his Ichor could save him. His air would eventually run out, and he would die.

'Where is that key, Caeculus?' he roared, thumping the glowing bars. 'Bring me the key!'

The interminable trek back towards the Forum was like something from a nightmare. Vesuvius had blasted so much rock and ash into the sky above Pompeii that it was now as dark as night. The only light left to guide them along the streets was the occasional flash of lightning coming from the plume above the volcano, and from the many small fires that had broken out across the city. It was clear countless lamps and braziers and torches had been knocked over while the city collapsed, setting fire to numerous buildings.

And then had come the next phase of the eruption. As they waded along through the ever-deepening layer of ash and pumice, Vesuvius had rumbled even louder than before, and then had begun spewing out great sheets of flame from its summit. Only minutes later, much larger, darker, more deadly pieces of rock had begun to fall from the sky, crashing into roofs like small meteorites.

Cassia was beginning to wonder whether she could make it much further. Her arms were aching from holding the buckler above her head for so long. And every so often, a large piece of rock would clang onto the shield, knocking her off her feet and onto the bed of hard, crumbling stones, which tore at her dress and her arms and her legs.

They passed other people in the street, dirty, haggard people trying to escape the city as they were. Some clambered about, frantically trying to move from one place to another, whilst others simply wandered about in a trance-like state, their terrified minds simply unable to deal with the shock of what was happening.

Cassia looked up ahead. The five of them were strung out in a ragged line, with Maximus, who was at the front, now almost invisible in the dark. With their heavy shields over their heads, they all looked as weary and as dazed as she now felt.

She just needed to rest, if only for a minute. She stopped for shelter under a large wooden awning at the front of a shop. It would normally have been high above the street offering shelter from the sun and the rain, but now, she had to duck to move underneath, so deep was the layer of pumice under her feet. She glanced up anxiously at the thick wooden beams above her head, but they still looked solid enough. It had no doubt avoided collapse because it sloped steeply downwards, the pumice bouncing off it and down into the road.

At last, the stones had stopped pinging off her shield, so she could finally lower it and rest her aching arm. She had barely finished letting out a heavy sigh, when a hand slapped over her mouth. Another wrapped around her chest. She was unable to breathe, to move. She tried to wriggle, to struggle against her assailant, but her strength had already been waning for some time.

Unable to fight back, she watched helplessly as Zak, Maia, Dexter and Maximus drifted away and vanished into the blackness, unaware of her fate.

'We should rest here a moment,' declared Maximus, stopping under a large protruding balcony. 'Let the others catch up.'

Exhausted, Zak did not need to be told twice. He slumped under the thick wooden beams of the balcony and sat down to rest with his back against the wall of the building. Moments later, Dexter dropped down beside him, so weary his eyes looked to be almost shut.

'Is that Caeculus' weapon?' asked Maximus in his deep voice.

Without realising, Zak had been fiddling with the chunky wristband. He looked at it and nodded. 'I picked it up after he ran away.'

'Well, you might as well throw it away now,' the gladiator growled.

'Why's that?'

'Only one of *them* can use those things. Not us humans.'

'I thought ... I assumed you were one of them,' said Zak. 'What with all your fighting skills.'

The gladiator grunted. 'No. I'm just human like you,' he replied. Then seeing Zak's obvious surprise, he added: 'I come from a long line of men and women who have been trained by these beings to assist them.'

Zak smiled. Having seen the man fight, he was now glad Maximus was on their side. 'When you chased me the other day, were you going to kill me?' he asked.

The gladiator gave a brief chuckle. 'If I'd wanted you dead, I would have thrown a knife into your back before you'd even gone twenty paces.'

'Then why chase me?'

Maximus sniffed while he considered this. 'You had seen me talking to Minerva. I needed to make sure you weren't going to tell anyone what you'd seen or heard.'

At that moment, Maia appeared out of the gloom, her head hanging low under her shield. She looked ready to collapse onto the ground.

'You took your time,' said Zak with a weak grin, looking up at her.

'Where's Cassia?' she asked suddenly, looking around.

'I thought she was with you,' replied Zak, feeling a sudden, horrible drop in his stomach.

'And I thought she was with *you*,' said Maia, looking horrified.

A black rock the size of a human head thumped into the thick layer of pumice, sending a cloud of dust and smaller stones into the air. Not far away, another one flew down and embedded itself into the loose ground. Yet despite these almost invisible missiles raining down, Cassia's captor dragged her by the arm on and on, causing her to stumble every few paces. She was just too weak to resist.

A pair of figures staggered past them, arm in arm, nothing more than silhouettes. Cassia called out for help, but the shadows just carried on as before until they melted into the blackness.

She tripped and fell onto the layer of small stones, causing the man to release his grip on her arm. In a flash, he bent down and yanked her back to her feet.

'What do you want with me?' she demanded, her voice cracking with a mixture of fear and anger.

A small fire nearby flared and cast a golden glow across his face. It was the boy she had thought was Caius, but who had turned out to be the man called Caeculus.

'I suggest you get a move on, before a rock smashes that tiny brain of yours,' he snarled, his face grimy and unpleasant.

Once more, he pulled her along, holding her wrist so tightly it hurt. All the while, pumice and rock and ash continued to fall about them, getting thicker and thicker. It scratched her legs and arms, one of which she held over her head in an almost futile attempt to protect it.

A nearby roof collapsed as they stumbled past, the terrible crashing momentarily rising above the constant din of the falling rock and the distant growl of the volcano.

Even Caeculus seemed to slow down for a moment, perhaps beginning to realise just how pointless and dangerous remaining out in the open was, when every moment could be their last. While still holding her firmly in his grasp, he bent down and began banging furiously on the closest door, which was already half buried, looking more like a square wooden hatch than a door. Without waiting long for a response, he pulled her along to the next door, and then the next. He was calling out for help, pleading with someone to let them in.

A face appeared at a window, a faint glow from a lamp lighting up the lined features of an elderly man. 'In here, friend,' he said in a kindly voice. 'We have room. But hurry.'

Cassia knew that Caeculus would accept the offer and go in. She had a split second to think. She feigned another stumble to the ground, managing to break free of his grip. He swore at her and bent down to grab her once more. But she was already fumbling with one of her long earrings. She slid it out of her ear and briefly thought of stabbing him with the tiny hook on the end. But she quickly realised it would cause nothing worse than a scratch. So instead, while Caeculus was yanking her back onto her feet, she stabbed the earring into the half-buried wooden door next to the window. It was too dark for Caeculus to see what she had done.

Wasting no more time, Caeculus thrust Cassia through the open window and followed close behind. She had to be helped down on the other side, since street level was now over a metre above the floor of the room. Once inside, they were ushered towards the centre of the house and into a windowless room. Five or six other people were huddled on the floor in the weak glow from several small oil lamps. One or two turned to look at the newcomers, whilst the others continued staring into space, indifferent to their arrival.

'Would you like some water?' the elderly man asked. 'I have only a little to spare. But hopefully the anger of the gods will pass soon and then we can go out for more.'

Caeculus downed the cup he was offered and gave nothing to Cassia.

'Could I possibly ...?' she began, before Caeculus turned and struck her across the face. She fell onto the floor and slumped against the wall.

'That's for hitting me earlier,' he spat.

'She is your slave, I presume,' said the owner of the house, a slight disapproving frown on his face. Though whether he disapproved of slaves or her treatment by Caeculus, Cassia could not tell.

'Yes,' said the son of Vulcanus. 'And she has tried to escape several times.'

'I am not a slave,' said Cassia, through gritted teeth. Maybe there was a chance she could persuade the others in the room who she was. Surely, at least some of them would have heard of her father or her uncle.

But then creaking and groaning sounds filled the house, getting louder by the moment. Outside the room, there was a mighty crash and Cassia expected the roof to come caving in on them at any moment. All eyes were glued to the ceiling as small pieces of plaster fell down around them, skittering on the patterned floor.

The sounds of destruction soon abated. Somehow, mercifully, the ceiling above them remained in place. The elderly man rushed over to the door and carefully, slowly, eased it open. Even in the dim light, it was clear to see the adjacent room had gone. Just a few paces from the doorway, there now stood an impenetrable wall of rubble, with large wooden beams jutting out from countless bricks and tiles. And as Cassia gaped at the sight, she could see thousands of small pumice stones flowing through the rubble like small cascades of water.

Tears began to sting her eyes. She just sat there, wiping them from her face, and prayed the others would find the earring. It was a slim hope. It was impossibly dark outside, and maybe the earring would be buried soon anyway. But that small glimmer of hope was all she had left.

'This is impossible,' said Maximus. 'I'm afraid we may never find your friend.'

Still gasping for breath, Zak looked up at the gladiator's grim face. 'I'm not giving up,' he said firmly.

They were sheltering from the ongoing bombardment of pumice under the still intact eaves of a large building. For the last few minutes, they had been darting from one shelter to the next while the large black rocks continued to thud into the thick layer of pumice around them. But it was hard to move fast, hard for their feet to gain purchase in the deep covering of small stones. Several times, Zak had put all his effort into an attempted sprint but had just ended up wading and stumbling no more than a few metres.

'It is too dark to see,' continued Maximus, the only one of them who seemed not to be breathless.

'You promised Minerva you would look after us,' said Zak, pointing a finger at him. 'And Cassia is one of us. We *will* find her.' The thought of not seeing her again terrified him. And the guilt, the terrible, all-consuming guilt he felt at not having checked sooner that she was still with them gnawed at him.

'Zak,' said Dexter quietly. 'He's right. There is no way to know where she is in this. We could all die trying to find her. I'm not sure that is what Cassia would want.'

A large piece of pumice crashed into the overhanging roof above them, sending a cascade of pieces of rock and shattered tiles over the edge like a sheet of water.

'If she lost her footing in this,' said Maximus, glancing at the clattering stones outside, 'she would be buried by now. I am sorry, Zak, but my duty now is to look after the rest of you.'

Zak studied the gladiator's set features, and then it dawned on him.

'Buried — of course! Maia!' he said, suddenly turning to his friend. 'I think I know where she might be.'

'How can you possibly know?' she asked, hope flickering in her eyes.

'Remember Mrs Sullivan showed us that picture of the bodies uncovered in a recent excavation? One of them was a girl with distinctive jewellery, just like Cassia's. That must be where she is now.'

'Of course!' cried Maia. 'She said it was in the northeast of the city ...'

'Near a fountain of Neptune,' added Zak, now bursting with hope. 'Dexter, Maximus — where is there a street fountain of Neptune?'

The two of them looked at one another uncertainly, before

Maximus spoke. 'I think I know where that is. But it is too dangerous to go there.'

'Fine,' said Zak. 'You can stay here. Maia and I are going to look for Cassia. Coming Dexter?' he added, as he stepped back out into the dark street.

Dexter shrugged and then followed. Behind him, Zak heard Maximus let out a huge sigh and then begin pounding his large boots into the ground.

With bucklers raised over their heads, the four of them set off through the darkened city once more. They scrambled through the shifting ground from one sheltered spot to another as fast as they could, while stones, large and small, continued to fall around them.

Zak's heart was thumping fast with anticipation. He had to be right. For if not, there would be no hope of ever finding Cassia again.

Chapter XIX

The Search for Cassia

As she sat on the floor in the pale light of a sputtering oil lamp, listening to the never-ending bombardment on the roof, wondering when and not if the ceiling was about to collapse on top of them, Cassia began to lose hope. She was losing track of time, too. Perhaps she had been there only a short while, or maybe it had been hours already. But then again, it hardly seemed to matter.

Another terrifying explosion hit the roof, shaking the walls and the ceiling. More fragments of plaster floated down. The others in the room huddled together in their family groups, some burying their faces to shut out the apparent inevitability of their impending fate. At first, the elderly man whose house it was, had offered words of encouragement, of reassurance. But even he was quiet now, apparently resigned to what was to come.

Only Caeculus was on his feet, pacing up and down, glowering at nothing in particular. He had tried a few times to dig his way through the rubble on the other side of the door. But it was so loose, so precarious that even he seemed to soon realise he was more likely to be buried alive in the attempt.

'Sit down,' she said calmly, as he passed close to her. 'There's nothing more we can do.'

He stooped down to snarl at her. 'You might have given up, but I haven't.'

'Are you not scared?' she asked.

'Scared of what?' he scoffed. 'None of this can kill me. It will kill you, but not me. I am the son of a god.'

She returned his cold stare, wondering how she had ever liked him. 'Then why did you take me? At least tell me that.'

He gave her a short, thin smile. 'Because you were at the back, left behind by your so-called friends. When they find out I've got you, they'll come running. That's when I can get that key to free my father.'

She remembered seeing the forlorn man in the mysterious cage under Vesuvius. Had his dejected appearance all been an act as well? 'Why did you take us to see your father?' she asked.

'I wanted you to feel sorry for him, for me. That way, you would be more inclined to trust me and to help me. And it worked, didn't it?' He leered at her once more.

If they were all going to die, she thought, at least this horrible young man would die with them.

'And why didn't you just take that wristband thing off Zak when we first met?' she asked. 'You could have stolen it at any time.'

'Because I realised very quickly that he could help me solve that riddle. He's clever, that Zak. In fact, I'll let you into a little secret: he's not at all what he seems.' Caeculus then let out a short, unpleasant laugh, which drew startled looks from the others in the room.

'What do you mean?' demanded Cassia.

But Caeculus did not reply. Instead, he walked away, a smirk etched across his face.

Maia was so tired she could barely think straight. She was worried they might never find Cassia again. And she was worried the longer they spent traipsing back and forth through the city, the less likely they would ever find the portal in the Forum and a way out of this nightmare.

And whenever she tried to force herself to think about something else, her mind would wander back to everything that Minerva had said. Her whole life felt like it had been a lie. She was not really Maia Jones at all, but the daughter of some mad scientist whose ancestors came from another planet. It was all too much to take in.

She felt in the pocket of her cape and fished out the Key of Portunus. It shimmered in her hand like a piece of burning coal, casting a faint but warm glow around her. With her other hand still holding the heavy shield above her head, she used the key as a torch in the oppressive blackness around her. The light did not project far, but it was better than nothing.

The black shape of Maximus had stopped up ahead, shield over his head like an umbrella. 'I think the fountain should be about here,' he said, looking down at the impenetrable carpet of pumice around his feet. 'But it must be buried.'

They were clearly standing at a crossroads, with narrow streets disappearing off into the dark. But the roads themselves, the pavements, even some of the buildings had gone completely. All that remained was the top half of several houses and shops poking up through the ash and pumice, dark and lifeless. It looked as though all the buildings were slowly sinking into the ground.

A rock flew out of the blackness and hit Maximus' upraised shield with a clang. Yet he barely moved or reacted, as though nothing more than a fly had just landed on it.

'Cassia!' yelled Zak. 'Cassia!'

Like her and Dexter, he was leaning tightly against the side of a building, trying to stay out of the remorseless cascade of pumice. But then she watched him shine a faint pool of light on the ground. He was using the *Temporum* to scan the surroundings. Maia immediately followed suit with the key. The two of them crisscrossed the road junction, dashing as best they could between sheltered spots under overhanging roofs.

'Cassia! Cassia!' they were all yelling now, while they searched.

But no reply came, just the endless drumming of stones and the continuous rumble of Vesuvius.

'Over here!' cried Zak suddenly.

Maia looked up and saw him crouching down under the battered remains of a wooden awning, which jutted out like the rib cage of a long-dead beast. In the light cast by the *Temporum*, she could see him holding something that sparkled. She waded across to him.

'That's Cassia's earring!' she said, with a leap of excitement. 'She must be nearby.'

'It was stuck in this door,' said Zak. He was pointing at a wooden door set into the wall behind him, although only a short section of the actual door was still visible above ground. 'She must have left it there on purpose.'

'Let's look in here first,' said Dexter. He rushed to the side of the awning, which by now was only a short distance above ground level, and, using several of the collapsed wooden beams as steps, clambered easily onto the roof of the building. Maximus and Zak followed him up and were soon out of sight. As weary as she was, Maia decided she was better off staying with the others, and so scrambled up after them.

Only the outer edge of the roof was left intact. Below them, a large hollow sloped downwards like a crater on the moon. Here and there, mangled roof joists were poking up at odd angles out of a thick layer of grey stones.

'I would guess that is an atrium that has collapsed,' said Maximus, rubbing his chin.

'Let's take a look,' said Dexter. Before anyone could utter any words of caution, he was sliding down the slope of pumice to the blackness below. Once at the bottom, he stood up and beckoned the others to follow. He then began calling out Cassia's name again.

By the time Maia had joined them, they could all hear voices coming from inside the house.

'It's her!' cried Zak. 'I can hear her calling.' He was on his knees already, digging with his bare hands, having cast aside his shield.

Out of the inky blackness above, a piece of rock flew down and thudded into the crater of pumice, sending up a shower of tiny stones into the air. But Zak ignored it and continued clawing at the ground.

Maia hesitated. She could hear the muffled voices, but whether one of them was indeed Cassia she was not so certain. Maybe it was just wishful thinking on Zak's part.

Dexter was now beside him, and the pair of them were digging out pieces of rock and roof tiles, casting them aside, while the massive frame of Maximus stood over them, a shield in each arm to form a roof.

When Maia moved in closer, the gladiator turned to look across at her from under his makeshift shelter. 'Remind me,' he said gruffly. 'Apart from the earring you just found, why is it you think your friend is here?'

'When they dig up Pompeii in the future,' she began, 'they find a group of bodies buried somewhere here, one of which has the exact same earring that Cassia wears.'

Maximus gave her a piercing, unnerving stare. 'So she dies here, tonight?'

'Well, yes. But not if we save her.'

'If she is meant to die tonight, then you should let her die.'

'What?' said Zak, turning around to look up at Maximus, sweat running down his grimy face.

'Minerva said you should not interfere with time,' growled the gladiator. 'There could be dire consequences.'

'Well, you can wrestle with your conscience all you like, but I'm going to save my friend,' said Zak, and returned to digging on his hands and knees. 'Besides, we've already messed with time, just by being here.'

Eyebrows knitted fiercely, Maximus glanced at Maia, who was not sure what to say.

Then, without warning, Maximus lunged forward between Zak and Dexter, brushing them out of the way. 'Move aside,' he ordered.

Although the boys were momentarily stunned, Maia thought

they were about to pounce on the fearsome warrior and start fighting. But then Maximus began digging into the ground, using the edge of his shield like a spade.

'You're taking too long,' he growled.

With rocks continuing to rain down around him, he worked at a ferocious speed, throwing aside pieces of wood and bricks like they were matchsticks. As he dug, he bellowed to the faint voices inside the house, commanding them to begin digging from their side, too.

A short while later, with Dexter's help, he moved a huge wooden beam to one side. A hand appeared out of the pile of pumice stones in front of them, scrabbling at the ground. A hole opened up quickly, until a face appeared.

'Ah, Maximus. Good. Help me out.' It was Caeculus, a sneering, superior look on his dirty face.

'How many of you are there in there?' demanded Maximus.

'Oh, I don't know,' replied the young man impatiently, still pulling at the hole to make it larger. 'Seven or eight, I guess.'

Maximus shoved one of his huge hands into the gap, thrusting Caeculus backwards and out of sight. 'In that case, you're coming out last. Women and children first.'

A girl of no more than six or seven was squeezed through the hole.

'We need to make this hole bigger,' yelled Maximus.

Immediately, Zak and Dexter leapt to his side and began pulling wildly at the debris. They were well below what had now become ground level, and every time they scooped away a handful of stones, more would flow back into their place. But at last, Maximus was able to dig down further, till he was standing up to his knees in dark grey stones and masonry. He bent down and lifted something large from out of the debris. It was another roof joist, stuck in the ground at one end, but now free and held aloft at the other. By so doing, he had created a gap big enough for people to crawl through on all fours. An elderly woman came first, followed by another woman.

'Is there a girl in there?' asked Zak anxiously. 'About thirteen with blond hair.'

'There's a slave girl,' replied the elderly woman rather pompously. 'But she'll be coming out last.'

'I am *not* a slave!' cried an indignant voice from within.

'That'll be Cassia,' said Dexter, grinning.

Maia felt an incredible surge of joy well up inside her.

Maximus barked an order to send her forward. Moments later, she appeared, her long hair in a tangled mess about her head. She clambered out of the hole and straight into Zak's arms, tears running down her cheeks.

'I knew you'd come,' she sobbed.

'Hurry up!' roared Maximus. His whole body seemed to be shaking, as he strained every muscle to keep the beam aloft. All around him pieces of the house and countless stones were falling down, threatening to block up the hole at any moment.

'We should leave Caeculus in there,' said Zak, peeling himself away from Cassia.

But while Maximus was struggling to keep the exit open, Caeculus suddenly barged past the owner of the house, as the elderly man was emerging through the gap. In no time at all, the young man was scrabbling his way up the slope towards the rim of the crater. Dexter darted after him, until Caeculus turned around and shoved him back down the slope amid a tumble of loose stones.

Silence filled the air, as abruptly as waking from a nightmare. Nothing moved, even the ghostly shapes of falling pumice hung in the air as if suspended on invisible string. Maia's eyes shot up to the roof, where Caeculus was just reaching the top. Four other figures were standing like statues along the roofline, no more than silhouettes against the coal-black sky.

'We followed Maximus here, sir,' one of them was saying, addressing himself to Caeculus.

'Get down there after them,' snapped the son of Vulcanus. 'You two, bring me the girl. You two, that boy,' he added, pointing at Maia and Zak.

'Maia!' cried Zak. 'The ring!'

'I know,' she yelled back. She had already dropped her shield and was now fumbling frantically in the dark with the large stone set into the ring on her finger.

Caeculus' voice was booming across the rooftops. 'Join me, Zak. I always knew Maia would be my enemy. But you. Well, we are the same, you and I. We are brothers, did you know that? Join me.'

Zak was ignoring him. He was facing Maia, calling urgently to her to use the ring. Her fingers felt fat and swollen, had lost all their co-ordination.

The four Vulcani were sliding down the slope towards them, almost surfing on a wave of pumice stones, their cloaks as black as batwings flying behind them. One of them was almost on top of her, his hooded face emerging out of the shadows.

The stone in the ring twisted like a dial on a small radio. The noise returned; the pumice fell once again, momentarily checking the progress of the Vulcani. The other people freed from the house were scrambling about in all directions, unaware of the Vulcani, just desperate to escape what they had thought would be their tomb. One of the Vulcani knocked a woman to the ground in his haste to get to Maia.

With a sickening crash, the beam above Maximus collapsed in a great cloud of dust. She heard him yell out in pain. Or was it Dexter? Or was it one of the Vulcani? She could not see a thing. It was dark, dusty, and pieces of pumice were blocking her view, were grazing her body.

A hand grabbed her wrist, a hand so powerful she felt like a tiny child in its grip, tossed one way, then the next. She was on the ground, on her knees, gasping for breath, her head swimming, disorientated.

'I'll take that,' said a voice snarling close to her ear. She was shoved away, was sliding down on her back.

She shook her head, trying to regain her bearings. There was almost nothing but blackness and endless stones falling from the sky.

Then she saw Caeculus at the top of the slope, his features distinct and glowing red as though he were staring gleefully into the embers of a dying fire.

In both hands, clutching it like a precious jewel, he was holding the Key of Portunus.

Chapter XX

The Weapon of a God

To his right there was nothing but a cloud of dust. To the left of it were two Vulcani swooping down the slope towards him. Zak could only see one other person. So he grabbed Cassia's wrist and yelled: 'Run!'

Thrusting his feet into the loose stones, he began pulling her up the slope to his left. Yet as fast as his legs were pumping, he found he was hardly moving. It was like trying to climb up a steep bank of pebbles at the seaside, his feet sliding back down with almost every step he took.

A hand grabbed one of his legs, pulling hard. He fell face first into the layer of stones. With sheer desperation bordering on panic, he lashed out with his other foot, struck something hard. There was a grunt from behind him, followed immediately by his leg being released.

With Cassia's help, he scrambled up the slope on all fours. Not stopping to look back, he leapt off the roof into the dark below, still holding onto Cassia. The drop was now little more than a metre, so they merely tumbled onto the thick layer of pumice below, scraping ankles and shins, yet somehow remaining on their feet.

As he steadied himself, Zak chanced a look behind him. Just above them, one Vulcani was poised ready to jump down, whilst the black shape of another rose to the top of the building, silhouetted against the sinister, lightning-scarred plume from Vesuvius.

Zak ran down the street, pulling Cassia along with him. Ahead of him, it was impossibly dark, nothing but large, angular shadows jutting out of the endless sea of pumice. It was impossible to see where he was going, to see where they could hide. So he just ran blindly, bounding awkwardly through the shifting stones, as though he were trying to run through deep water, or run in a dream.

Large volcanic rocks were still falling all around them, almost invisible in the dark. He could hear them more than see their shapes, crashing into the ground. If one landed on his or Cassia's head now, they would be flung to the ground, injured and at the mercy of their pursuers.

While his pulse raced faster and faster, the panic rising, he briefly considered throwing the time machine back at the Vulcani. If he gave them what they wanted, perhaps they would just leave him and Cassia alone. But no, that was not an option. It was the only means they had of escaping the erupting Vesuvius.

He turned sharply at right angles, down a different road. Just ahead, flames were leaping from the roof of a building, casting long, dancing shadows all across the ground. He quickly realised that light was not his friend. It might help him to see where he was going, but it would also signpost their whereabouts just as easily as if spotlights were trained on them. So he made yet another abrupt turn, straight into a rectangle of blackness to his right, praying it was an alleyway or some other gap they could run down. As he turned, he glanced over his shoulder. The two Vulcani were closing fast, their knees pumping high in the air in an effort to move quickly through the moving ground.

Beside him, Cassia was struggling, gasping for air, the pain etched across her grubby face. A lifetime of easy living had not prepared her for running for her life. But he was not prepared to leave her behind again. So he pulled at her arm, tugging her along, even though it must have been hurting her.

The way ahead was nothing but blackness. Yet he strode on and on, his feet sinking with every step he took. At any moment, he expected to fall into an unseen hole or collide with a wall.

A brief flicker from the nearby fire, cast a fleeting glow across a railing to his right. He realised it was a wooden balcony, only now it was at street level, so it looked more like a veranda than a balcony. Hoping, praying that the blackness was as impenetrable to their pursuers as it was to him, Zak lunged towards the low balcony wall and clambered over, pulling Cassia with him. The roar from the volcano, the crashing of thunder in the distance, the unceasing pounding of the pumice on the city easily drowned out the noise of them collapsing onto the wooden floor.

He lay there panting furiously, holding Cassia close in an attempt to cover the sound of her frantic gasps for breath. Above them, the overhanging roof was still intact, sheltering them from the falling ash and stones.

Through the thick slats of the balcony wall, Zak saw two ghostly black shapes bound past them. One of them cursed when a black rock the size of a tennis ball hit him. After a brief pause, he moved on and quickly melted away into the inky blackness.

'Come on,' whispered Zak. 'We can't stay here.' He rose to his feet, pulling Cassia with him. Still unable to speak, she just went on panting heavily.

Feeling his way along the outer wall, Zak soon found the door to the house. Once inside, he turned on the *Temporum* to give them some light, albeit faint. The room was a mess. There were signs of a hurried exit, with overturned trunks and tables, and clothes and other valuables strewn everywhere. A small part of the roof had collapsed in one corner of the room, where a steady pattering of pumice was trickling in. There was a danger the whole roof could collapse on top of them at any moment. But to venture back outside now would have been just as dangerous. Hiding for a short while in the house was, Zak quickly decided, a risk worth taking.

He turned around and pushed at the balcony door till it was almost closed, then told Cassia to cross the room to the opposite side. He then lowered himself to the floor next to Cassia, making sure he had a clear view of the balcony in front of him. He sat with his back to the wall, utterly exhausted.

Maia was lying on the ground, still dazed. Slowly, she realised she was instinctively holding an arm above her head, shielding herself from the falling pumice. A piece of black rock had already hit her arm; blood was trickling down her forearm onto her face. But there was no pain, and she could tell the wound was already healing. She was, after all, the daughter of an alien, with special blood that could heal her wounds at speed.

The thought almost made her laugh. Why had she not realised it before? When she was eight, she had fallen off her bike, been hit a glancing blow by a passing car. Yet she had walked away without a scratch. A miracle they had said at the time. A chance in a million. Except that now she knew it had had nothing at all to do with chance.

And then there was the time she had been playing chase in the playground. She had collided with another boy who was coming around the corner of a school building. They had both been running at full speed, had hit one another and then gone sprawling across the concrete. The boy, a horrible bloody mess, had gone to hospital, while she had walked away unscathed. And now she knew why.

The last few silhouettes to escape from the house were shuffling away up the slope. Only one tall figure remained next to her, prowling about the bottom of the slope under his dark hood.

'Where are you, Maximus, you traitor?' she heard him mutter.

A shorter, thinner figure crept up behind the man, a long stick raised above his head. The two figures were nothing more than shadow puppets against the dark grey sky and the frequent flashes of lightning. Then the stick of what she presumed was wood came swinging down onto the man's head. He toppled to the ground with a grunt.

Realising it was Dexter who had struck the remaining Vulcani, Maia scrambled to her feet to help.

'Maia!' he cried, still holding his stick. 'Are you all right? Where are the others?'

'I don't know,' she replied, looking around. 'Zak! Cassia!'

There was no reply.

Then, with a sudden gasp of despair, she remembered what had just happened. 'Dexter — Caeculus has got the key! One of them took it from me.'

'Then we have to go after him. Perhaps that's where Zak has gone already.' He turned to head up the slope.

'Wait! We don't stand a chance on our own. We need Maximus. Where is he?'

She was on her hands and knees again, clawing through the stones and pieces of masonry in the dark. Dexter was beside her, feeling about, tossing indistinct shapes over his shoulder.

'He's here!' he shouted at last. 'Help me.'

The two of them cleared away the rubble from around the gladiator, who lay on his front, unmoving.

'Is he dead?' asked Maia.

Dexter was rolling the massive, muscle-bound man onto his back. 'No. He's still breathing.'

'Not for much longer,' growled a voice from behind them.

Maia spun round and saw the Vulcani whom Dexter had just struck, looming over them. He reached for his sword and, with a metallic scrape, pulled it from his scabbard.

'You all right?' Zak asked Cassia, who was sitting next to him on the floor.

In the pale light, she looked thoroughly dishevelled and stared blankly into space. She nodded at last and swallowed hard. 'We're not going to make it, are we?' she mumbled, her voice shaking.

Zak wanted to quickly contradict her and promise that everything was going to be all right. But he instantly knew that would sound ridiculous. 'I don't know,' he said in the end. 'But I haven't given up just yet. Anyway, what's wrong with you?' He gave her a playful nudge with his elbow. 'You're supposed to be the cheerful, optimistic one.'

'Am I?' she sighed, her breathing at last beginning to return to normal. 'Well, at least I won't have to get married, if we don't get out of this.'

Zak shot her a startled look. 'You're getting married? When?'

'Next month, supposedly,' she replied, her voice full of bitter resignation.

'But you're only thirteen.'

She shrugged. 'That's quite normal for a Roman girl.'

'Wow!' replied Zak. 'Your uncle mentioned something the other day about your betrothed, but I didn't really think much about it. Is he ... nice, the boy you're going to marry?'

'Oh, Zak,' she chuckled rather sadly. 'You really do come from a completely different world to me, don't you? I don't get to choose whom I marry. My parents chose for me. I'm nothing but a commodity to them. They see me as something to sell, something to further my father's political career. I barely know the man I'm to marry. He's in his forties. A senator. A horrible man, by all accounts.'

Zak hardly knew what to say. 'Cass, I'm so sorry. I never realised.'

'I'm always cheerful,' she continued with a weak smile, 'because I wanted to enjoy the last few months of my freedom. You see, it won't be marriage — it'll be servitude. I'll be stuck at home having countless babies, if I survive childbirth, and weaving on a loom, or some such. I know you think I'm sometimes hard on Dexter, but he and I are just the same really. We're both just slaves. But at least if we get out of this, I promise to give Dexter his freedom. He's earned it. You and Maia have opened my eyes a little. Made me see the world differently.'

'Cassia,' he said, and waited until she turned to look at him. 'If we do get out of this alive, most people will think you're dead. Including your parents. If you want them to, that is. You'll be free.'

She stared at him a while, then broke into a wry smile. 'I suppose you're right. But what about you? You look as sad as me.'

Zak laughed, but then his smile evaporated quickly. 'I think I might be ... Vulcanus' son.'

'What? Don't be daft.'

'It's some of the things that Caius or Caeculus has said. And things I'm able to do.'

'That evil boy was just trying to goad you into handing over that ... that thing you have, that's all. You can't believe a single word that comes out of his poisonous mouth.'

'Maybe,' said Zak absently.

'Anyway, how old are you?'

'Thirteen. Why?'

'Well, there you are, then,' she said brightly. 'Vulcanus has been imprisoned since at least the Great Earthquake, seventeen years ago. So you can't be his son, can you?'

He wanted to believe that was the end of it. But in this weird world of time travelling gods and aliens into which he had been suddenly thrust, he doubted that anything was ever quite that simple. For now, he did not want to say any more on the subject, or even think about it. Because something inside him, in the pit of his churning stomach, told him it was true.

Creaking noises crept into the room. They looked at one another with fear in their eyes. Feet were crunching about in the pumice close to the balcony outside. Unless they moved, they would become trapped in the house.

'If only I had a weapon,' whispered Zak. Then it occurred to him. He took out Caeculus' wristband from his pouch, turned it over and over in his hands. Maximus had said no human could use it. But if he truly was the son of Vulcanus ...

'There is one way to find out if I really am the son of a god,' he muttered, sliding the strap over his wrist.

Caeculus had wasted no time. No sooner was the Key of Portunus in his possession than he had hurried away towards the walls of the disappearing city, leaving the Vulcani to find the time machine while he went to free his father.

Although not as tall as before, thanks to the deep carpet of ash and pumice, the thick stone walls of the city still loomed high into the dark sky above him. He found some steps and clambered up the short distance to the top. Once there, his eyes scanned the desolate scene before him.

Vesuvius, dark and brooding, stood on the horizon, belching out black clouds as thick as before, while the ground between the city and the volcano was now nothing more than a barren wasteland. The vast, featureless plain was a gently undulating sea of blacks and dark greys. Every so often a flash of lightning would send a momentary sheet of pale light across the landscape, highlighting the tops of dying trees or the roof of a crumbling house, which still protruded above the surface like people drowning in the sea, gasping for air.

As his eyes raked across the dead landscape, he noticed a faint glow in the distance, off to the left towards the coast. Something large was glowing red and orange and yellow, like the flames from a fire. He smiled to himself, then hurried along the wall until he reached a tower. From there, he climbed out of a narrow opening and managed to jump down onto the field of pumice stones. After dusting himself off, he began wading across the plain towards the shimmering light, towards his imprisoned father.

Now more than ever, Zak was convinced there was someone lurking outside in the shadows near the balcony. Above all the creaking and groaning of the roof and the drumming of stones, he could hear what sounded like footsteps crunching on gravel.

Doubts began to flood his mind. What if it was not a Vulcani at all, but an innocent person out looking for shelter? What if it *was* a Vulcani, but he was not able to fire the strange weapon on his wrist?

He decided to aim it well away from the noises outside. He held up his arm as he had seen Caeculus doing, pointed his clenched fist at the wall nearby, then dipped his hand down.

A dart of fire shot out horizontally from the device. It barely made a noise, until it plunged into the wall, tearing pieces of the thick plaster off and exposing the brickwork underneath. He immediately tried it again, punching another hole in the plaster. Cassia started violently and yelped, as if someone had just poured a bucket of cold water over her. But for a few moments, the exhilaration of having such a powerful weapon at his disposal made him forget everything else, all the anguish and fear. Then a thought made him wince. If he could fire this weapon, it meant he was not human.

Shoving those thoughts to one side, he rushed towards the door, pulled it wide open. Flames from the burning roof just around the corner were casting a dim light across the road in front of him. And there in the shadows stood a hooded man, frozen to the spot, as motionless as if time had once again stopped. But Zak knew it was shock this time that had momentarily paralysed the man.

Zak held up his other wrist, the one with the *Temporum* around it. 'Did Caeculus send you to get this?' he asked in a confident, aggressive tone.

Another figure appeared nearby, also hooded, also threatening in his demeanour. One of them took an uncertain step forward.

Zak fired his weapon across the street, taking care to miss the Vulcani, but close enough to spook them. They flinched nervously. Oh, how he wished he could see their faces at that moment, to see the indecision, the growing anxiety he knew they must have been suddenly feeling.

'Well, come on,' he taunted them. 'Come and fetch it.' He then fired again, and again. The bolts of fire sped towards the two men, narrowly missed their ducking heads and exploded into a roof behind them.

Their hoods twitched, as if they were exchanging a nervous look. And then they turned and hurried away, wading through the pumice in the same frenzied panic that Zak himself had felt only a short while previously.

Cassia moved next to him onto the remains of the balcony. 'At last,' she sighed. 'We don't have to run anymore.'

'Come on,' said Zak. 'Let's find the others.'

Before the man could swing his sword down, Dexter flung himself straight at him, striking him in the midriff and sending them both staggering onto the ground in a tangled heap. While Dexter wrestled with him, Maia turned back to Maximus, trying to rouse him. As brave as Dexter was, she knew he would not last long against a trained soldier. But the gladiator was unconscious, as though fast asleep, and barely breathing.

Perhaps she would be better off helping Dexter. She turned around and saw him throwing his fists wildly at the Vulcani, who lay on his back, frantically trying to block everything that was being thrown at him.

The man's sword was lying next to him. She could reach it if she were quick. But then what? Could she really stab a man?

The Vulcani shoved Dexter in the chest, sending him flying backwards as easily as if a rope were yanking him away.

She lunged for the sword, felt its cold handle in her sore and cut fingers.

A foot slammed onto the sword blade before she even had time to see how heavy the weapon was. The shock jarred along the sword, and she released her grip with a yelp. A hand pressed against her forehead, thrusting her away, until she toppled onto her back, crashing painfully onto the stones.

The dark shape of the man rose massively above her, sword in hand. He moved away from her, stood over Maximus, the point of the sword moving close to the gladiator's body.

A hand shot up towards the Vulcani like a striking snake, grabbing his wrist. Maximus rose up onto one knee, struggling with his opponent. With grunts and groans the two men swayed this way and that, both trying to unleash a punch here, a kick there.

With both hands now on the sword, the Vulcani was pushing down on the gladiator, who was still on his knees, leaning further and further back, his strength still not fully restored.

Maia was about to leap forward to offer what meagre, pathetic help she could, when a finger of fire shot through the air and landed with a puff of dust at the Vulcani's feet. Another fizzed past his nose, making him jerk his head round, a startled look on his shadowy face.

'Leave him alone!' yelled a voice. A voice she knew well.

'Zak!' she cried, and turned to see him standing at the top of the slope behind her, an arm outstretched before him.

In the blink of an eye, Maximus had wrestled the sword from the man's hands. With a flash of panic, the man turned away and scrambled up the opposite slope, constantly looking over his shoulder as he moved, until he had disappeared out of sight.

Zak came sliding down the slope, holding Cassia's hand. He helped the dazed Dexter to his feet, and the four children embraced.

'By Jupiter!' said Maximus, brushing himself off. 'You children attract trouble like flies to horse dung.'

Maia burst out laughing. A laugh of pure relief, which spread through the small group, except for Maximus who stood shaking his head with a puzzled and rather disapproving look on his face.

It was only then that Maia realised the rain of pumice had stopped. How long ago it had ceased, she could not tell, but it was at least one less thing to worry about.

They all clambered back up the slope to stand on the remnants of the roof. As they stood looking out over the dark, lifeless landscape, the distant Vesuvius exploded once more, spewing great geysers of flaming lava into the night sky.

As spectacular as the sight was, Maia knew it signalled the start of the next phase of the eruption.

As if reading her mind, Zak said: 'We need to move. Before those pyrotechnic splurges race down the side of the volcano.'

Maia laughed. 'I think Mrs Sullivan called them pyroclastic surges.'

'That's the one,' chuckled Zak, looking down at the *Temporum*. 'The dot is still pulsing in the Forum. We need to get there in the next couple of hours or we're toast.'

Chapter XXI

The Return of Vulcanus

Vesuvius was roaring like a never-ending peal of thunder. Lit by regular flashes of lightning, the column of black smoke and ash was now so enormous it was impossible to see where it ended and the night sky began. And the top of the mountain itself could be seen in silhouette every time a burst of lava erupted from out of the crater.

Yet as terrifying as it was for Caeculus being so close to an erupting volcano, he feared his father's wrath infinitely more. So he pressed on, wading through the vast expanse of pumice stones towards the distant chink of glowing light, which looked like the dying embers of a great bonfire.

As he drew slowly nearer, he heard a terrible rumbling sound, looked up and saw something happening on the western slopes of the volcano. It was hard to make out in the dark, but the side of the mountain appeared to be crashing down the slope towards the sea. In the short moments of light afforded by the lightning and the spouts of lava, he could see great clouds of billowing ash swarming down the side of Vesuvius like an impossibly large avalanche. Moments later, the few tiny pricks of light there had been on the coast were snuffed out in the blink of an eye.

The frightening sight spurred him on, just when his muscles had been aching with tiredness and urging him to rest a while.

The corner of his father's cage was now clearly visible, a triangle of glowing reds and oranges, jutting up out of the black ground. The small section still above ground was now barely as tall as a person. If his father had been human, Caeculus realised, the man would have been dead by now.

'Where have you been?' roared Vulcanus as his son approached. 'Get me out — now!' He was crouching in the remaining corner of the cage, his long, matted hair running across his face like streaks of black blood.

'I—I'm sorry, father,' stammered Caeculus. 'I was held up—'

'I'm not interested in your excuses,' bellowed Vulcanus, his thick beard quivering. 'You do have the key, don't you?'

'Y-yes, of course.'

'Then use it!'

Caeculus fumbled in the folds of his cape and took out the large, glowing key. 'What do I do with it?'

'Give it here.' A large hand shot through the bars and snatched it from his grasp.

For a moment, Vulcanus turned it over in his hands, staring at it wide-eyed, savouring the moment he must have dreamt of for so many long years. He then plunged the fist holding the key into one of the bars in front of him. A thousand tiny, white sparks flew in every direction, like startled insects. Then, one by one, the bars began to shrink and fade into nothingness.

Moments later, the light from the cage had all gone. The large, imposing silhouette of Vulcanus rose up to his considerable height, looking down on his nervous son.

'Did you bring the belt?' he asked, the impatience of earlier beginning to fade.

Caeculus reached inside his cape and handed over a large, bulky belt. 'Yes, father. I left it in the sun as instructed. It should be fully charged by now.'

'Good. Then let us have some light.' He circled it round his waist, snapped the buckle shut and began touching different parts of the outer surface. 'You are too young to have ever seen me wearing this,' he added in his deep, gravelly voice as he worked. 'It is the source of my considerable power.'

A moment later, a ball of fire appeared in his outstretched palm, floating just above the hand. The size of a small child's head, it was a perfect sphere of intermingled, tiny flames, shimmering like a miniature sun rising in the morning sky. The glow from it lit up Vulcanus' face, highlighting every crease in his weathered features, every line in his smug expression.

Mesmerised beyond words, Caeculus just stood staring at it. It was the most astonishing, the most beautiful thing he had ever seen. And it had been created by his father.

Vulcanus began striding forward, away from Vesuvius. 'Come,' he said. 'We have work to do.' Using it as a torch, he held the ball of fire before him. 'Where is Bellona?' he asked as Caeculus hurried alongside him.

'She's in the villa, making preparations for your return.'

'Excellent. And what of the *Temporum* made by that cur Janus?'

'The boy still has it.'

Vulcanus shot his son a fierce, disapproving look.

'He—he's still in Pompeii with Janus' daughter, somewhere. The Vulcani are out looking for them now.'

'You travelled forward to their time, did you not?'

'Yes, father, we did track the device to—'

'Then why not track them now?'

'When the boy activated the device, we were able to find his location using the staff Bellona found in Janus' villa.'

'So where is the staff now?'

Caeculus swallowed hard. His father's impatience was growing by the second. 'We—we have lost it,' he said, then began talking quickly before his father could berate him. 'Maximus is a traitor. He was Minerva's spy. He turned on us. He killed some of the Vulcani. The staff was lost in the confusion.'

'Maximus — a spy?' bellowed Vulcanus. 'How could you let yourself be so easily deceived?'

He had stopped abruptly in the vast field of black pumice, glowering down at his son. Caeculus trembled and, for a moment, feared for his life. But before he could respond, his father's face softened a degree.

'No matter,' he growled through clenched teeth. 'He will pay dearly for his treachery, I promise you that.'

The mini sun in his hand started vibrating, as though it too seethed with as much anger.

'We must find the boy, and quickly,' declared Vulcanus. 'Before he escapes through your fingers once more.'

Just then, the ground began to shake, and a rumbling sound grew behind them. Caeculus spun round. To his horror, he could just make out an enormous, billowing cloud descending the dark southern slopes of Vesuvius, heading straight for them at great speed. As he watched, it grew and grew like swirling smoke in a gale, expanding towards them faster than the fastest galloping horse.

'Father!' he yelled in panic, above the growing din.

Vulcanus stood calmly. He gave his son a disapproving glance, before raising both hands towards the approaching storm. The vast maelstrom rose high above them until even the massive Vesuvius was obliterated from view.

Just as it seemed about to envelop father and son, fire appeared all around them. A dome of leaping, curling flames settled all about them, shielding them from the fast-moving clouds of searing ash.

Vulcanus turned to his son. 'What is wrong with you? You're as nervous as a timid mouse.' His words dripped with bitter disappointment, which stung Caeculus to his bones. 'My own son has no idea what I'm capable of. Now that I am free again, there is nothing on this planet can stop me. Not even an erupting volcano.'

Now that only the occasional small piece of pumice was falling from the night sky, the long trek back to the Forum was at least a little easier than before. However, progress was still painfully slow, owing to the enormous quantity of pumice and ash, which now lay across the city. Almost every step Zak and his friends took seemed to sink deep into the ground, such that trying to move quickly was impossible and merely sapped their already diminishing strength. So they stuck to a slow and steady pace, trudging in near silence, so exhausted were they. However, this time they stuck close together, determined not to let another of their number be picked off in the dark.

All round them, there were signs of life. Now that the bombardment seemed to be over, people were crawling out from their houses, some in small groups carrying flaming torches and bundles of possessions. Others wandered about aimlessly, stumbling in the dark, apparently unsure what to do or else beginning a futile search for friends or relatives.

As the night wore on, they saw more and more people moving about. Names were being called out, loved ones sought. A child cried incessantly. Zak felt their pain in the pit of his stomach. He wanted to help them all, but knew that was impossible. After all, just helping his immediate group of friends was going to be hard enough.

Somewhere along the way, Maximus had picked up a burning torch, which he now brandished like a sword in front of him, lighting the way. It was strange seeing the city like this. It was as though every building had sunk into the ground up to at least the height of the first floor. Any building that had only been one storey high had now vanished, been erased from the map. And a good many of the taller buildings now lay in ruins, their roofs caved in, their insides crushed. Their inhabitants most likely dead.

It occurred to Zak that two thousand years would pass before people walked these streets again. He resolved there and then to visit the ruins of Pompeii if and when he finally got back home.

While he traipsed along, lost in his thoughts, a burst of what looked like fast-moving flames shot over his head and disappeared up the road, like a swooping, blazing bird. Another followed moments later. The five of them tumbled to the ground.

'Zak! Zak Scarlett, come here!' The voice, deep and gravelly, boomed out behind him. As he struggled to see in the dark, the voice continued. 'Oh, don't worry, Zak. If I had wanted you dead, you'd be dead already.'

Maximus, crouching low, had hurried up beside him, torch in one hand, shield in the other.

'I think it's Vulcanus,' said Zak.

'Oh, it is,' replied the gladiator simply. 'The rest of you keep going. I will delay him as long as I can. Now go.' He handed the flaming torch to Zak, and drew his sword as slowly, as silently as an assassin.

As Zak led the other three away down the street, he kept looking back over his shoulder, straining to see anything in the dark beyond a few smudges of indistinct light here and there, where small fires flickered in the gloom.

'Don't run away, Zak,' bellowed the voice once more. 'You have something I need.'

Zak turned around again to see if he could see how far away Vulcanus was now. Just as he did so, another ball of fire flew through the air. This time it was low to the ground, heading straight for them. The broad silhouette of Maximus thrust his shield in the air, striking the ball of fire, altering its trajectory at the last second. It veered off and crashed into the side of a nearby building, instantly setting it ablaze.

But deflecting the missile had clearly taken its toll on Maximus, for he was now lying on his back, thrust backwards by the force of the impact.

'Here, take this,' said Zak, handing the torch to Dexter.

'Where are you going?' demanded Cassia, the light from the torch catching the anguish in her face.

'To help Maximus.'

'And what exactly can you do that Maximus can't?' demanded Maia.

Zak was already hurrying back down the road towards the gladiator. 'I have this,' he said over his shoulder, holding up his right arm to show them Caeculus' weapon. 'Head to the Forum as fast as you can. I'll join you there.'

More fire fizzed past him, so close he felt the heat on his face. In the distance, he could just make out two dark figures approaching along the road. They plodded steadily forwards, wading awkwardly through the sea of pumice and ash.

A man appeared out of the gloom, close to Zak, his face a mask of fright. 'Get away while you can,' he said, glancing fearfully back at Vulcanus and his son. 'The gods have come to punish us.' He scrambled away, falling over every few paces in his haste to get away.

Just in front of Zak, Maximus was scrabbling back to his feet, slipping and sliding in a desperate attempt to move quickly.

As Zak approached, the gladiator seized his arm. 'What are you doing? I told you to get out of here.'

'You need some help. And I've got this.' He pointed his right arm into the darkness, towards the ghostly silhouettes coming towards him, and fired. He dipped his wrist twice, sending two fiery darts off into the gloom. They momentarily lit up the buildings one by one on either side, as they shot down the road, like the light from a train passing in the night. But ultimately, the darts were too small, the surroundings too dark, for Zak to see if they had struck his pursuers.

Vulcanus responded with a cry of what sounded like anger rather than pain. Moments later, a much larger fireball was rushing at great speed towards Zak and Maximus. The gladiator shoved Zak to the ground, thrust his shield into the path of the crackling sphere, deflecting it off into the night. But in doing so, the force threw him off his feet, and sent him flying through the air until he crashed into the shifting ground with a grunt.

'Is that the traitor Maximus with you, Zak?' Vulcanus demanded. 'Oh, I shall enjoy exacting my revenge on you, Maximus, you treacherous dog.'

Moving quickly sideways, Zak launched more of his own fire in response, aiming blindly down the road. His own flames might have been puny in comparison, he realised, but they were at least enough to distract his opponent.

He helped Maximus back to his feet, and then the two of them waded quickly down a side street where the tops of the buildings were barely higher than they were.

'Let's have some more light, shall we?' said Vulcanus in a chilling, mocking voice. He then fired another fireball into the building on the corner, instantly setting fire to its roof. Flames leapt into the night sky, sending shadows and pools of orange light dancing in every direction.

Although Zak could see his surroundings much more clearly now, he also knew the light made them far more vulnerable than before. He turned to face Maximus, who stood against the side of a building, breathing heavily. In the flickering light from the fires, Zak could see his face covered in dust and scars and sweat. He looked exhausted.

'I'm not sure I can hold him off much longer,' the gladiator said between gasps. 'I don't have the powers.'

Zak studied his face for a moment. The man had given everything to get them this far, but now he looked spent.

'You don't need to,' he said. 'Go back. Join the others. I have an idea.'

Maximus looked like he was about to object. But then he must have seen the steely determination in Zak's eyes and thought better of it. 'What's your plan?'

'He wants this,' replied Zak, holding up the wrist with the *Temporum* strapped to it. 'I can use that to buy us some time. Go to the Forum and wait for me there.'

For a brief moment, Maximus gave Zak a piercing stare, as though he were trying to decide whether the boy was brave or simply mad. In truth, Zak was not sure himself which he was. He just knew that at that moment, his was the only option they had left.

'Don't do anything foolish,' said Maximus. 'And I'll see you shortly.' He hobbled off into the dark with his battered and blackened shield, leaving Zak alone and suddenly wondering whether he had made the right decision after all.

Vulcanus and Caeculus were standing at the corner just a few paces away, peering down the side street. Though he could not see their features, Zak knew instantly which was which. The much taller and broader Vulcanus, with his mass of wavy long hair, stood oozing menace, while the slender Caeculus stood cowering a step or two behind, as though afraid his own father might turn on him at any moment.

Zak fired off three flaming darts and ran as best he could to the other side of the road, diving into the shadows. As he shuffled along the side of the building, one of Vulcanus' mini suns tore into the building just above him. Ash and pumice and fragments of tile flew about him like a swarm of bees. Somehow, he managed to stay on his feet, and just kept moving, knowing that every step he took was a step he drew his opponent further away from his friends.

'Zak!' boomed the voice of Vulcanus behind him. 'This is futile. You cannot win, you cannot escape. Instead, I give you the chance to join me. You are one of us, after all. Or did you not know? You do not belong with them; you belong with me.'

More fire erupted around Zak. He lost his footing, fell to the ground. Above the crackle of flames, he could hear heavy footsteps crunching towards him. Desperately, he crawled away on all fours, the warm pumice scratching at his hands.

He rolled onto his back and fired blindly down the road. Several bursts of fire shot out from the weapon on his wrist. He watched them racing towards the two dark figures. But then the darts suddenly froze, suspended in mid-air like a collection of small lamps strung out on a wire. The tall Vulcanus was holding out his hands, palms facing the floating flames. With a swift, sudden movement, he flicked his fingers, and then the darts were flying straight back towards Zak.

Zak flung himself to one side as they struck the wall next to him, dislodging great chunks of plaster.

Vulcanus was laughing, an echoing and thoroughly unnerving laugh. 'Did you, a mere boy, think you could defeat me, the god of fire? Fire is my element, boy. Now hand over the *Temporum* before I burn you alive.' His tone had suddenly changed, was no longer the calm but unsettling voice, trying to coax Zak onto his side; it was now full of impatience and anger.

'Ha!' scoffed Zak in defiance. 'You wouldn't risk destroying the *Temporum*, would you?'

He had leapt back onto his feet, creeping backwards through the stones, a hand constantly steadying himself against the wall of a building as he moved.

A sudden burst of flames and smoke from a burning building leapt between them for a moment, obscuring Zak's view of the other two. He wasted no time, turned and bounded down the road. An opening appeared to his left, the entrance to a dark alleyway. He headed straight for it and plunged into the darkness. As he ran awkwardly through the pumice, he glanced at the two devices on his wrists. In the dark, it was hard to tell them apart, even this close. So from much further away, would Vulcanus be able to tell the difference? He knew he was running out of time. It was now or never.

A fireball flew down the alleyway, exploded into a low-lying roof nearby, setting it ablaze. Light flooded the alleyway, orange, flickering light which sent shadows leaping in all directions like a cave of disturbed bats.

'There is no escape, Zak,' thundered Vulcanus. 'This is your last chance. Join me — or you will die.'

Zak stopped, turned round. 'All right,' he said, holding up his hands in submission. 'You win.' He took the weapon off his wrist. 'How do I know you won't just kill me once I hand it over?'

The bearded face of Vulcanus was staring at him a short distance away. The nearby flames were glinting in his piercing eyes, which now stared at Zak with nothing but malevolence.

'You will just have to trust me.'

Zak glanced to either side of him. The buildings were half buried, their pumice-covered roofs only a little taller than a man.

'I do not trust you,' he yelled. 'And I will *never* be one of you.' With all his might, he hurled the weapon over one of the low-lying roofs. 'If you want it, go and find it.'

He turned and ran, not bothering to check whether they had fallen for his ruse. For even if they had, they would soon be after him anyway, when they realised what he had done. But as he stumbled along the alleyway, Vulcanus' booming, angry voice was receding.

'Go and find it, you fool!' he was shouting at his son.

Zak kept on running, jumping, bounding through the pumice, stumbling every few paces till his palms and his knees were covered in blood from falling on the stones. But nothing would stop him now. Time was precious. He had bought himself a few minutes, nothing more. He had to make them count.

Somehow, he managed to gain his bearings. Then he realised the sky was beginning to lighten to the east, nothing more than a smudge of light grey against the black of night, but enough to guide him through the city.

In front of him, the ground was opening out. A row of massive stone pillars jutted out of the pumice. He was in the Forum. His heart leapt for joy.

Several people staggered past him, moving frantically in the opposite direction, fear written in their faces. A rumbling noise was growing and growing. He looked up and out of the city towards the cone of Vesuvius. Except that Vesuvius was no longer there. A huge, swirling cloud stretching as far as he could see in both directions was rolling, tumbling, billowing towards the city across the plain. A pyroclastic surge.

With the speed it was travelling, Zak could tell he had a matter of mere seconds before it hit Pompeii.

Chapter XXII

The End of Pompeii

'I think it was about here,' said Maia. She was standing in the middle of the Forum, or what was left of the Forum. Some of the buildings, weakened by the earthquakes, had collapsed under the weight of pumice and disappeared from view altogether. All that remained of others were large pieces of wood or stone pillars poking out of the ground at odd angles. But to one side, the upper storey of one long building was still largely intact, the many pillars of its upper colonnade still visible, like a row of cracked and decaying teeth.

'How do we get to it?' asked Dexter, moving the burning torch to cast some more light across the building.

'I guess we're going to have to dig,' replied Maia. 'Oh, where is Zak? He could at least tell us exactly where the door is.'

'What is that?' cried Cassia suddenly, pointing down the length of the Forum.

Maia turned and immediately saw it. The roiling clouds, the tumbling mass of greys and black were just like the animation of a pyroclastic surge that Mrs Sullivan had shown them. For a moment or two, she stood and stared as it raced towards the city. She felt strangely detached, as though she were back in the teacher's office watching a video on a giant screen. She remembered being told that such surges travelled at over a hundred miles an hour and were unimaginably hot. Those still alive in Pompeii at the time, Mrs Sullivan had said, would have been killed instantly.

As it sped towards the city, rising up like a great sandstorm in a desert, she knew she had but seconds left. They had come so far, and yet had fallen agonisingly short.

By now, Zak had joined them out of the gloom, a terrible look of resignation on his weary face. As the noise grew and grew, they all huddled together, even the bulk of Maximus, and hugged. Cassia looked terrified, while only Dexter's eyes betrayed his fear. Maximus remained as inscrutable as ever.

Maia closed her eyes. She was at least with some of the best friends she had ever made.

When the great crash came, it seemed oddly far away. The sound quickly subsided. A rush of hot, acrid air blew across their faces, ruffling their hair, making them break apart and cough. Maia opened her eyes, scarcely daring to look towards the cloud.

The end of the Forum was strangely still, the top half of the temple still visible.

'The walls!' Dexter cried out. 'The city walls stopped it.'

In the distance, above the roof of the temple, thin wisps of grey smoke swirled about like dancing ghosts. The silhouette of Vesuvius had reappeared in the distance.

They all began laughing, a strange laughter born of sheer relief at having escaped what had seemed like certain death only moments earlier. Once more they hugged, and began dancing round in circles, all except Maximus who watched on in bemused silence, although Maia knew he had to be as relieved as they were.

'Right. We need to get out of here,' said Zak. 'Vulcanus will be along soon.' Maia saw him staring into the small screen on the *Temporum* on his wrist. 'The light is still there. It's about here,' he added, rushing forward, pointing to the dark ground.

Maximus marched towards the colonnade and immediately began digging his shield into the layer of pumice, scooping out large amounts with each attempt. The others joined him, kneeling down, and dug with their bare hands.

After barely a minute or two, Dexter stopped and stood up. 'This is not working,' he said. 'Look. As we scoop away the stones, almost as many fall back into their place. We're getting nowhere.'

'He's right,' agreed Maia.

They all stopped and stood up, gazing at the small, insignificant depression they had made in the ground.

'Of course,' said Zak, suddenly brightening. 'How stupid! The building is still there. We just have to climb inside and dig out the door knocker from the other side.'

They looked along the colonnade for a way in. In some places, the pillars had fallen over, bringing down whole sections of the roof, blocking off windows and doors.

'Look! There's a door over there,' said Cassia, pointing.

They hurried towards a small wooden door, buried up to knee-height. Zak and Dexter tried to open it without success, until Maximus ordered them to stand aside. With a swift kick of his right foot, the door flew open. A brief trickle of pumice stones flowed into the gap.

Holding the torch in front of them, they entered the dark room in single file. The place was a mess. Chunks of plaster lay all over the floor, mingling with dust and pumice and spilled pots of paint, abandoned when the workmen had fled the site. The wooden floor was barely visible under so much debris.

Maia eyed the ceiling nervously, worried it might cave in on top of them at any moment. Then, when the floor creaked disconcertingly, she glanced around her feet. The whole building was likely to collapse, she realised, but then, what choice did they have?

Treading gingerly across the floor, they made it to the landing and from there to a flight of wooden stairs. Down they went, the light from the flickering torch chasing away the shadows before it. The ground floor was in total darkness. After all, realised Maia with mounting unease, it was now completely underground.

As they gathered around the torch in the middle of a large room, Maximus appeared out of the gloom holding two more unlit torches. Using their torch, he then lit both of them and placed them in sconces on opposite sides of the room.

Zak was already looking at the *Temporum*, trying to locate the head of Janus. 'It's over there,' he said, pointing off into a darkened corner.

Maia's heart sank when the light from the torch swung towards the direction in which Zak was pointing. Sloping up from the floor to a point well above their heads was a wide incline of pumice stones. It was immediately apparent that a huge amount of stones and ash had burst through the door and the ground floor windows and had poured into the room. There was no sign of the door, which must have been torn from its hinges and now lay buried under the slope.

Zak puffed out his cheeks and stood scratching his head. 'The door must be under that lot somewhere.'

'Well, best we get started, then,' said Dexter. He then shoved the blunt end of the torch into a pile of stones nearby and began shovelling handfuls of pumice out from the slope in the flickering light.

The others joined in, including Maximus with his shield. But Maia soon realised it was not going to be easy. As fast as they scooped out stones, more and more poured in after them, undoing the work they had just done, until it felt like they were trying to shovel water.

'Remind me why we are doing this,' asked Cassia, wiping her brow.

Zak continued digging as he replied. 'We need to find that door knocker with the head of Janus on it. We won't be able to pass through this doorway, but hopefully we can just rip it off and then re-attach it to a different door.'

'And then what?' asked Maximus, as he scooped up a large mass of stones with his shield and tossed it over to the far side of the room.

'The only way we can escape Pompeii now,' replied Zak, 'is to use the *Temporum* to get out of here.'

It was then that Maia heard something. 'What's that noise?'

she asked.

They all stopped digging to listen. A faint rumbling sound was coming from their left, growing louder and louder.

'I'll go and look,' said Maia. Feeling decidedly uneasy, she ran across the room and climbed up a ladder left by the workmen, which led up to an upper gallery running the length of the room. Along the wall were several small windows, none of which had glass, just a thin wooden cross. She pressed her face into the nearest gap and peered out. Straight ahead, to the east, the sky was a pale grey as the sun tried to pierce the enormous ash cloud from Vesuvius, which still hung over the city.

She turned to the left, towards Vesuvius. And gasped.

Another pyroclastic surge was racing down the slopes of the volcano. Giant clouds of ash were swelling out as they moved, inflating like an endless series of huge, dark grey balloons.

'Another one of those clouds is coming,' she yelled out to the others down below.

'Oh, great!' said Zak. 'How long do we have?'

Maia's mind was already racing as fast as her breathing. She knew Pompeii was about five miles from Vesuvius and that the surge was travelling at over one hundred miles per hour. But some of the distance had already been covered by the cloud. She tried to suppress the panic rising inside her while she did a quick calculation.

'Two minutes, maybe,' she said, her voice cracking. 'At most.'

Zak stopped digging and stared up at her, horror written across his face. 'Right, keep digging everyone,' he said. 'Maia, give us regular updates.'

With renewed urgency, they resumed their digging, flinging stones behind them with frantic desperation, filling the room with the sound of a stormy sea pounding a beach of shingle. Yet still there was no sign of the wooden door.

Maia's eyes kept flitting back and forth from the growing cloud outside and down to her friends, who were now working in their own thin cloud of ash caused by their desperate attempt to unearth the buried door.

She looked out of the window once more. Vesuvius had vanished once again, hidden by the sheer size of the approaching cloud. With every second that passed, it grew and grew, rising and falling, swirling and rolling. Great bulges were growing out of it as it neared, like thick smoke billowing from a raging, unstoppable fire.

She looked down again, through the haze of ash, at the others working in the guttering light from the torches.

And then she knew. Knew they were never going to make it. The door was still buried, with not even a corner showing. The surge of super-hot ash was only seconds away. Even if they suddenly yelled out that they had found it, there would be no time to fix it to another doorway and escape.

Time really had run out this time. The oncoming cloud was far greater than the one before. She knew it was the one that would finally bury Pompeii and all those people still left alive in the city.

She wanted to cry. For the second time in the last hour she was resigned to death. Should she tell the others? Or just let it happen. The end would be so quick they would never know. Perhaps it would be better that way.

She looked out of the window. The surge was rising above the city walls, three, four, five times their height. Any second now, the walls would be breached. Their time was up.

Time.

The thought flashed through her mind. She grabbed the large stone in the ring given to her by Minerva. If the Vulcani had a device for slowing down time to a crawl, and the stone could block its signal, what if their device were still active? All she had to do was stop the ring from blocking the signal.

She twisted the stone back and forth by small increments, her thin fingers trembling almost uncontrollably.

Then there was silence.

Her heart leapt. She peered outside. At the end of the Forum, just beyond the temple, the cloud was frozen, looking like a distant range of mountains in the gloom. She wanted to cry.

'What's happened?' asked Zak.

Maia ran along the gallery and down the ladder, talking as she went, tears dripping off her face. 'I used the ring, Zak, to stop time,' she sobbed. 'I had no choice. We were running out of time.'

At the bottom of the ladder, she threw herself at Zak and burst into tears on his shoulder. 'I thought we were all going to die.'

'That was great thinking,' said Zak, patting her on the back. 'I think you might just have saved our lives.'

'Come on,' said Maia, sniffing and pulling away. 'We need to find this door. We don't know how long we have.'

Dexter, Cassia and Maximus were all frozen in mid-movement, striking unusual poses, while dozens of pumice stones hung in the air. Even the flaming torches stood motionless, like mere paintings of fire, hanging on the walls.

Maia and Zak began digging once more, using Maximus' heavy bronze shield to heave piles of stones out of the way. Maia's muscles were sore and so terribly tired. But somehow, adrenaline just kept her going.

'Look!' cried Zak, pointing at the slope of stones. 'I can see it.' He stepped forward, his feet crunching and slipping on the uneven surface. A corner of thick wood was protruding out of the pumice.

Zak let out a whoop of joy. But Maia stilled him almost immediately. 'I can hear voices,' she whispered.

Zak rolled his weary eyes. 'You have got to be kidding me.'

Maia strained her ears. The world was so silent at that moment that every little sound stood out. Footsteps were crunching on the pumice outside. More snippets of muttered conversation drifted down to them. Maia and Zak exchanged a look of dismay.

'Find a suitable door,' whispered Zak. 'And a way to attach

the Janus head. I'll try to dig it out as quietly as I can.'

Maia nodded and crept back past the large statue of Maximus. Every footfall she made seemed to echo like the beat of a drum in the quiet. Her heart was beating so fast she even began to worry that those outside must surely hear that, too.

Zak was slowly scooping away stones from the wooden door, trying but failing to do it silently.

She found a doorway at the opposite end of the room. To her relief the door opened without any difficulty. It would do.

The sound of a sudden rush of stones filled the room. She spun round and saw Zak lying on his back, half buried under pumice, with most of a wooden door lying next to him, flat on the ground.

'In there!' shouted someone. To Maia it sounded like Caeculus. 'There's someone in there.'

She hurried over to Zak who looked dazed. One of his legs was buried. She pulled him free. More stones came tumbling down in mini cascades, now clattering noisily on the door.

'I can see them!' shouted the voice from above. 'In here, father.'

Maia looked up and saw a head peering through one of the small first-floor windows, looking down at them. The head of Caeculus.

Zak was pulling at the half-buried door, straining with all his might to free it. 'Get Maximus' sword,' he yelled, just as the small head of Janus emerged out of the stones.

Maia dashed to the back of the room, where Maximus had put down his sword belt. Behind her, she could hear the breaking of wood. When she hurried back to Zak with the sword in her hand, she could see one of Caeculus' boots kicking in the wooden lattices in one of the window frames. He had one leg through the small opening, was climbing through.

She gave the sword to Zak, who began frantically hacking at the door knocker. He tried kicking it, then started prising it off with the blade of the sword.

Caeculus was on the upper gallery, glaring down at them. Then he was rushing towards the ladder.

With one final, desperate grunt, Zak removed the door knocker. He tossed it straight to Maia. 'When I give the word, twist the stone in that ring. We won't have long.' He ran towards the ladder.

Without waiting to see what he was going to do, Maia turned and headed for the doorway. She looked over the door, frantically trying to think of somewhere to put the head of Janus. Did it have to be on the door itself or on the frame or somewhere else? Her scrambled, terrified mind was just not sure.

She glanced round to see Zak at the foot of the ladder, Caeculus on the first couple of rungs at the top. With his shoulder, Zak barged the ladder, then barged it again.

She tried to focus on her own problem. The door knocker in her garden they had attached to the frame of the gate, she remembered. So surely it did not matter where it went as long as it was close by. She placed it on the floor, right in the gap between the door and its frame.

Behind her, the ladder fell to the ground with a clatter. Maia turned round in time to see Caeculus flailing his arms in the air, as he fell a short distance to the pumice-strewn ground.

'Stop this!' roared another voice from above. Vulcanus' head was now protruding through one of the windows, his angry, bearded face snarling down at them.

'Now, Maia!' yelled Zak.

She twisted the stone in her ring. 'Have you programmed the watch?' she cried.

'Already done,' he shouted back.

Noise filled the room. The roar of the approaching pyroclastic surge, the crackle of the torches, the clatter of dozens of pumice stones flying through the air.

Zak grabbed Cassia roughly by the arm as he ran towards

Maia. At the same time, he was yelling at Maximus: 'Go to that door! Go to that door!'

Maia in turn seized Dexter by the arm and yanked him towards her. The others looked startled, as though their faces were still frozen in time.

A ball of fire raced into the room. It exploded into the wall between Zak and Dexter. Dust and pieces of masonry flew out in all directions. Maia felt the building shudder.

She looked up as she moved towards the door. Vulcanus, wide-eyed and teeth bared like a rabid animal, had his hands together, then began spreading them slowly apart. Fire was forming between his palms.

'Hold hands!' screamed Zak. 'Hold hands!'

The five of them converged on one another. Hands shot out grabbing whatever part of each other they could get hold of.

Vulcanus was about to unleash his next ball of fire, when the surge hit him, tearing him sideways and out of sight.

The deafening roar of destruction was all around them.

They lunged as one towards the open doorway.

There was a blinding flash of light. And Maia felt herself lose consciousness.

Chapter XXIII

Consequences

Zak's head was spinning. He was not sure whether he was awake or dreaming. Strange indistinct shapes of varying colour were floating in and out of his vision. His mouth was desert-dry and his whole body ached, and he felt as if he were unable to move.

Slowly, his vision returned. He was lying on his side, staring at blades of grass. Sunlight was warming his face. It was not hot, perhaps from a setting sun, but it felt so pleasant to feel the sun on his face after what had felt like days in the dark. And the smell of grass and flowers drifted into his nostrils, sweet and oh so nice.

His head began to clear, and then suddenly he remembered the events of a few moments ago. He sat up abruptly, looking around him. He was on a small patch of lawn in what appeared to be a well-maintained garden. Maximus was pushing himself up off the ground, while the others lay on the grass around them still dazed. Just behind him, in the shade, stood a small stone archway at the edge of the lawn. He guessed it must have been the portal through which they had just come.

He turned back to his friends and helped Maia and Dexter to their feet while Maximus helped Cassia. They all stood looking at one another in a circle, weary, vacant expressions on all their faces. Without exception, they were all covered in dust and dirt, and their clothes were torn and hanging loosely. Their arms and legs were covered in cuts and bruises. They looked like a group of ghosts or half-dead zombies.

Zak looked at Maia and smiled. She looked just as shabby as he himself no doubt looked, with her once dark hair now a grey matted mess. She smiled back and then he started laughing. 'We did it,' he said. 'We actually made it back home.'

Maia began laughing, too, smiling warmly back him.

'Are we sure they can't follow us here?' asked Cassia. She was barely recognisable behind the layer of grey all over her face and hair. Her once pristine blond ringlets had long since turned into a dishevelled tangle of Medusa-like snakes.

'I think we're safe here. They don't have one of these,' replied Zak, showing the *Temporum* on his wrist.

'They did track us here once before, though,' said Maia, her smile dropping.

Maximus sniffed loudly. 'We used the staff of Janus to find you on that occasion. That is now buried somewhere in Pompeii. We don't need to concern ourselves with that anymore.'

'So we can finally relax,' sighed Maia, dropping her shoulders and closing her eyes with relief.

'And surely that cloud killed them, anyway,' said Dexter.

'Neither Vulcanus nor Caeculus will be dead,' said Maximus gruffly. 'They are like gods, remember. It would seem only their own technology and old age can kill them.'

'And lack of air,' said Cassia. 'Minerva said they breathe like us. So if they are now buried, perhaps they will suffocate, with any luck.'

'I hope you're right,' said Maia, while Maximus looked doubtful.

'Well, I don't know about the rest of you,' said Zak cheerily, 'but I have no intention of going back to find out what happened to those two.'

Maia smiled wryly, whilst the others stood in what Zak thought was rather a sombre silence.

'Guys,' he said, looking pointedly at each of them in turn. 'We're free, all of us. Dexter, you're no longer a slave. Cassia, you don't have to get married. Maximus, you don't have to work for anyone, good or bad.' He expected to see more joy on their faces. 'Look, I can take you all back to your time if you want,' he continued with wide-eyed enthusiasm. 'Or we can have some fun together. We now have a time machine. We can go anywhere, at any time. How cool is that?'

'Sounds good, Zak,' said Maia. But she looked at him forlornly, and he immediately realised he was missing something. 'But where did we leave the head of Janus we took from Mrs Sullivan.'

'On your back garden ...' His heart sank to his feet.

'And, before we left Pompeii just now, what time did you set the *Temporum* to?' continued Maia.

Zak studied the watch closely, praying he had made some simple mistake. 'I set it to the day we left your garden, just a few minutes later. Oh no.' He looked around. Wherever they were, it was clearly not Maia's garden, even though the *Temporum* showed the correct date and time.

'Is there only one door knocker in England?' asked Maia, moving closer to look at the time machine.

Zak looked at the map. 'Yes, but …' he mumbled. 'I don't understand.'

'Hey! You lot!' shouted a voice. 'What are you doing here?'

Zak turned sharply around and saw a man striding towards them. He was wearing a red tunic with an elaborate gold pattern around the hem.

'The museum is closed,' yelled the man, waving his arms in the air.

Maximus braced himself, looking ready to strike the man. Zak put a hand on the gladiator's arm to check him. 'Okay. Sorry. We were just leaving.'

'Hey, you're not escaped slaves, are you?' asked the man, looking them all up and down through narrowing eyes.

'What? No!' said Zak, thinking he must be joking.

But there was no humour in the man's face, only a look of revulsion, as though a bad smell were drifting up his nostrils. Even given their shabby appearance in his immaculate garden, the man's reaction troubled Zak.

They hurried out of the garden, the man close behind them. He used a small handheld device to remotely open a pair of large gates, and then ushered them out onto the street.

Zak turned around to look at the man again. 'Sorry. Just a moment. We got lost. We didn't mean to go in there. Could you tell us what this place is?'

'Are you from another planet?' scoffed the man. 'It's the Villa of the Renegade.'

'The renegade? What renegade?' asked Maia.

The man looked at them aghast and spread his hands out in disbelief. 'Janus of course. Who else?' He then closed the gates, tutting to himself as he disappeared from view.

Zak ran a hand through his hair. Dust and small pieces of pumice fell out, causing him to cough. 'What is going on here?'

But the others did not reply. They were all now standing in silence, gazing at something behind him. Zak turned to see what they were looking at. They were up on a hill, looking down onto a huge, sprawling city spread out across the plain before them. A wide river cut the city in half, its twisting curves looking somehow familiar to Zak, even if none of the buildings did. There were skyscrapers and great glass buildings, which glowed orange and bronze as the setting sun glinted off their polished surfaces.

A plane flew over. Yet it was almost silent and looked nothing like any plane Zak had ever seen. It swooped over the city like a giant eagle rising the thermals, before heading for an airport in the distance, on the edge of the city

'I think you got the wrong year, Zak,' said Maia, as she watched a strange, sleek vehicle pass by on the road. 'We've travelled into the future, surely.'

Zak shook his head with bewilderment and studied the watch once again. 'No. If this thing is still working as it should, this is the same day we left.'

'But it can't be,' said Maia.

Zak had no idea what to say. It made no sense at all.

Cassia, Dexter and Maximus had not spoken for some while. With their covering of grey dust, they stood like stone statues, gazing at the city below. If the sight was stunning for Zak and Maia, then for the three Romans the futuristic city must have looked like an astonishing, magical world created by the gods.

Zak was shaken abruptly from his confused thoughts when a vehicle pulled up in front of the museum they had just come from. It was long and windowless and had a large door on one side which then slid smoothly open. A stern-looking man stepped out, again wearing a tunic, and then began barking orders at a group of five or six men and women who tumbled out of the vehicle. They all wore simple tunics and each had a thin metallic ring around the neck. They all looked downcast and forlorn.

As they came out of the vehicle, the last man to exit fell over onto the pavement. Immediately, the stern-looking man rounded on him, shouting insults and orders. He then took out a small device from his pocket and pressed a button. The ring around the fallen man's neck glowed red, and he let out a yelp of pain, before scrambling back to his feet.

'I thought you told me you didn't have slaves in your time,' muttered Dexter in Zak's ear.

'We don't,' replied Zak uneasily.

'I know a slave when I see one, Zak.'

Zak was lost for words once more. He watched the group of people being marched into the museum, while the man in charge barked orders at them to clean the place quickly yet thoroughly. If they failed to do so, he yelled, they should expect punishment.

'Zak, look!' said Maia. She was pointing up the hill behind them. On the top of the gentle rise, stood a marble statue of a man, many times larger than life-size.

With a growing sense of disquiet, Zak followed Maia the short distance up the hill to the foot of the statue. The enormous, muscular and bearded man looked down over the city with fierce eyes and a curl of the mouth.

Maia was reading the inscription. 'To commemorate the accession to the throne of his highness, Vulcanus XIII, the senate and people of Londinium have erected this statue. May his reign be as long and as prosperous as each of his eminent forebears.'

She turned and looked up at Zak with a mixture of puzzlement and fear.

And then it hit him. He felt sick, felt faint, the air draining from his lungs. He sank to his knees. 'Oh no!' he said. 'No!'

'What? What is it, Zak?' asked Maia.

'We've changed history, Maia.' He covered his face, barely able to breathe. 'When we saved Cassia, we also saved Caeculus, didn't we? He was meant to die with her in that house. When he got out, he saved his father. Vulcanus must have then seized power and his family has been ruling ever since.'

'That's ridiculous,' said Maia, though there was a growing doubt in her eyes. 'Isn't it?'

Zak shook his head. 'It's the only thing that makes sense.'

'What can we do?' asked Cassia.

'We have to go back,' said Zak. 'We have to go back and make everything right.'

'We can't go back and change what we did,' said Maia. 'Minerva said it never works.'

Zak took a couple of deep breaths. He could already feel himself becoming a little calmer after that terrible, initial shock. He knew there was no point cursing their luck or wishing they had done something differently. What was done was done. What they needed now was a plan, a way to make amends.

'We won't go back to change what we did,' he said at length. 'We'll go back to just after we left. Not to Pompeii obviously, but somewhere else. We then have to find a way to defeat Vulcanus before he takes over. If we can do that, perhaps history will resume as it should have done.'

'And just how do you propose to do that?' asked Maximus.

'I don't know,' snapped Zak. 'But I have to try. I won't force any of you to help me. But I hope some of you will.'

'Well, of course I will,' said Maia.

'And I've got nothing else to do, have I?' said Cassia with a grin.

A wry smile crept onto Dexter's face. 'I shall go wherever my new master wants me to go.'

Zak smiled back at them all, then turned to Maximus. 'And what about you, big guy?'

The gladiator's face was as impassive as ever. 'I shall come with you. After all, someone needs to make sure you lot stay out of trouble.'

Zak smiled. 'Right, that's settled. Let's go.'

'Could we please make our first stop somewhere with a lovely warm bath?' asked Cassia. 'I'm filthy.'

'Yes, you're right,' said Zak. He paused before adding with a grin: 'You are filthy.'

They all looked at one another and burst out laughing.

As they strolled back towards the museum, with the idea of breaking back in after dark and passing through the archway back to ancient Rome, Zak smiled to himself. He knew there would be tough times ahead, but there was no better group of friends he would rather have around him.

Vulcanus stood with his arms folded, drumming his fingers. Frowning, he sighed heavily once more, waiting for the ash storm to pass, while all around him the flames danced, leapt and twisted like thousands of coiling snakes. He had created the sphere of fire all around himself to act as a shield against the mass of ash and pumice that had surged over him. Now he was simply impatient to get out.

At last, the roar of the cascading clouds had stopped. His entire flaming sphere was now buried. He wafted his hands into the air, and immediately, the sphere began rising up with him still inside. The ball of fire bored through the layer of ash, until it burst through the top and hovered over the ground. He snapped his fingers and another ball of fire appeared over the ground nearby. With casual hand movements, he directed the second sphere towards the ground. It plunged into the loose layer of steaming ash and disappeared.

Moments later, it reappeared. Inside, red-faced and coughing, was Caeculus. Vulcanus brought the two spheres together until they merged into one. His son collapsed at his feet, gasping for air and looking exhausted.

'Oh, pull yourself together!' snapped Vulcanus. 'It's only a bit of hot ash. It won't kill you.'

'Sorry, father,' said Caeculus.

Vulcanus looked down at him. He was sure he could see fear in the boy's eyes. How could a son of his be afraid? Caeculus could be very disappointing at times. He was not like his other son. Now, *he* really was brave.

'They got away,' said Caeculus.

'Evidently,' growled Vulcanus. 'No matter. It's time for change. Enough hiding. We should be ruling this planet, not hiding in caves.'

'I agree, father. But are there not others who will stop us?'

Vulcanus snorted. 'After all this fighting, there are hardly any of them left now. We are free to do as we wish. These primitive people think we are gods. So let us start behaving like gods.'

'I have a feeling the daughter of Janus and her friends will return,' said Caeculus.

'So do I. And when they do, we must make sure we are waiting for them. I still want that time machine. When we get our hands on that ...' The thought made him laugh. 'Well, no one will be able to stop us then, will they ...?'

End of Book One

The story continues in Book Two

The Prophecy

available on Amazon now.

If you would like more information on any of my books as well as news on new releases, please visit **www.johndfennell.com**

I really hope you enjoyed reading this book. If you did, I would be very grateful if you could add a rating and a short review on **Amazon** to let others know what you thought.

Many thanks,

John D. Fennell

Printed in Great Britain
by Amazon